Ransom stared at the lifeless body that lay at his feet.

"Did you notice anything peculiar about her?" he said.

"Peculiar?"

"Look at her."

Gerald did so. He searched her lifeless form with his eyes, knowing that his partner must have seen something of note. Whatever it was, it escaped Gerald.

"I don't see anything out of the ordinary."

"Look at her face. There's something very peculiar about it, given the unusual nature of her visit to my office."

"What's that?"

"She looks surprised."

———————— ★ ————————

"Works very well..."

—*Booklist*

"[An] enjoyable series..."

—*Wilson Library Bulletin*

FRED W. HUNTER

RANSOM FOR AN ANGEL

WORLDWIDE®

TORONTO • NEW YORK • LONDON
AMSTERDAM • PARIS • SYDNEY • HAMBURG
STOCKHOLM • ATHENS • TOKYO • MILAN
MADRID • WARSAW • BUDAPEST • AUCKLAND

RANSOM FOR AN ANGEL

A Worldwide Mystery/January 1997

This edition is reprinted by arrangement with Walker and Company.

ISBN 0-373-26224-8

For Dr. Jane Stedman, my mentor and friend

ONE

A Murder Foretold

"I WANT YOU to investigate a murder."

She stood framed in the doorway looking as if she had just stepped out of a novel by Dashiell Hammett. The lack of a fur was the only concession to current social consciousness. She wore a miraculously unwrinkled beige silk suit, with a white ruffled blouse that remained dry and fresh despite the stifling July heat.

"Do you know something we don't know?" asked Ransom, looking up from the clutter of reports on his desk.

"I beg your pardon?" said the woman.

"It's normal police procedure to investigate all the murders we know about."

The woman's lips betrayed the barest hint of a smile as she removed her dark green sunglasses, revealing the clearest ice blue eyes Ransom had ever seen. Had he been a few years older, he would have described her as a striking woman. She had scored a direct hit with him.

Despite her smile and her piercing eyes, it was clear that she was troubled.

"You *are* Jeremy Ransom, aren't you?"

"Yes. And this is my partner, Detective White. You can rest easy with him. Unlike me, he's not inclined to facetiousness."

Gerald nodded to the woman.

"May I sit down?"

He indicated the chair with a nod.

The woman entered the office quietly, with only the slightest sound of rustling silk. As she lowered her slender frame onto the wooden chair facing Ransom's desk, her right hand absently brushed the wide brim of her hat, almost as if she were brushing wisps of hair from her face. The movement betrayed a nervousness that was incongruous with her otherwise calm exterior.

"I suppose that was a melodramatic way to begin a conversation," she said.

"It was a surprise. Murders don't normally come to us, we go to them."

Again the faint smile played about her lips. "I'm afraid you're making fun of me," she said with a trace of sadness.

Despite Ransom's reputation for hardness, he turned a deep crimson at the tone in her voice. He was ashamed. Gerald mentally noted this historic occasion.

"I'm sorry, it's the heat. Chicago is no place to spend the summer."

The slight tilting of her head told him that he'd been forgiven. He cleared his throat and continued, trying to instill a note of professionalism in his voice.

"However, what I said before really is the truth. If there's been a murder, I assure you that we're already investigating it."

"But it hasn't happened yet!" Her face looked startled, her eyes wide, as if she had surprised herself with the statement. Her fingers tightened around the spaghetti strap of the small tan purse that hung loosely over her shoulder, the color draining from the knuckles. She rose quickly and quietly from the chair she'd just accepted and turned away from the bewildered detectives. Both Ransom and Gerald were surprised by the force of the desperation beneath her immaculate exterior. Still gazing at the woman's back, Ransom fingered a pencil that lay amidst the piles of paperwork, rolled it between his thumb and forefinger, and tapped it lightly on the top of his old, scarred desk.

"Do you have reason to believe that someone is going to be murdered?"

"I have no...rational reason...to believe such a thing." Her shoulders trembled slightly.

Ransom glanced at his partner, whose face betrayed no emotion.

"And yet you think someone is going to be killed."

"Yes."

"And who is the intended victim?"

She turned and looked him squarely in the eyes.

"I am."

It was to Ransom's credit that he didn't bat an eye or raise an eyebrow during the silence that followed these two words. The pleading look in the woman's eyes demonstrated her seriousness. What remained for Ransom to discover was the cause of her certainty of her impending murder, in the absence of what she herself had called a *rational* reason. He gently guided her back to the desk, and she returned to the hard wooden chair.

An embarrassed smile brightened her face.

"I seem to be discovering an untapped talent for melodrama."

Ransom smiled at her but said nothing. Gerald, seated on the vinyl couch along the wall of Ransom's office, stared at the floor.

The woman sighed. "It really is very hot, and I haven't been sleeping well. I haven't slept since Monday. Today is Thursday."

"What happened on Monday?" asked Ransom gently.

"My name is Angela Stephens. I think I should tell you that now because they'll want to know it when you put me in the mental ward."

"I'm sure that won't be necessary," said Ransom, attempting his most engaging smile.

"You haven't heard my story yet. The man downstairs looked at me as if I were crazy."

"The man downstairs?"

"The desk sergeant I think he was called. I started to tell him the problem and he told me to see you."

Gerald stifled a laugh and avoided Ransom's annoyed glance.

"Is it *Mrs.* Stephens?"

Angela nodded.

"Mrs. Stephens, what makes you think that someone is going to kill you?"

Angela hesitated and lowered her head as if embarrassed to face him. "I've been told that it will happen," she said quietly.

"Told?"

"Mr. Ransom, I want you to know that it took all the courage I have to come here. It took courage because I know you'll think I'm crazy...or worse, stupid." She glanced up at him quickly, checking his expression. Seeing nothing, she lowered her head and continued, nervously tugging each finger of her left hand with her right. "As I said, it took all my courage. It's taken me from Monday until today to be upset enough and scared enough to come to you."

"What happened on Monday?"

"I'm emphasizing all this because you *will* think I'm crazy."

"Mrs. Stephens..."

Angela sighed wearily. "I went to a woman named Melina. Her 'office' is on Ohio Street. She's a 'reader-adviser.' That's exactly the expression I was afraid I'd see on your face," she said, the right corner of her mouth twitching upward attractively.

"You went to a fortune-teller."

"And you think that's crazy?"

Ransom's normally taut face relaxed into a smile that was almost warm. Gerald shifted uneasily on the couch, recrossed his legs, and returned his gaze to the floor.

"Looking at you I should say it was out of character," he said.

"That was a very judicious reply," said Angela, with a gentle laugh that filled the room with music. She was relieved beyond her own understanding to have her declaration treated with dignity by the detective. Dignity and something else. She was, in fact, a little puzzled as to just how she *was* being treated. But Ransom's attitude did make it easier for her to continue.

"I really do believe…" Angela began hesitantly, then taking a deep breath, she started again firmly. "I really do believe that some people are gifted to see into the future. I'm not talking about pseudogypsies that do up their heads in scarves and have big gold loops dangling from their ears. You know what I mean, the ones that gaze into crystal balls. But there are others—people who can seriously plot astrological charts, or see into your character through the palm of your hand, or can, with the assistance of the tarot, see into the future."

Ransom smiled inwardly but was careful not to reveal his amusement at the fact that so intelligent a woman would place gypsies in a separate category from palmists and card readers.

"And of course, there are genuine psychics. Even the police have used them on occasion…so I've read." She blushed slightly at reverting to this tactic but quickly recovered herself. "If you are a true believer, and reasonably sensitive, you get a sense for the genuineness of these various practitioners. You can tell charlatans from the truly gifted." She stopped suddenly and looked at Ransom, searching his face for some reaction. "I suppose you find it hard to believe that I could classify myself as intelligent and still believe in fortune-tellers."

But Ransom didn't find it hard to believe. Chicago is a city of sparkling normality, where the bizarre and the commonplace peacefully coexist in a way that makes the bizarre seem normal. Well, if not normal, then not something to be feared. From time to time fringe elements will flare up and be splashed across the front pages of the daily papers, as fringes are wont to do, and public furor of one kind or another (for or against the fringes) will erupt overnight. But furor in Chicago comes and goes like California earthquakes, leaving far less damage in its wake. Furor dies away quickly, and life goes on. Fringes are, after all, a part of the whole: and a decorative part at that. Generally there is a refreshing attitude of "live and let live" in Chicago that allows almost everything, within limits, to exist together without so much as a nod or a wink from the neighbors. It is quite common to find psychics, psychiatrists, lawyers and hookers practicing in the same pricey Michigan Avenue high-rise: all maintaining a quiet, dignified, upper-middle-class sensibility.

Ransom suddenly realized that Angela was waiting for a response. Without changing his expression, he said, "I've worked long enough in homicide to realize that some very intelligent people do some very amazing things. Sometimes with amazing results. I try not to judge what people believe as long as they don't use their beliefs as an excuse for breaking the law."

Angela looked at him thoughtfully. "That's very sensible," she said finally.

"But you haven't really answered my question."

"Which was?"

"What happened Monday? What exactly did Melina say to you?"

Angela's pale white hands tensed slightly, and after a moment's consideration, she spoke matter-of-factly.

"She reads tarot cards, you know. You shuffle the deck and then she lays the cards out and can tell the shape of your future from the pattern they form. I've always thought—some readers will also say this—that the fact that you shuffle the cards means that there is a certain amount of chance involved in what the cards show—that maybe it's just one possible future—but Melina denies this. She says that the cards never lie."

She looked to him for prompting to continue, and he responded with a noncommittal "Mmmm."

"I'd...rather not go into detail about the things she told me as she laid out the cards—she told me things about my past and especially my present—personal things—that were...accurate. Accurate enough to convince me that she was the real thing. When she got to the last three cards, she suddenly tensed and laid the cards facedown on the table, covering them with her hands. She said, 'I'm sorry, I can't go on.' I'm afraid I made a bit of a fool of myself, but…she had been able to see so many intimate details of my life in the cards that I pleaded with her to tell me what she'd seen.''

"And she told you," said Ransom with an irony he regretted the moment he'd spoken.

"She offered to give me my money back rather than tell me, but I kept pleading, and she relented. I wish I'd taken the money.''

"What did she tell you?''

Angela paused as if unsure whether or not to go on. She coughed lightly into her right hand and then continued. "She laid out the last three cards. They were death, the fool, and the hanged man. She told me the death card—a skeleton wielding a sickle—was *my* death. My impending death. And she said the fool would be responsible.''

"And the hanged man?''

Angela released a sigh that, instead of sounding relieved, sounded tense and choked.

"The hanged man is the figure of a man being hung upside down by one foot. It can mean many things, depending on its position in the pattern and the rest of the fortune. But Melina told me that for me, having this card fall in the last position is a good sign.''

"A good sign?'' said Gerald incredulously. Angela started in her seat, having forgotten that he was in the room. He had a singular talent for making people forget he was there.

"A sign that my killer would be brought to justice. She said…she said…'' Angela faltered, and her eyes welled with tears. She bowed her head and held the bridge of her nose between her thumb and forefinger. She seemed to call upon her years of good breeding and inner strength to dispel the tension in her mind and body. Before the eyes of the onlooking detectives, her muscles relaxed and her composure was restored. When she raised her eyes to Ransom, they were once again crystal clear.

"Melina said that knowing my killer would be brought to justice might not be much, but it might help me to rest easier in my grave."

"Big of her," said Gerald disgustedly.

Ransom looked at the woman with a concern that he himself was at a loss to explain. Of course, her story was absurd, and he dismissed it immediately. But what he could not dismiss was the sincerity with which she believed it.

He also could not dismiss a stirring he felt somewhere between his neck and his knees: a feeling that seemed centered in one area of his body and then traveled to another the moment he tried to analyze it. As Angela had spoken, he became vaguely aware of a sensation of both warmth and emptiness that at first seemed to settle in his chest, then sank to his stomach, then continued its descent. He realized uncomfortably that he was allowing his mind to wander into fields through which he hadn't allowed himself to travel for far too long. He sat up abruptly to dispel the unwanted feelings.

"This Melina seems to have told you a great many things, but you can't possibly believe her."

She smiled wanly. "I know it's difficult for you to understand. You're a detective and you deal in facts. But I do believe her. She told me things she couldn't possibly have known if she weren't...yes, I believed her. All I can say to you is 'there are more things in Heaven and earth than are dreamt of in your philosophy.'"

Ransom glanced at a picture in a small silver-plated frame on his desk and smiled. "*Hamlet*. I have a friend who's fond of quoting Shakespeare to me."

He pushed his creaking swivel chair back and stood up. He walked to the front of the desk and sat on its edge, running his hand over the blond hair that he'd had cut close-cropped against the summer heat. He looked down at Angela and spoke firmly.

"Mrs. Stephens, you *do* seem to be an intelligent woman. And you're right, I don't understand how you could believe a fortune-teller. Tell me why you do."

"What do you mean?"

"You must have some reason for believing that what she told you will happen."

Her good breeding forced her to look him in the eyes, despite her embarrassment. "She told me things about certain aspects of my life that she couldn't possibly have known. Things I've kept...well, things of which I'm not particularly proud. She seemed to know everything."

"Did she happen to know who the killer is?" said Ransom, unable to hide his mounting frustration.

"She couldn't give me a name."

"How irritating of her."

Angela looked up sharply. "She described him."

"And?"

She sighed. "It is a man who is well off in the world, and well thought of. He is attractive, well dressed, and graying at the temples. He appears to be in his late thirties or early forties..." she faltered, remembering, "...his hands are large and strong."

She emitted a faint, choking sob from somewhere deep in her throat and stopped speaking, but did not break down.

"And you believe you know this man?"

"She described my husband."

"And about a million other men, I should say."

"What possible reason could she have for telling me these things if they weren't the truth?"

Ransom thought for a moment, then continued.

"Has your husband ever threatened you?"

"No."

"Has he ever given you reason to believe that he might want to kill you?"

"No."

But she had hesitated, however slightly, before answering him this time. Ransom paused for a moment, looking at her thoughtfully.

"Have you ever given him reason to want to kill you?"

Both Angela and Gerald were surprised by this question.

Angela thought a moment before answering, as if carefully choosing her words.

"I don't believe he knows of any reason," she said slowly.

Ransom pushed himself off the desk and heaved a frustrated sigh. His desk chair creaked loudly as he plopped down onto it.

"Mrs. Stephens, you must know that there's nothing I can do about this story you've told me. We can't arrest a man because a tarot card reader told you he was going to kill you. I can't put you under surveillance—the sergeant would laugh me out of his office."

"I understand that," she said quietly.

"Then why have you come to me? What did you hope to accomplish?"

Her face calm, she raised her eyes to his and held him transfixed. When she finally spoke, her voice had taken on an unmistakable tone of resignation.

"I came to give the future a hand."

"WHAT DO YOU make of that?" Gerald said as Ransom watched the retreating figure of Angela Stephens.

But Ransom was lost in thought. Thoughts of cool silk and warm nights, as well as thoughts of the limitations of his job.

Gerald scratched his stiff, mousy brown hair and contemplated his partner. They had been paired for almost a year now, and he had yet to see this facet of Ransom's personality. Ransom had seemed to be made up of snap judgments and remarkable intuition, but never had he exhibited anything resembling libido. In his partner's eyes, Ransom's emotional range was limited to anger, self-satisfaction, or complacency. This was something different, and Gerald found it confusing. He cleared his throat.

"Ransom...what do you make of that?"

Ransom awoke from his near trance and looked at the excessively pale face of his partner.

"What do I make of it?" Ransom paused and gazed out the door. "I wish the rules were different."

"Come on, you don't believe she's going to be killed?"

"Of course not," said Ransom with marked hesitation. "And yet, if I had only to go by how strongly *she* believed it, I would send a whole squad to watch her."

Gerald stood up and stretched his legs. The back of his pant legs were damp with sweat.

"I wonder why she believes it."

"'Ah, that is the question'…there's something more behind this. Something's wrong."

"Well, what does your world-famous intuition tell you?"

Ransom shot him a warning glance. He was in no mood for their usual banter.

"My *guess* would be that she's done something, maybe even something rather minor, for which she thinks her husband might want to kill her. Look at how she hedged when I pressed her on that. Minor or not, she was too embarrassed or ashamed of herself to tell us what it might be. She was also very cagey when she said she didn't believe her husband *knows* of any reason to kill her."

"I caught that."

"So, we know two things: She's done something wrong—or thinks she has—and she's not sure whether or not her husband knows about it."

Gerald said with a short laugh, "And then up pops this fortune-teller, who knows all about it."

Ransom pushed back his chair, which creaked more quietly, as if not wanting to disturb the somber atmosphere that had overcome the office. He walked to the door and gazed out through the squad room as if he could still see the silk-swathed figure retreating through the sea of aging desks.

"But it's frustrating. I've heard thousands of stories of murder and reasons for murder over the years—all after the fact. Whether or not you understand it, at least after the murder's been committed there's something you can do about it.'' He shook his head. ''There's nothing we can do about *this*.''

Gerald crossed behind him and followed his gaze. ''Jer...you know that if someone had come to us with a *normal* story—if a wife came here and said that she *knew* her husband was going to kill her—even if she had good reason to believe it—there wouldn't be much we could do about it. Not unless something happened.''

''I know.''

''There's nothing we can do until after the fact. It *is* frustrating, but it's true.''

''You know what's even more frustrating?'' said Ransom, glancing at his partner over his shoulder. ''She knew that. That's what she meant by 'giving the future a hand.' She wants us to find her murderer after it happens.''

TWO

A Murder in Waiting

RANSOM PULLED UP in front of the wood-frame house, which was no longer the fading gray it had been when he'd first seen it. A slight ache in his shoulder reminded him in equal parts of his newly acquired age fixation and of the free time he'd spent, when the weather was fine, fixing up the old woman's home. The exterior had been greatly improved by a fresh coat of powder blue paint, which, he thought with a smile, matched Emily's eyes (which had also seemed gray when they'd met).

Emily was a gentle but tough elderly woman who had proven instrumental in helping Ransom solve a previous case. Since then he had adopted her as a sort of surrogate grandmother in lieu of living grandparents of his own. It was not merely out of loneliness that this adoption had taken place but out of a sincere respect they felt for each other. Ransom had never met a sharper old woman, so that in addition to her serving as an ersatz grandparent, Ransom considered Emily his personal Miss Marple. It was not unusual to find him having a Sunday dinner with her, discussing the cases in which he was involved and mulling over the meaning of life in general over their after-dinner tea.

Part of his fondness for Emily Charters stemmed from the very fact that she was the only person about whom Ransom was willing to admit to having had an erroneous first impression. Up to that time, he'd been proud of his ability to form an accurate assessment of a person almost on first sight. In Emily he'd been fooled, though through some form of convoluted logic he'd been known to claim that Emily was the exception that proved the rule.

Ransom had often thought with a certain degree of humility and amusement of the day Emily had come to his office and asked him to investigate the death of her elderly friend: a death put down to natural causes, which had turned out to be one in a series of murders. At first, Ransom had taken Emily to be a quaint if bothersome old woman whom a sympathetic ear and a kind word would placate. He couldn't have been more wrong. Emily had held the key to the murders. Though Ransom was not one to readily admit when he was wrong (since it so seldom happened), he'd been unable to avoid it in her case. She was sharp, and he admired that in anyone.

But there was something else that Ransom couldn't avoid in Emily's case. In the normal course of a murder investigation, Ransom routinely became entrenched in the lives of the people involved, both guilty and innocent, in an entirely clinical fashion. In his darker moods he was known to consider it a kind of rape, stripping strangers of all decency and leaving them to heal themselves. When in this frame of mind, he salved his conscience by reminding himself that his job, though distasteful, was necessary. In his better moods, he considered the end of a case like the curtain coming down at the end of a play, or closing the cover at the end of a book. The relationship with the players has ended. He often thought of himself as an audience to real-life drama: actually, not audience so much as critic. But whichever term he preferred, he held the firm belief that the players should not intrude into the lives of the audience.

But he had broken this unwritten law with Emily. Admiration had given way to attachment. His own grandmother had died when he was barely five years old, and he had only a dim recollection of her as a horribly wrinkled woman, somewhat resembling one of those dried-apple witches, who was almost blind and scared him by feeling his face to identify him when he accompanied his parents on their periodic, obligatory visits to her. He had been relieved that his parents felt so obliged only once or twice a year. In Emily, he had found something resembling the grandmother he would have liked to have had. As time passed, he'd revived his long-lost childhood tradition of a normal Sunday dinner with the old woman, and she'd routinely dealt out strong tea and strong advice in equal measures: the advice more often than not appearing in the form of iambic pentameter cribbed from Shakespeare, Emily's literary passion.

For her part, Emily seemed to have grown younger over the past year. On the not-so-rare occasion that she was of a wistful mind, she attributed this rejuvenation to the growth of new friendships. The death of Meg Ferguson, Emily's last lifelong friend, had served not as an ending, as it might have for a lesser woman, but as a beginning. It brought Emily together with the detective, and she had grown to accept him in the role of substitute grandson.

Ironically, Emily was to suffer another great loss less than a year later: Her cat, Fedora, had finally aged to the point of no return and had willingly shed the last of her many mortal coils quietly one afternoon as Emily made her tea. Emily had called Ransom, who came immediately to her side. The two friends had stood solemnly over the immobile body of the animal, which lay comfortably curled up in her basket. Ransom had suddenly become aware that this was the first nonviolent death scene he'd been called to since his father had passed away from heart failure almost ten years earlier. It was not a thought that sat well with him.

The loss of Fedora hit Emily harder than Ransom would have expected. It brought her closer to depression than he thought she could go. Because she was naturally resilient, her depression hadn't lasted long, but it had left an indelible impression on the detective. Emily, for all her strength, was human. It was to assuage Emily's loneliness that Ransom had taken to visiting her more often. At least, that's what he told himself.

"It was very curious," said Ransom vacantly as he

rested the blue cup that had become his own on its saucer. He would normally have preferred a mug, but somehow that would seem out of place in Emily's house.

"I beg your pardon?" said Emily.

Ransom suddenly returned to the present.

"What?"

"You said it was very curious."

"Oh, yes, I'm sorry. I was just thinking of something that happened at work."

Emily's questioning glance prompted him to continue.

"A very attractive young woman—very well heeled, as you would say—stopped in to my office today to give me the results of her tarot card reading."

Emily's thin gray eyebrows slid upwards and peaked at their middles. "That *is* curious. Did you know this woman?"

The phrase "not as well as I'd like to" rose unbidden in Ransom's mind. He dismissed it and responded with a simple "no."

"Then why on earth did she think you'd be interested in her fortune?"

He cocked his eye at the old woman and said pointedly, "Because it involved a crime."

"Oh, my," said Emily. It was impossible to tell from her tone whether or not these words were meant to convey any irony, but her character-lined face showed that she was thinking.

"Am I to understand," she said after a long pause, "that this fortune has come true?"

"Not yet."

"I see."

Not quite sure what it was she did see, Ransom began to drum his fingers lightly on the table.

"And what exactly did this woman expect you to do?"

"I'm sure I don't know."

"Did she think you'd be able to prevent the crime?"

"I don't know," said Ransom more irritably than he intended. "What really puzzles me is that she seemed like a highly intelligent, well-educated woman. I don't see how anyone with an ounce of intelligence could believe in that kind of nonsense."

Emily gave a little shrug. "Yes, but that's because you're so young."

Ransom was stopped short by this. "You don't believe in fortune-telling!"

"Oh, no, my dear, not for a minute. It may very well be that there are people who for some reason or other can see things before they happen—in fact, I would venture to say that that's more common than we think—but I don't think I could ever bring myself to believe that someone could see anything helpful in a deck of cards, no matter how artfully the cards were painted. But that's not what I meant by 'That's because you're young'—I didn't mean young in years, I meant because you were born later than myself. You see, when I was young spiritualism was a much more accepted pursuit."

With the uncomfortable feeling that she was lumping herself into this category, Ransom said with a wave of his hand, "People were less educated then."

"Really?" said Emily with an indulgent smile. "I'm afraid that it's a common foible in the younger generations to mistake information for knowledge. I will admit that people today are exposed to much more information than we were, but I wouldn't say that they're any more *educated*." She stopped and adopted her most puckish expression. "Why, some of us can even quote Shakespeare."

"Emily, I didn't mean to imply…"

"And…" she continued with a raised hand, thoroughly enjoying herself, "…I assume that you would consider Sir Arthur Conan Doyle an educated man, and he was one of the stoutest proponents of spiritualism in the early part of this century. He even wrote a history of it."

"All right, all right," said Ransom, laughing ruefully, "call off your dogs, Emily, I concede: An educated person can believe in spiritualism. But that doesn't explain why they would."

Emily took a sip of her tea and nodded thoughtfully to herself. "Well, of course there is always the possibility that something precipitated it."

"What do you mean?"

She cleared her throat and straightened herself in her chair in a way that resembled a schoolmarm preparing to teach. "I believe in the case of Doyle the death of his son in the war was the catalyst. It was at that point...I assume in his grief...that he really started delving into it. I've read that he even participated in séances to try to communicate with the boy."

Ransom made a sound like "harumph," then said, "Given that explanation I would say that the loss of his son sent his mind a little out of balance."

"Perhaps," said the old woman slowly, "but the point is that that can happen to an educated person just as easily as an uneducated one."

Ransom rested an arm on the table and was lost in thought for a moment; then he turned to Emily and said, "So what you're saying is I need to find out what caused this woman's belief in the fortune-teller."

Emily sat back in her chair and eyed him quizzically. "I'm not saying anything of the kind. I can't see that it matters at all."

"What?" said Ransom, taken completely off guard.

"What I mean to say is, it is interesting as an example of how inexplicable human behaviour can be, but...well, there hasn't *been* a crime committed, has there?"

"No."

"Then what does it matter?"

"Oh...it doesn't matter," said Ransom vacantly, raising his cup to his lips, "it doesn't matter at all."

AS HE SLID the key into the lock, his sweat-moistened forehead drooped against the door. Hot to cold, hot to cold. The lobby had been almost frigid with air-conditioning. The elevator and hallway were stifling—not really hot, but no air circulating. He knew that once inside the apartment he could turn on his air conditioner, but the rooms would take time to cool off, and somehow he could still manage to sweat even after the apartment had reached a comfortable temperature.

The lock clicked, and Ransom swung open the door, switching on the lights with an automatic gesture. He kicked the door shut, slid his right hand under the knot in his tie, and pulled it loose and out of his shirt collar with one tired movement.

He stripped down to a pair of black jockey shorts—which he wore not for style, but so that he wouldn't have to separate his laundry—and turned the knob on the air conditioner to "on." As usual, it emitted a comforting hum, but when he waved his hand over the vents, the air felt warm and dry. He was sure he was the only man in Chicago whose air conditioner didn't blow cold until it warmed up and always smelled musty even though it was used almost every day during the summer.

He sighed heavily, lumbered into the bathroom, and turned on the taps in the bathtub. He had lately taken to staring at himself in the mirror while the bathtub filled, looking for signs of aging, all the time telling himself that an obsession with growing old was unnatural in a man of thirty-seven. But he'd been spending more and more time in front of the mirror since the day he'd discovered one gray hair amidst the sparse hair on his chest. He hadn't been fazed by the few gray hairs that had long since graced his temples, especially since they were difficult to see in his blond hair, but finding one on his chest he was sure was the first step into a nursing home.

However, this obsession was merely indicative of a more deep-seated problem. Ransom would never admit to having given up on life, but it always remained in the back of his mind that his life had reached a plateau—and one that was not much higher than sea level. Like millions of people, he had had expectations for his life when he'd been in his twenties: expectations that, unlike millions of people, he had realized. But those achievements somehow no longer seemed important or worthwhile. He now tended to see the future stretching out before him like an endless highway with no scenery, road signs, or off-ramps. And despite the impeccable reputation he'd achieved along the road for solving seemingly unsolvable cases, he saw his past the same way. On occasion it struck him as ironic that he could see his life as uneventful, even though his days were spotted with murder and mayhem, not necessarily in that order.

It was for this reason that his emotions were so mixed about the stirring his loins had undergone by the beautiful woman who'd interrupted his paper shuffling. On the one hand, he was more than pleased to note that he was still capable of being aroused. On the other, the fact that she was unattainable (she was, after all, married, and Ransom had standards) merely served to accentuate his loneliness.

Loneliness. That was the word his mind had been avoiding as it replayed Angela Stephens's every word and gesture. A great toll had been taken over his decade on the force as he had developed his persona as a loner, and it didn't help to remind himself that he had actively courted his current lifestyle. He smiled to himself. Sherlock Holmes had agreed: Emotional relationships could only cloud your mind.

But even as this thought crossed his mind, he had to modify it. He had allowed one emotional attachment to take root in recent days: his relationship to Emily Charters.

He shook his head again. A surrogate grandmother was no substitute for a mate. To make matters worse, he was annoyed at his own humanity. The heroes of detective novels, loners and mavericks one and all, did not suffer from any such human frailty as loneliness. For the first time in recent memory, he was aware of being flawed.

The water splashed loudly into the tub, which was almost filled to overflowing. He shook himself to clear his head, reached down to turn off the tap, and pulled the plug to let a little of the water drain out.

He wasn't wrong, he told himself firmly. The presence of mind he so proudly possessed could only be hampered by romantic entanglements. Or could it? Other detectives seemed to manage wives and lovers and still perform their professional duties. But Ransom was not like other detectives.

After a moment, his face melted into a smile. He was being too hard on himself. It was the nearness of forty, and the pressure to settle down (like an adult) with a wife and raise children. A family. Isn't that what someone his age should be doing? Isn't that what everyone said? He was painfully aware of the high cost of being a maverick when he'd been in the presence of Angela Stephens.

He shook his head again to clear his mind. He stepped out of his jockey shorts, letting them lie where they fell on the bathroom floor, then went out to the living room to retrieve his book. He was still rereading the works of Dickens, and was now starting *A Tale of Two Cities,* a book he remembered enjoying when he'd first read it in college. "It is a far, far better thing that I do, than ever I have done" were words he remembered vividly. They stirred something in his mind and heart at the time, and still did: the desire to know a love like the characters find in Victorian novels, love so deep and abiding it was worth dying for. He sincerely doubted that that kind of love existed in twentieth-century Chicago. Actually, he doubted if it had ever existed anywhere outside fiction.

THREE

Death

THE SUN GLOWED dull and hot, like a flame through gauze, on the following morning. The temperature was already eighty-eight degrees at seven-thirty when Ransom left for work. Beads of sweat had appeared on his forehead in the time it had taken him to unlock the door of his tan Nova. An aptly named car in this heat, he thought as he turned the key in the ignition.

It promised to be the fifth day in a row with temperatures in the hundreds and humidity to match. He wouldn't have been surprised to hear native drums and the cries of cockatoos in the background. It was impossible to believe that a mere four months earlier there had been blizzards and subzero weather. This was normally part of what he loved about Chicago: The city runs hot or cold, always in extremes. Ransom had no use for the middle road.

But today, after a bad night's sleep, the air seemed not only oppressive but foreboding. A bad omen. As he entered area headquarters, he tried to shake the nightmares that had made him wake in sweat-soaked sheets, despite the fact that his air conditioner, hyperactive once it had started working, had left the apartment almost frigid.

In his dreams, the figure of a woman called to him from across a ravine, pleading for his help. As he frantically tried to find a means to cross the gap, the earth shook and the ravine widened. The woman faded farther and farther into the distance, her cries fading with her. In one last, futile effort, he had run—it had seemed like miles—and tried to leap the ravine. But the gap had widened, and he fell far short of the other side, plunging deeper and deeper into blackness. As he fell, he heard a woman's quiet, derisive laughter from the cliff from which he'd flung himself. And in the laughter, one whispered word: "fool."

He had awoken, sitting bolt upright, sweat pouring down his chest and back. Even as he remembered the dream, his heart beat faster and his breathing grew shallower. He shook his head briskly to dismiss the memory. As with many nightmares, the memory faded, but the haunted feeling remained. He swept by the desks of busy detectives without a word and threw himself into his chair. He wanted nothing more than to intertwine his fingers behind his head, lean back, and close his eyes, not to sleep, but to rest.

It hadn't occurred to him before this oppressive Friday morning how at home he felt in his office. He could only attribute this momentary feeling of peace to the interrupted night he'd just suffered. His previous evening of navel-gazing had left him with the uncomfortable feeling that his apartment, where nobody awaited his return, was merely the place he went to sleep. Robbed of that sleep, it didn't seem like home at all.

I really have to stop doing this! he thought.

He leaned back in his chair, closed his eyes, and took several deep breaths, which he released slowly. Gradually he began to relax and quiet his mind.

"RANSOM." A FAMILIAR voice called to him from the blackness. He was aware, and yet not aware, of his surroundings. His eyes snapped open involuntarily, and he saw that the red numbers of the digital clock on his desk read 8:15. He had been asleep for about ten minutes.

"Are you all right?"

Gerald stood in the doorway, his face a question mark the color of Elmer's paste despite the unrelenting summer sun.

Ransom cleared his throat. "I'm fine. I just didn't sleep well."

"I'm sorry to hear that," Gerald replied, with more concern than Ransom would have thought the occasion called for.

"What? What is it?"

"A call just came in. Newman is sending Robinson and Wilke out on it. I thought you'd want to know."

The sense of foreboding Ransom had felt earlier returned.

"What?"

Gerald hesitated, fearing the coming reaction. "Angela Stephens was murdered."

For a split second, Gerald doubted whether his partner had heard him. Ransom's face registered nothing. Then, without changing expression, he leapt out of his chair and shot past Gerald, almost knocking him into the door.

"Don't leave!" he yelled at the bewildered Robinson and Wilke as he sped through the room and into Sergeant Newman's office, slamming the door behind him.

"Newman! A case just came in and I want it!"

Mike Newman sat with his feet up on the desk and his continually graying hair dropping over his forehead. A small bit of egg yolk clung to the point of his red-and-blue-striped tie. His face was a picture of surprise, his eyes staring widely at the overheated detective.

"What?"

"The Stephens case. The murdered woman. It just came in. I want it!"

"I just sent Robinson out on that," the sergeant managed to sputter in blank amazement.

"They haven't left yet! They're waiting out there. Don't send them, send me!"

Newman dropped his feet to the floor, the last few words helping him regain his composure.

"They're waiting? What the hell for?"

"I told them to."

"You *what?*" With this, Newman was on his feet. "Are you out of your goddamn mind? I didn't send them out for sandwiches; this is a murder!"

"I know that! I want the case."

"What the hell's the matter with you—and why the hell are we having this conversation? *I'm* the one who decides who goes."

Ransom almost smiled despite his anxiousness. "That's why we're having this conversation."

"Look, this isn't a difficult case. The body was found in her apartment''—he glanced impatiently at his watch—"about twenty minutes ago now. For God's sake, the husband probably did it."

Newman swept the hair out of his face again with his right hand as he crossed from behind the desk to his door. "And I want Robinson to get his ass over there before I hear any more bad press about how slow our response time is."

Newman began to open the door, but with a swift move Ransom slammed it, the sergeant still holding the knob.

"Mike, please..."

The sergeant was brought up short by the uncharacteristic note of pleading in Ransom's voice.

"Let me have this case." He said it simply, but there was the barest hint of embarrassment in his voice. Newman looked at him searchingly.

"Do you know this woman?"

Ransom hesitated. "No."

"No? Then why—"

"All right," said Ransom. He pushed himself away from the door, crossing over to Newman's grime-smeared window. "It's not a simple case. At least...no, I'm sure it's not."

"What are you talking about?"

"She told me she was going to be killed."

There was a loud silence, the type one would expect to follow an announcement of this sort. After a moment, the silence was penetrated by the frowning Newman.

"You said you didn't know her."

"She came here...she came to me yesterday to ask for help."

"Oh, Christ!" said Newman, with a growing certainty that he wasn't going to like what he was about to hear.

Newman listened quietly while Ransom, with something bordering on embarrassment, related the highlights of Angela Stephens's visit. It was uncharacteristic for Ransom, who had spent so much time carefully cultivating the persona of a loner, to open up to anybody. It was especially unusual for him to open up to a "superior" whom he thought of, with affection, as a minor annoyance. The importance of this event was not lost on Newman. When Ransom had finished, the sergeant said nothing. The two men stood across from each other in the dingy office, silently contemplating each other. Finally, Newman twisted the doorknob and pulled open the door.

"Robinson, Wilke, forget this one."

The two detectives shrugged and returned to their desks. Ransom stopped briefly in the doorway.

"Thanks, Mike," he said quietly.

Newman averted his eyes and pushed the gray hair out of his face as he went back to his desk. Then he said with an attempt to regain his authority. "Just see you get results."

"Gerald!" yelled Ransom as he charged across the squad room. Gerald smiled, following Ransom out the door. He half expected his partner to yell "the game's afoot!" Gerald knew that no matter how much a loner Ransom imagined himself, he needed his assistance. With his customary faith in his partner, Gerald had already retrieved the address of the murder scene from the other detectives.

Ransom stopped suddenly when he reached the stairs and went back to the squad-room door.

"Newman! Who found the body? Who called?"

Newman poked his head out of his office.

"The husband."

AS A DETECTIVE, Ransom had always seen himself as something of an avenging angel, working on behalf of the deceased. But this was the first time in his career that he'd been "hired" by the deceased, and the determination to avenge her death burned inside him like a furnace stoked by an unseen hand. As Gerald drove him to the scene of the crime, Ransom was already uncomfortably aware that this determination, rather than working for him, could work against him, narrowing his vision and blinding him to possibilities he knew he'd have to consider.

"You couldn't have prevented it," said Gerald, turning the car onto Lake Shore Drive.

"Hmmm?"

"Nobody would have taken her seriously."

Ransom was silent.

"When it comes to that, nobody would have taken her story as seriously as you did."

"I can do what she wanted, Gerald," said Ransom as though through a fog.

"Huh?"

"She didn't want me to prevent her murder. She knew I couldn't. She wanted me to solve it."

"That shouldn't be too hard. Do you think the husband did it?"

"You know me better than that. We haven't even seen him."

"Well, I mean, this Melina character was right about the murder. Maybe she was right about the murderer."

"It would hardly be admissible evidence."

Gerald swung the car into the semicircular driveway of the fifteen-story Lake Shore Drive apartment building in which Angela Stephens had lived, and died. A black doorman, in his shirt sleeves and loosened collar in a concession to the heat, ran down the short flight of cement stairs to greet them as they climbed out of the car.

"You the police?"

Ransom nodded.

"They're in thirteen-oh-one," the doorman called over his shoulder. He had barely reached the bottom step before he was hurriedly preceding the two detectives back up to the front door. He grabbed the huge brass handle on the heavy glass door, pulled it open for them, and pointed down a hallway on the right.

"Elevator's at the end of that hall."

Leaving the doorman behind, they walked down the hall to the elevator. Their shoes made no noise on the thick red carpeting that covered the floor. A marble bench was discreetly bolted to the floor near the elevator, and the walls surrounding it were mirrored. Ransom caught a glimpse of his face as they waited and was shocked to realize that his jaw was so firmly set and his eyes so determined that he looked as if he'd been carved in stone.

He closed his eyes and said to himself, "I have to keep my perspective."

With that, the elevator doors opened.

They rode up in silence. Gerald rarely tried to second-guess what his partner was thinking and was even less inclined to do so now. Familiar as he was with Ransom's moods and eccentricities, he had sensed something during the interview with Angela Stephens that was completely unexpected. Gerald wasn't sure he wanted to know what it was. One thing he was aware of was the heightened determination in his partner's manner—if it were possible for it to be heightened.

Number 1301 was the corner apartment at the south end of the hallway. They approached it silently, and just as Ransom raised his hand to knock, the door swung open.

"She's dead," said the bleary-eyed man without preamble.

Frank Stephens would ordinarily have been thought handsome by anyone's standards. He had very dark brown hair, olive skin, and pale green eyes that no painter could have done justice to. It gave the impression that he had been color-coordinated at birth. Although in his mid-forties, the white hairs at his temples could be counted on one hand. He wore a very expensive gray Italian suit that, despite the early hour, looked as if it had been sweated in all day. Around his neck was a gray tie with thin, widely spaced diagonal red stripes. The top button of his shirt was open, and the tie was askew. Ransom involuntarily glanced down at Stephen's hands, which were well manicured, tremulous, and large.

Flipping out his badge, he said, "I'm Detective Ransom, this is Detective White."

"She's dead!" The words seemed to spring out of him involuntarily.

Shock, thought Ransom.

"Where is she?"

Stephens turned and headed wordlessly into the apartment. The detectives followed him down an unlit hallway whose floor was so highly polished it glowed in the dark. Ransom made a mental note that most surely there were one or more people employed to clean this place, and he would need to talk to them.

They went through an archway into the perfectly appointed living room of the duplex apartment. The Early American furniture may not have been new, but was close enough, and the center of the floor was covered by a spotless, deep-pile white rug. Two walls of windows met at the southeast corner of the room, offering a view of the lake that gave the feeling of being surrounded by water. The dining room was visible through a huge archway cut in the west wall. Directly above this archway was a balcony that looked down into the living room from the second floor. It explained why the room appeared to be so enormous: The living room stretched upward, the combined height of the first and second floors.

Below the balcony, partly hidden from view by one of a pair of matching couches, was the body of Angela Stephens. She wore an ivory-colored nightdress. Her left leg was straight, and the other bent at the knee and twisted to the right at an angle that no conscious—or living—human could bear. Her eyes stared up at the ceiling. Her hair fanned out around her head like a golden halo, looking almost as if it had been arranged for a picture. But the picture was marred by a small pool of blood extending to the right from beneath her head.

Ransom glanced up at the balcony as Gerald bent down to feel Angela's pulse, already knowing what he would find.

"She's dead all right." He stood and turned to Ransom to add quietly, "Looks as if...at some point...she went over the railing up there. But look at her neck."

Ransom didn't need to look. He had already noticed the bruises.

"Call the crime lab."

Gerald looked at Frank Stephens, whose glazed eyes hadn't left his wife since they'd entered the room.

"Mind if I use your phone?"

He didn't respond. Gerald went off in search of a phone.

The room took on a funereal silence. Ransom and Stephens stood together like two mourners who had come to view the remains of someone they'd known from completely different points of reference, strangers to each other.

Ransom closed his eyes and silently mourned the loss of a thing of beauty from a world that needed all the beauty it could get. He wondered, not for the first time, if perhaps it was actually better for beauty to be suddenly snatched away than it was for it to slowly wither and die. Sudden death would at least save the Angelas of this world from the ravages of time.

He opened his eyes and saw once again the crumpled corpse with its painfully splayed legs. No, he thought, no one is elegant in death. This would be his memory of her. He made a mental note to have his head examined.

Frank Stephens stood over his wife, his moist eyes wide and terror stricken. He was mumbling.

"You *are* Mr. Stephens, aren't you?" said Ransom quietly. Stephens didn't move or reply.

"What happened here?"

"She's dead," he mumbled, still staring at the body. "I don't know...she's dead."

Ransom's face hardened as he searched Stephens's eyes. In an ordinary domestic crime, the husband would be the prime suspect. But an ordinary crime does not have fortune-tellers pointing the finger at the guilty party before it occurs. No, thought Ransom, I cannot...I cannot act on what a fortune-teller has said. He tried to clear his mind of its racing thoughts and decide on a way to get the husband to speak. After a moment, he said gently:

"You found her."

Stephens jerked his head up as if startled, and he seemed almost relieved.

"Yes, I found her," he said, his voice seeming to come from the bottom of a pit. Tears welled up in his eyes. "I came home...she was...there."

"You came home?"

"About half an hour, forty minutes ago."

"From where?"

"The Hyatt."

"Have you been out of town?"

"The Hyatt downtown."

Ransom's eyes narrowed. He knew what was coming, and his heart sank at the thought that the prediction had been right. It couldn't be this simple.

"Why did you stay at a hotel last night?"

Tears streamed down the husband's face. Hot, flowing tears that seemed out of place from this businessman.

"We quarreled."

"You had a fight?"

"We quarreled," Stephens said through his tears. "She's been so...odd this past week. She's been...she's been even more odd."

This sparked Ransom's interest. "Even more odd than what?"

Stephens wandered aimlessly into the living room. "This past year she's grown away from me...she's become distant."

"But more so this week?"

Stephens didn't respond.

"What brought about this argument?"

"It's been worse this week. Every time she looked at me, her eyes glazed over. If I didn't know better, I'd have thought...but last night, I confronted her about it. I was tired. I have a lot of responsibilities. I'm under a lot of pressure. I was tired of the way she was acting."

"Did she tell you what was wrong?"

Stephens shot him a rueful glance. "No. Well, yes."

"Which is it?" said Ransom sharply, trying to control his frustration.

"She said...oh, God, I know how this looks...I know how it will sound...it didn't make any sense..." He took a deep breath and shuddered as if trying to regain control. "She said she was afraid of me." Then he added quickly, "But it didn't make any sense! I've never given her any reason to be afraid of me. But...I could see it in her eyes...she was really terrified! I was so angry and confused, I stormed out of here and checked into the Hyatt."

"What time was that?"

"I don't know. About eleven, I think."

"And this morning?"

Stephens closed his eyes. Tears continued in a steady stream from under his lids. "I came home, just a little while ago. I didn't bring a change of clothes with me last night. I didn't bring anything. I was just going to change and go to work. Then I found..." His knees seemed to buckle. He wobbled and then sank to his knees on the floor by the couch.

Gerald appeared in the archway to the dining room. Ransom went over to him.

"The techs are on their way."

Ransom stared at the lifeless body that lay at his feet. Then his eye caught something that had been left lying on an occasional table to the right of the archway, the only other occupant of which was a pale green Princess phone. He picked it up and unfolded it. It was an advertising flier of the type commonly pushed under apartment doors, though the paper was of a heavier, more expensive stock. It was tinted blue and printed in letters large enough to be impressive but not so large as to be garish. It advertised Melina, a reader-adviser who could "accurately read your past and present, and predict your future through the amazing power of the tarot.''

Ransom looked back down at the face of the dead woman.

"Do you notice anything peculiar about her?" he said.

"Peculiar?"

"Look at her."

Gerald did so. He searched her lifeless form with his eyes, knowing that his partner must have seen something of note. Whatever it was, it escaped Gerald.

"I don't see anything out of the ordinary."

"Look at her face. There's something very peculiar about it, given the unusual nature of her visit to my office."

"What's that?"

"She looks surprised."

FOUR

The Investigation Begins

"SOMETHING IS very wrong here," said Ransom, slipping the flier into the inner pocket of his jacket.

Gerald continued to study Angela's face and finally realized that Ransom was right. If it were possible, the dead woman *did* look surprised. Stephens continued to weep quietly, his face buried in his hands.

Gerald kept his voice low as he spoke to his partner. "You know a face can screw up in all sorts of ways when a person's dying, especially in pain. You don't think it's just that?"

"Hmmm. Perhaps. Perhaps it's just like hearing of the death of someone who's been terminally ill: No matter how much you expect it, it always comes as a shock."

They were silent for a moment.

"Stay here and watch our friend. I'm going to do the upstairs, downstairs bit."

Ransom went through the archway into the dining room, which was occupied primarily by a long mahogany dining table and a matching sideboard. To the left was another archway leading into a hall that stretched back through the entire length of the apartment into the kitchen.

Immediately inside the hallway was a tan-carpeted spiral staircase, which he mounted two steps at a time. He passed through a doorway at the top of the stairs and found himself on the balcony he'd seen from below. He looked down into the cavernous living room where Gerald stood silently gazing out at the lake, while Stephens sat crumpled on the couch, at sea in his opulent surroundings.

"'It was the best of times, it was the worst of times'," Ransom muttered to himself.

As Ransom watched, Stephens's hands tightened on his knees, his knuckles showing white. In Dickensian terms, thought Ransom, Stephens was the picture of the "ruined" man. Though of necessity distracted, Ransom couldn't help but marvel at how entirely appropriate Victorian terms still seemed to be. For a moment, he longed wistfully for the day when he might retire to his bathtub with Mr. Dickens forever (and of course, in his present state of mind, he felt that day to be not very far off).

Directly beneath Ransom lay the body of the dead woman. To the casual observer, the scene was reminiscent of a decidedly Scandinavian Don José overlooking the body of an incongruously fair Carmen; or perhaps somewhat more accurately, an inverted balcony scene with a dead Juliet. He pushed himself away from the railing.

The balcony fronted a wide hallway with doors on either side, leading to bedrooms. Ransom opened each door in turn and gave the rooms a cursory glance. At the end of the hall was the master bedroom, its door open wide. The room was feminine in its appointments, bearing the imprint of Angela's tastes, which, thought Ransom with disappointment, ran rather predictably to satins and creams. The only evidence of Frank Stephens's presence was a pair of men's dress slacks draped carefully over the back of a chair.

Ransom moved slowly and soundlessly across the white shag carpet to the closets that lined the west wall. He slid open the door, revealing a wide variety of very expensive women's clothes. Hat boxes were piled high on the shelves above. He slid the door closed and opened the next. In it were several men's business suits in varying shades of blue and gray, and one black suit, which, Ransom thought sardonically, would soon be put to use.

So, he thought, they did share the room. The basic femininity of the decor could probably be attributed to the husband desiring nothing more than the comfort of his wife.

As he slid the door closed, he tried to disregard the pang he felt.

Ransom moved to the white vanity. Beside a pearl-handled comb and brush stood a double frame. He picked it up gingerly, assuring himself with a rueful smile that unlike the frame on his own desk, this one was certainly solid silver. The right picture was of the husband, and Ransom was startled to realize that this picture served as evidence that the man downstairs was far more affected by the death than even Ransom had thought. The man in the picture was indeed handsome and in control, though his smile gave no indication of the arrogance that so often accompanies self-assurance.

The left side of the frame contained the face that had haunted him for the past twenty-four hours. (Had it even been that long?) Her eyes smiled out at him from beneath a different wide-brimmed hat from the one she'd worn when they'd met. She looked, in fact, much as she had the day before. Her eyes shimmered at him, evidence of a much happier time than she'd known recently. They seemed to twinkle with amusement and knowledge. They seemed to be challenging him to find her murderer.

If she hadn't been sure who her murderer was before, thought Ransom, she was now.

RANSOM FOUND the doorman cooling his heels, so to speak, just inside the glass front doors.

"Looks like it's gonna be another hot one. I'm like to melt," he said with a toothy grin as the detective approached. "You gonna take him away?"

"Who?"

"The Stephens man. He's the one that did it, in't he?"

"That's what I hear," Ransom sighed. "What's your name?"

"Walter, sir. Walter Lyman."

"Tell me, Walter, when did your shift begin?"

"Just at seven o'clock. Some damn way to start the day,

in't? Him screaming the wife been killed. I never worked in a building where there's been murder goin' on.''

"Did you see Mr. Stephens come home this morning?''

"Yes, I did! Just right on about seven-thirty.''

"You looked at the time?''

"Yeah—good thing I did, too, in't? I looked at my watch because here I was opening the door to let him in, and it seemed like about the time I oughta be opening the door to let him out! So I marked the time—you bet I did. Damn good thing, as it turned out.''

Ransom smiled to himself. Walter was so obviously pleased with having something to do with the event that Ransom couldn't quell the desire to throw a little scare into him.

"Hmmm. One would think you knew something was going to happen.''

Walter's eyes widened, the large whites covered with a bright red web of blood vessels, making them look like a rather repulsive geological map.

"No, sir! It was just different—to see Stephens—Mr. Stephens—coming in when he did. That's why I marked it!''

Ransom stifled a laugh with some difficulty.

"I'm sure that's it. Is there any way that the residents can get in or out of the building without you seeing them?''

"Yes, sir!'' said Walter, with a touch of pride that Ransom found mystifying. "I'm responsible for opening the front door, and that's all! They don't have some fancy monitor or surveillance cameras hanging up around here. Never had need for it. Till now.''

"How else can people get out?''

"They can drive right out the back. See, everybody lives here got a security key that opens all the common doors. They can use it to open the garage door that opens on the alley out back. And there's a back stairway going down to the back door of the building. Key opens that, too. I only see 'em if they come out the front.''

"Hmmm,'' said Ransom thoughtfully. So even if Stephens had left as he said he had, it would have been easy enough to come in the back way, climb the stairs—it would be too risky to use the elevator, but he wouldn't have been likely to run into the type of people who live in this building on the stairs—and then simply return the front way later, looking as if he'd been gone all night. Ransom frowned.

The more Ransom thought about it, the less he liked it. It was possible that Stephens had checked into the Hyatt, returned in the middle of the night, strangled his wife, then gone back to the hotel; but was it likely? What bothered Ransom the most was the argument. Why on earth would Stephens admit to the argument, knowing the light in which it would put him if he were the killer? Perhaps it was the fact that Stephens had spent the night at the Hyatt, an action that would be very hard to explain were there not something wrong between the man and his wife. Perhaps he had felt he had no choice but to admit to the argument, then play the bereaved husband who had lost his wife while they were on bad terms. The whole scenario struck Ransom as being a trifle too clever.

"You okay, sir?"

"What? Oh, yes, I'm fine," said Ransom to the perplexed doorman. "Who was on the door last night?"

"That was Herbert. Herbert Stickney. He's on nights."

"You have his number?"

Walter pulled a small spiral notebook out of his pocket and scribbled the number down with a blunt pencil. "Sure. I got to keep some paper handy because these people're always asking me to get their sink fixed or their toilet unstopped, and I got to call the management office. They're supposed to call the office theyselves, but you know rich people."

He tore the sheet out of his little notebook and handed it to Ransom, pocketing the pencil.

"Thanks. Two men will be coming from the crime lab. Send them right up."

"Yes, sir!"

Ransom started back for the elevator, then stopped suddenly and looked back to the doorman.

"Walter...did you like the Stephenses?"

Walter beamed his toothy grin at the detective.

"Same as all the rest."

GERALD WHITE WAS generally a comfortable man, but as out of place in the Stephenses' meticulous living room as Frank Stephens would have been at a dog fight. When Ransom reentered the apartment, Gerald was seated on the edge of a velvet-cushioned chair with clearly polished mahogany legs. He stood when Ransom entered and joined him in the entrance hallway. Stephens was now seated on a couch by the windows, staring out at the lake like a child who was never allowed to run and play.

"I've had a little look around while you were gone—he didn't look like he was in any condition to go anywhere."

"And?"

"And I didn't see any signs of forced entry. The doors aren't scratched at all."

"It doesn't surprise me."

"Well, this is a security building. So that makes it look pretty bad for him, doesn't it?"

Ransom smiled sardonically. "It isn't a very secure security building. There're a couple of ways you can get in and out quite easily with only a so-so chance of being seen."

"If you have a key."

"All right. But look at this place. They must have at least one maid and she'd most likely have a set of keys. And there may be others."

Gerald regarded Ransom for a moment. "Jer, I know you don't want to give any credit to those predictions she told us about, but it does seem logical that he killed her."

"Logical...' said Ransom slowly, turning the word over in his mind. "It does seem logical, doesn't it?"

Gerald sighed. He had long since become accustomed to

Ransom's habit of ruminating his way into obscurity, but being used to it didn't make it less irritating.

"No, it isn't logical," said Ransom finally. "There's something wrong here."

"You mean because of the prediction?"

"No. I mean there's something wrong *here,* and I can't quite put my finger on what it is. It's like what teachers used to do in school, remember? Hold up a drawing and say, 'Now, what's wrong with this picture?' and you had to figure out what it was. I feel like that now. There's something wrong with this whole setup."

Gerald watched Ransom with mounting concern. Over the past year he had learned to trust Ransom's unerring intuitiveness, but intuition was one thing, turning something simple into something complicated was another. Gerald knew that to Ransom, the prediction of murder complicated the case. But to Gerald, whose belief system allowed the possibility of coincidence, just because a fortune-teller said it would happen didn't mean it wasn't so. For the first time since their pairing, he doubted his partner.

Gerald leaned closer to Ransom and said quietly, "I don't know what you're thinking, but you *know* we've got to take him in, don't you?"

Ransom looked over his shoulder and sighed.

"Yes."

RANSOM HAD BECOME aware of the now familiar sense of irritation sometime around midafternoon. He wanted a cigar. But even Gerald wouldn't put up with his smoking in the small interrogation room.

But more importantly, at Emily's prompting, Ransom had been trying to give up smoking his beloved plastic-tipped cigars. Emily couldn't abide smoking of any kind and had made it her personal crusade to get him to stop, reasoning that a man in his late thirties should be expected to live longer than a woman in her late seventies (though Ransom, in his secret thoughts, found this reasoning dubious). Unfortunately, as for so many others, when he had tried to stop it had gotten worse: He had graduated to Coronellas, which were larger than his usual brand and untipped. He now started each day vowing not to smoke, but at the first sign of tension, his desire returned full force. And that desire manifested itself as irritability, which he would relieve as soon as possible.

The cause of his present tension was obvious. After the evidence technicians had arrived at the Stephenses' apartment, the detectives had brought Stephens back to area headquarters for further questioning, and all three of them were finding the proceedings rather heavy going.

Frank Stephens now sat before them on a hard wooden chair, his arms resting on the lone table, sticky with a thick coat of varnish, that served as the only flat surface in the interrogation room. His hands were cupped around a foam cup of tepid coffee. He bore the look of a man whose initial shock had given way to the realization of being in a nightmare from which he had no hope of waking.

The two detectives and their suspect had remained silent for some time.

"You didn't know her," said Stephens, suddenly breaking the silence.

Ransom was startled and his cheeks reddened. He resisted the impulse to reply, "I knew her better than you think," and repeated to himself, "You didn't know her, you didn't know her..."

"Angela's name really fit her. Angela. Angel. She was an angel."

Stephens's voice had taken on the tone of melancholy reminiscence.

"I've known her for more than twenty years," he said. "We met in college. We were both going for our MBAs at Northwestern. I was...on the road to success. Following in my father's footsteps. I mean...well, what I mean to say is I thought of little else other than my career. I didn't want anything else...any distractions. And then I met Angela...in an economics class...and she proved to be the biggest distraction of all. I know..." He faltered and looked embarrassed. He made a move as if to take a sip of coffee from the cup he clutched so tightly, then changed his mind. "I found out what they mean when they say that a woman 'turned your head.' Angela turned mine. And she gave me something to work for, other than myself. She gave me a reason to succeed other than just wanting success...if you can understand that."

Ransom was silent for a moment, then said:

"Did you both get them?"

"What?"

"Your MBAs."

"Of course. My wife...was...a career woman before it became fashionable." He took a sip of the coffee, holding the cup in both hands. His mouth twitched into an embarrassed smile. "Actually, my wife was a career woman before it became a necessity."

"For her?"

Stephens shook his head slowly. "For anyone."

"And how long had you been married?"

"It will be...it would have been fifteen years this June. The twenty-seventh."

"So you knew her..."

"I knew her for about five years before we got married."

"Long courtship."

"Oh, it wasn't a courtship," said Stephens, warming somewhat to the subject. "We knew we wanted to get married from the start. Our courtship...our courtship was interrupted by the death of her parents. They were killed in a head-on collision with a drunk driver who was on the wrong side of the road. It hit her pretty hard."

"I can understand that," said Ransom softly, "but five years is a long time."

"She wasn't in mourning or anything like that all that time. It was her sister."

Gerald quietly flipped the sheet of his notebook over and continued scratching his pencil against the new page.

"Her sister?" Ransom prompted.

"Eva," Stephens replied.

Ransom wasn't sure, but he could have sworn that Stephen's voice hardened when he spoke her name.

"Eva is five years younger than Angela, and was in her midteens when they lost their parents. From what Angela told me, Eva was already in the throes of teenage rebellion. Without their parents, she went wild, and the wildness was directed at Angela. Angela felt...she felt..." He faltered again, and his eyes became clouded with tears.

Ransom looked on Stephens with something resembling compassion and finished his statement for him.

"Your wife felt responsible for her sister, and decided to take care of her."

Stephens nodded through his tears. "She would, you know, she was like that." His right hand trembled, and he formed it into a fist. "She was the kindest person I've ever known."

I'll just bet she was, thought Ransom.

"Eva turned out to be more than Angela could handle. She got in trouble with the police. Petty crime type of things...and things like joyriding. But Angela kept trying."

"Taking care of this girl must have been a full-time job. How did your wife manage?"

There was a brief pause during which the change in Stephens's expression was barely perceptible, but unmistakable. He was clearly aware he was entering dangerous waters.

"There was no problem—there was no monetary problem. Angela's parents left all of their fortune to her—except for an amount to be given to Eva when she turned twenty-one, on the stipulation, of course, that she take care of Eva until then."

"So your wife's decision to take care of her sister wasn't entirely altruistic."

"She was a bright woman. She didn't need the money," said Stephens sharply.

"Hmmm."

"Their parents knew Angela well enough to know that

she would take care of Eva. They were right. Until she was twenty-one.''

''And then what happened?''

''Exactly what you'd expect.''

This time the tone was unmistakable.

''She took the money and ran. I think it was somewhere around fifty thousand dollars—I don't really know. Angela never went into detail about it, and I didn't ask. I think she was ashamed. I think she felt that Eva was the one failure of her life.''

He stared at his coffee cup.

''I don't think the money lasted a year,'' he added.

Ransom leaned back in his chair, which was on a par with the suspect's for discomfort. He extended the index and middle fingers of his right hand and tapped them absently against the table, as if he held an invisible cigar.

''This fortune that your wife received from her parents, was it considerable?''

Stephens shifted uncomfortably in his seat.

''Her father was what they called a self-made man back when that meant something. He built up a chain of stationery stores—Brinkley's. He made quite a bit of money which, along with the stores, was left to Angela. She sold the stores a couple of years after...after the shock of their deaths had worn off.''

''So it meant she was independently wealthy.''

''It meant she could spend her time managing her own money instead of managing other people's.''

''Hmmm,'' said Ransom thoughtfully. Then, after a pause, added, ''The sister will have to be informed. Do you know where she is?''

''Oh, yes. She's back. In Chicago,'' said Stephens wryly. ''Forgiven but not forgotten.''

Ransom searched Stephens's face. The chair squeaked beneath him.

''Mr. Stephens, now that your wife has died, who will get her independent means?''

Frank Stephens's head shot up, and for the first time he

looked as if he'd regained his senses. He stood up so abruptly his chair was knocked back against the wall, and slammed his fist down on the table with such force that Gerald dropped the pencil with which he'd been scratching his notes.

"I did *not* kill my wife!" he shouted.

"I didn't say you did."

"You must know"—his voice took on a pleading tone—"you must remember that I'm one of the vice-presidents of the Security National Bank. I make...my salary is fairly high. I have all the money I need."

"Need, need..." said Ransom absently, tapping his fingers against the side of the table. "Need is such a funny thing."

"What?" said Stephens, confused by this unexpected response.

Gerald surreptitiously retrieved his pencil and resumed his notes.

"Is it possible there is another reason you might have wanted to kill your wife?"

Stephens's face drained; he looked the very definition of dumbfounded as he deflated back into his chair. Ransom was immensely pleased with this reaction. He decided to press a step further.

"*Did* you have a reason to kill your wife?"

Stephens's eyes remained blank, but the left corner of his mouth twitched once involuntarily. When he spoke, his voice was hollow and distant as if it called out from deep inside his nightmare:

"No."

"Mr. Stephens, back at your apartment you said that you and your wife had 'grown apart' over the past year. What caused this estrangement?"

"Are you charging me?" said Stephens blankly.

"Not yet. Why did the two of you grow apart?"

"We didn't."

"I understood you to say..."

"I was being—politic. I guess I've been with the bank

too long. The truth is, Angela grew away from me. I mean, she'd become distant.''

"The cause?''

He hesitated. "Partly because of Eva. When Eva came back, she gave us the old sob story about having changed, being a different person. She said she met a man she's serious about—at least, that's what she says. Angela believed she'd changed: I didn't. Where people were concerned my wife was inclined to think—or hope for—the best, you know what I mean?''

"An admirable quality that often leads to disappointment.''

"Yeah.''

"A quality I admire,'' Ransom added sharply.

Gerald raised an eyebrow.

After a pause, Ransom continued. "Many couples disagree about their in-laws: it sometimes leads to estrangement, rarely to murder.''

Stephens shifted uncomfortably in his chair and wrapped his hands around his coffee cup once more.

"It's really very hard to explain. When do you first realize that someone has changed?''

"I'm not interested in philosophy, Mr. Stephens, I'm interested in the truth. Was there a change in her attitude toward you?''

"No. Only secondarily. There was a change within herself,'' he said crisply, then went on defensively. "I wasn't trying to be philosophical, I was trying to explain.'' His eyes became hazy. "You realize that someone is different, and then in retrospect you can see the signs were there. But it's hard to put your finger on when the change began. It's hard to see change when you live with someone day after day. It's much easier to notice change when you've been away.''

"Like Eva?''

"Oh, yes, Eva noticed.''

"How did your wife change?''

"I...I don't know.''

"You said she'd grown distant."

"Distant, but never unpleasant—as if something had come between us. Not something that I'd done or failed to do or anything like that, but something."

"Did you ever confront her about it?"

Stephens lowered his eyes to the floor. "No," he said almost inaudibly.

"And how long ago—in retrospect—do you think this change began?"

He paused for so long that Ransom thought he wasn't going to answer. But he said suddenly, "About a year, I guess. It's been going on about a year now. But lately she's been more and more odd."

"She didn't..." Ransom began warmly, then bit his tongue. He'd almost said, "She didn't seem odd to me," but didn't want Stephens to know they had met.

"How did she seem odd?

"My wife has always had a...passing interest in the occult."

"Passing?" said Ransom, furrowing his brow. This was not correspondent with the intense belief she had exhibited to him.

"She wasn't crazy. No black masses or secret societies or anything like that, but she enjoyed fortune-tellers, tarot card readers, that sort of thing. For fun. Just for fun."

Stephens's right hand swept up and brushed the hair back from his eyes, a gesture reminiscent of the way Angela had absently brushed the brim of her hat the day before. To Ransom it bespoke a deeper relationship between husband and wife than he liked to imagine.

"She would see a sign that said, 'Your cards read for five dollars' and she'd head right in. Never taking it seriously." His face clouded over. "But, in a way, I think she did sort of believe in it. The way you do when you read your horoscope in the paper. You believe it if it's something good, and laugh it off if it's something bad."

"Unless it comes true," said Ransom quietly.

"It was her only flaw. I know it doesn't seem very big—

and it didn't used to be. But lately, she seemed to believe in it more.''

"How lately?'' asked Ransom quickly.

"Oh...the past month or so, I guess.''

Ransom considered Stephens for a moment in silence. Some of the suspect's color had returned, presumably from concentrating on his wife alive instead of dead. The silence seemed to bring Stephens back to the present situation, and his face slowly fell.

Ransom reached into his pocket and pulled out the flier. "Have you ever seen this before?''

Stephens glanced quickly at the advertisement.

"No. But it's just the type of person she'd go to.''

"How odd,'' said Ransom, fingering the edge of the blue paper.

"What?''

"I found this on the table by your wife's body.''

Stephens stared at him blankly, then said, "I've never seen it before.''

RANSOM SAT WEARILY behind his desk, the usual creak of the chair providing added annoyance, and pulled a cigar out of his upper left-hand drawer. He lit it with a guilty glance at the picture on his desk. In his mind's eye he could see Emily waggling a wrinkled finger at him and clucking her tongue. He smiled as he took a long, satisfying drag and leaned back in his chair, releasing the smoke into the air.

During the breaks in the interrogation, the detectives had tried to reach the dead woman's sister, a process made more difficult, since Stephens didn't know for whom she worked. Ransom asked Detective Robinson to try and track her down.

The interrogation had continued without change. Stephens repeated his story several times with mounting tension and an increasingly uncomfortable awareness of how thin it sounded. But he didn't waver. Ransom adjourned the proceedings when he found that their interview had reached the point of diminishing returns.

"Well, what do you make of that?" said Ransom, his smile broadening as he savored the smoke.

"If he's lying, at least he's consistent."

"Hmmm."

"He doesn't change his story."

"Perhaps it's the only one he knows."

"I suppose that would make it easier to remember," said Gerald sardonically. "Word for word, over and over."

Ransom rolled the cigar between his fingers and thumb. "You really should try a Coronella. They're very relaxing."

"Huh?"

"I think it's the action of the smoke dissipating into the air. It gives you the feeling of your troubles—pardon the pun—going up in smoke."

Gerald eyed his partner for a moment. Ransom looked pleased with himself in a way that made Gerald want to kick him repeatedly. He did, however, take it as a good sign: For Ransom, smugness (for lack of a kinder term) was normal. It signaled a welcome return to normalcy after the disquieting differences of the past twenty-four hours.

"You think you know something, don't you?"

"Oh, it's far too early to say I *know* anything," said Ransom coyly, tapping the ash off the end of his cigar.

Gerald threw himself onto the couch that covered the left wall of his partner's office. "All right, what is it?"

Ransom continued to roll the cigar between his fingers.

"He repeats his story without variation—and I will grant you, it's a very thin story."

"He fights with his wife, goes away, comes back, and finds her dead. How very inconvenient for him."

"Gerald, you're beginning to sound like me!"

"You don't have to insult me," said Gerald with a smile. "You know his story is stupid."

"Ah, yes," Ransom smiled, "but idiocy is so often the truth."

"Ransom, I really hate it when you get in this mood. If you're onto something, let's have it!"

"Oh, I'm not onto anything in particular."

"But you don't think he killed his wife."

"No."

"Why not?"

"Because I think he's telling the truth." He paused. "Don't you?"

With extreme ill grace, Gerald replied, "Yes, goddammit, I do."

"Ah!" said Ransom, with a whimsically raised eyebrow.

"With reservations," Gerald added testily. "One thing he said bothers me."

"Only one?"

"When you pressed him on motive he said he didn't have a reason to kill his wife."

"Perhaps he's telling the truth."

"Oh, Ransom, everybody has a reason for wanting to kill their wives."

Ransom's smile grew wider. "Do you mean to tell me you've thought of killing Sherry?"

"Once or twice, but the feeling passes quickly." Now it was Gerald's turn to smile. "And of course, I know with you on my trail I'd never get away with it."

Ransom laughed for the first time since meeting Angela Stephens. The sound relieved the tension in the room.

"All right," Gerald continued, "I'll give you that his wife said he had no reason to kill her—"

"Actually, she said he 'knew of no reason.'"

"Right! So, like you said yesterday, maybe there actually was something he might kill her for if he knew about it. What's to say he didn't find out about it and do it?"

"You seem to want him to be guilty."

"I'm just trying to provide balance."

There was an uncomfortable pause.

"Are you sure," Gerald continued carefully, "that you're not being prejudiced?"

Ransom's eyes narrowed. "What do you mean?"

"The predictions. Angela Stephens's fortune."

"You don't mean to tell me you believe in fortune-telling?"

"I didn't say that!"

"You don't mean to tell me," continued Ransom, with exaggerated incredulity, "that you think he's guilty because a fortune-teller said so?"

"He might be guilty," said Gerald with exasperation. "He's the obvious suspect. And, I might add, the only suspect at the moment. You seem to think he's innocent *because* of the predictions."

Ransom was brought up short by this and fell into thoughtful contemplation of the charge. It was true that the fortune-telling aspect of it did bother him, but not for the reason Gerald thought. Ransom didn't believe in fortune-telling, and the sincerity of Angela's belief in it was incongruous. Perhaps he, like Angela's husband, considered her belief to be a flaw in an otherwise flawless woman. But giving his partner's accusation serious consideration, Ransom didn't feel that his disbelief in fortune-telling was keeping him from accepting the obvious conclusion in the case. He felt his doubts ran much deeper than that.

"No," he said finally, "I honestly don't believe that's the reason."

This was enough for Gerald, at least for the moment. He knew his partner well enough to know he was painfully honest with himself under normal circumstances. He ignored the voice at the back of his mind that told him these were not normal circumstances.

"Then what is it?" he asked.

Ransom rose from his desk and looked out the window, taking another leisurely puff of his cigar.

"I have the same problem with Mr. Stephens as I did with his wife. There is no concrete evidence for believing him—God knows, all fingers point in his direction—but I believe him...just as there was no concrete evidence to believe Mrs. Stephens would be killed, but it happened."

"But his story is stupid."

Ransom glanced at Gerald. "So was hers. His story is no more implausible than many true stories. It's so confoundedly stupid that I'm inclined to believe it."

"The business about staying in the hotel?"

"Well, that's just it. If he was setting it up as an alibi, it was a particularly weak one to choose. I mean, he's an intelligent man. He must know that it would be easy enough to check on this alibi. And you know as well as I do that you can wander in and out of any of these hotels without much fear of being noticed."

"So if it was premeditated," said Gerald, helping Ransom to think aloud, "it was a weak alibi—and given that the man is vice-president of a bank, you'd think he'd come up with something better."

"And yet..." said Ransom, taking up the thread, "he admitted that they'd argued. Another rather unintelligent thing to do while standing over the dead body of your wife. Now of course, he could be uncommonly clever and setting himself up as 'too guilty to be true,' all the time being up front about the argument and all, reasoning that it would look too much like a setup—and that we'd be inclined to look elsewhere for a suspect."

"He gives us humble police a lot of credit," said Gerald with a smile. "But you can't get away from it: It would have been easy as anything for him to come home in the middle of the night and kill her, then go back to the hotel. Then he has the opportunity of returning in the morning— to be *seen* coming into the building, and make a big, dramatic show of finding the body."

"With a night alone in a hotel room as an alibi? No, no, no, it just doesn't work." He tapped his cigar, and a large ash fell onto the windowsill. "The only way his story works is if it's true."

"But, Jer, you've got to look at the alternative. I mean, if Stephens didn't kill his wife, then you have to accept that they quarreled, he stormed out of the house at about eleven o'clock at night, and someone else happened along out of the blue and seized the opportunity to strangle her!"

Ransom swiveled around in his chair and gazed out the window reflectively. "Sounds beyond the realm of possibility," he said with a gleam in his eye.

"Yes, it does," said Gerald hesitantly, searching his partner's face.

"I wonder..." Ransom's voice trailed off, and a short silence ensued, which Gerald finally broke. "So what are we going to do with Stephens?"

Ransom thought for a moment. The cigar had burned down to a stub, which he tossed into the garbage can by his desk.

"You know, there is one *tangible* thing that makes me inclined to believe him."

"What's that?"

"His manner when we met him. What would you put that down to?"

"Shock."

"Exactly. Shock."

"But shock at having discovered the body or shock at having killed her?"

"Ah, there's the rub," said Ransom thoughtfully.

"Miss Emily would be proud of you."

Ransom smiled at this. Having a great respect for the woman and the part she had played in the Pennington Players case, Gerald always referred to her as "Miss Emily."

"What does that leave us with?"

"The evidence technicians. Maybe they'll be able to find something. In the meantime we can talk to the neighbors and see if anyone heard the argument or anything else last night. We'll hold Stephens a little while longer while we do it. Has Robinson found the sister yet?"

"Nope."

"Hmmm. We'll want to talk to her."

Gerald was aware of the frustration in Ransom's manner. "What are you thinking?"

Ransom sighed. "I'd like another cigar."

THEY KNOCKED on the door and waited. Walter, the doorman, had prepared them for the wait by telling them that

1302 (like many doormen, he was in the habit of referring to the residents by apartment number instead of name) used a walker and it would take her some time to get to the door. Walter had also prepared 1302, at Ransom's instruction, for the detective's arrival by calling up to tell her they were on their way.

Before leaving his office, Ransom had called Herbert Stickney, the third-shift doorman, who said he had seen Stephens leave the building at about eleven and had not seen him return. This at least verified part of Stephens's story. They were left with the annoying fact that a resident could easily come and go through the garage or back door without being seen. Further questions to the sleepy night doorman had revealed that nobody except residents had gone into the building last night, at least through the front door. Ransom sighed when he hung up the phone, realizing that the absence of strangers again pointed the finger of guilt at the husband. Who else but a resident could have gone in the back way? You needed a security key for every common door except the front, and there'd been no signs of a break-in anywhere.

On their return to the Lake Shore apartment building, the detectives questioned Walter about the Stephenses' neighbors. Ransom was always a little surprised by how much the average doorman knew about the comings and goings of the tenants and wondered if the tenants found it comforting or unnerving that someone always seemed to know where they were. Walter had explained that 1201, the apartment directly below the Stephenses', was vacant, and 1401 was on vacation in Cancun. That left little miss 1302, as Walter called her.

"She old. She never goes out" was the sum total of Walter's knowledge of her life.

They heard the approaching clink of the walker, assuming that the old woman had passed from carpeting to the hardwood floor of the entrance hallway.

"Who is it?" said a thin voice through the door.

"Detectives Ransom and White, Chicago Police Department."

"Oh!" said the voice, sounding surprised even though she'd been told they were on their way up.

The detectives heard what sounded like the walker being thrust up against the wall, and after a pause, the clank of the two dead-bolt locks. The door opened a crack, and a wide-open, gray eye stared at them through the space.

"May I see your identification, please?"

The detectives glanced at each other, then dutifully pulled out their badges and showed them to the woman. The wide eye stared at the badges as if they were some unidentifiable foreign matter, blinked once, and looked back at Ransom.

"Oh, well, then, I'd better have you in."

The eye retreated from the opening, and the door opened slowly. The woman struggled to extricate the walker from behind the door. Ransom pulled the door closed a little to help her, and the walker popped out of the recess. Startled, the woman almost went over backward, pulling the aluminum contraption down on top of her, but Ransom was quick enough to steady it and its owner.

"We'll go in here, gentlemen," said the old woman, only momentarily shaken and then starting down the hallway. The effect was not unlike that of an aged cat that could leap in fright one moment and fall asleep the next.

They followed her down the hallway like an excessively slow funeral procession. Ransom noticed that the old woman's knuckles were white from hanging on to her walker for dear life. Though in the hallway the apartment seemed to be much like the Stephenses', the living room couldn't have been more different. The room was filled to overflowing with large, heavy cushioned furniture that was old but too shabby to qualify as antique. The chairs and two sofas were mismatched and topped with cheap, white, lacelike doilies, all of which were turning brown around the edges. The wall-to-wall carpeting was brown and in bad need of a vacuuming, and Ransom realized with disgust that the walls, which he at first thought were tan, were actually white, but darkening through years of neglect.

The room smelled of age, but not the age of wisdom, experience, and love of life that Ransom had come to attribute to his friend Emily. This room had the musty odor of death and decay: of clinging tremulously to life before returning to dust. Ransom had the fleeting impression that this woman was slowly disintegrating and becoming one with her surroundings, her dust mingling with the dust of her environment until the two became one. It was the scattering of her ashes through a process of osmosis. He was almost afraid to breathe. He was suddenly seized with the desire to talk to Emily.

"I'm sorry I can't offer you anything. I didn't know you were coming. Of course, there's water if you don't mind getting it yourselves. The glasses are in the cupboard by the stove."

"No, thank you, Mrs. Percy," said Ransom, sure that he didn't want to see the kitchen.

She gave him a frightened glance, as if trying to figure out how he'd known her name. Then the explanation seemed to come to her and she relaxed.

"Please sit down," she said, struggling to lower her frail frame onto a sofa in the middle of the room.

Ransom sat directly opposite the sofa on a large chair covered with well-worn, mustard-colored corduroy slipcovers. Gerald tried to sit discreetly in a corner on a ladderback chair whose straw seat had several snapped strands. The loud crackling noise it made as he sat robbed him of his customary invisibility and made him wince.

Ransom studied Mrs. Percy as she finally pushed herself away from the walker and plopped onto the sofa. She was a picture of dishevelment. Her faded blue floral-print housedress was badly in need of ironing; her hair, which was gray but seemed to be yellowing with age like old parchment, was tied with a faded pink ribbon at the nape of her neck. Unfortunately, large bunches of her hair had come loose and shot away from her head like misdirected spurts from a faucet with a clogged filter. The withered skin of her face was interrupted by the bright red lipstick that she had sloppily smeared on her chapped lips. She looked like an excessively timid cat, nervous and frightened, but with an instinctive stealth and low cunning. The overall impression was decidedly unfavorable.

The old woman rested her tiny clawlike hands on the top rail of her walker. Her eyes shined. She licked her lips. Ransom felt uncomfortably like a mouse.

"I can't keep the place up like I used to when my husband was alive. Don't have the money," she said apologetically. "I'm just lucky he got it paid off before he decided to die."

"Paid off?"

"The mortgage."

"These are condominiums?"

She smiled with a craftiness that was unnerving. Once again, Ransom was reminded of a cat. "You didn't know that? You can't be too good a detective."

"I've been busy," said Ransom. The fact that these were condominiums did, however, explain to him Mrs. Percy's incongruously low-class existence in this high-class building. Presumably with the mortgage paid off, she could afford to exist in this building on her Social Security and perhaps her husband's pension. Exist and not much else.

"I suppose you know why we're here?"

The old woman's withered face clouded over. "It's about last night, isn't it?"

Ransom nodded. "Did you hear anything?"

"Would...would I have to go out?" Her nose wrinkled as if she were sniffing around something unfamiliar.

"I beg your pardon?"

"If I heard something...would I have to go out? There would be a trial. Would I have to go there?"

"We don't know exactly what will happen yet," said Ransom carefully.

"I haven't been out in a very long time. My friend Mrs. Miner—actually, she's not a friend, she's just a longtime acquaintance—her husband, when he was alive, was a friend of my husband's, so I guess she feels some sort of obligation even though we never much cared for each other, ourselves—she brings in my groceries. Everything else I can get through catalogs."

"I don't know that you'd have to go out," said Ransom gently, "but the truth is important, you know. A woman's been killed, and finding out the truth about her murder is our responsibility, and the responsibility of anyone with information."

He hoped this would have the desired effect of stirring a sense of responsibility in someone old enough to remember the meaning of the word. He was disconcerted to hear her reply.

"But *he* killed her, didn't he?"

"Who?"

"Her husband."

"Why do you say that?"

The crafty look returned. It was apparent that she was the type of woman who, despite her fear, couldn't help but pass on a piece of gossip.

"Did you hear them arguing?" Ransom prompted.

"Oh, yes! I heard them! They were arguing all right! I couldn't actually hear much of what they said, because this is an old building, you know, and the walls are thick." She looked disappointed. "But they argued, and the one thing I did hear her say, very clearly, was 'I'm afraid of you! I'm afraid!'"

She sat back, satisfied and searching Ransom for a sufficient reaction. Ransom half expected her to lick her lips.

"What time was this?"

The satisfaction was replaced by vagueness. "Time? Time…about…a little before eleven o'clock."

"What happened then?"

"When?" she asked, confused.

"After they argued."

"He slammed right out of there, didn't he?"

"He?"

"The husband."

"How did you know it was him? Did you look out the door?"

"Oh, no," she said, the idea obviously scaring her.

"Then how did you know it was him?"

"Well, *she's* dead, isn't she?"

Ransom glanced at Gerald out of the corner of his eye. Gerald coughed lightly into his hand and then continued to jot down notes.

"Did you hear anything else last night?"

"I hear lots of things," she said. "I don't sleep through the night anymore. Haven't for years. I wake up, and sometimes I get up and look out the window, or have a drink of water, but most of the time I just lie there and think, or listen. And I hear a lot of things: comings and goings, doors opening and closing…voices."

"And last night?"

"Last night?" the old lady repeated, the wrinkles on her forehead deepening like unevenly plowed rows in a parched field.

"After Mr. Stephens left," Ransom continued patiently, "did you hear anything else?"

"I heard him come back!" she said, baring her teeth in a cunning smile that Ransom found particularly revolting.

"I should ask you again, how did you know it was him?"

Her smile quickly waned, "Like I said before, I didn't look out the door. I couldn't…" Her voice trailed off and her eyes traveled to her walker. She ran her hand lightly over the top of it.

"It's not easy for me," she said vacantly.

"I understand. So you heard someone—possibly Mr. Stephens—come to the apartment."

"Yes. She came to the door and let him in."

"She let him in…" Ransom mused.

"He knocked on the door and she let him in. He must've forgot his keys."

"Do you know what time that was?"

"I have a clock right there on my nightstand. It was about eleven-thirty. I can't speak...heh-heh...I can't speak for the accuracy of my clock or my eyes at that hour of the night."

"Did you hear the person leave again?"

"I don't...I don't..." Mrs. Percy suddenly looked very confused. "I'm not sure." She thought for a minute and then smiled nervously at Ransom. "You see, I drift...I drift...in and out of sleep. It's hard to say...but I sometimes wake up."

"And did you?"

"What?"

"Wake up again last night?"

"Oh...I might have, but I didn't hear anything else. And I wasn't listening in on them. I didn't think anything was wrong. There was no reason to. It was really no different than any other night, really."

"You mean Mr. and Mrs. Stephens were accustomed to having these arguments."

"Oh, no, I don't mean that at all—I meant the comings and goings."

Ransom looked at her with sudden interest. "What do you mean?"

"What?"

"About the comings and goings—this was usual activity for the Stephenses?"

The old woman eyed him slyly. "I couldn't say exactly what they *do*, but they do come and go at odd hours."

"Such as?"

"Well, you see, sometimes he comes home in the middle of the day to see her—home from the bank, I mean—he's some sort of banker, you know. And sometimes—not any different from last night—he, or the two of them, leave and then come back not much later, and then leave again. I think it's very strange. When my husband was alive, when we went out, we stayed out for a while. But those people always seemed to be opening and closing doors."

"Yes…" said Ransom slowly, "…and that's what was going on last night?"

She nodded her wrinkled head eagerly. "Oh, yes, oh, yes."

"But you can't be sure of the time?"

"It was very late," she said defensively. "I'm sure…I'm sure he came back at eleven-thirty, but I drift…"

"So you didn't hear anything else after that? You didn't hear Mrs. Stephens at all?"

"I didn't hear anything more until this morning when I heard that Stephens man yelling 'She's dead, oh, God! Oh, oh, oh!'" She said this last with such an unpleasant note of mockery that Ransom couldn't help but curl his lip in distaste. A momentary look of fear passed over her eyes, as if she was suddenly reminded she was in the presence of strangers and that making a mistake in their presence could prove cataclysmic in some unknown way.

"Well!" said Ransom, standing up so suddenly that it made the old woman gasp. "Thank you very much, you've been most helpful!"

Gerald folded his notebook and stuck it and his pencil into his shirt pocket. He tried to rise quietly from his chair, but was foiled by a loud crack from the straw seat, which elicited a startled "Oh!" from Mrs. Percy, who had completely forgotten he was in the corner. Ransom repressed the smile of satisfaction he felt at startling the unpleasant old woman. Mrs. Percy grabbed her walker and began to struggle to an upright position, but Ransom stopped her.

"No, don't get up. We can see ourselves out."

"Oh, well. It was very nice to see you. Come again, if you need to."

"ALL THAT PROVES is he could have done it exactly the way we thought," said Gerald as they climbed back into the car.

"It proves that someone came here last night a little less than an hour after Stephens left."

"Someone?" said Gerald impatiently, "In a high-security building?"

"High security? You make it sound like a form of Catholicism."

Gerald exhaled forcibly. "It's either the front door or a key, Ransom. You can't get by it."

"Oh, I don't know, I can think of at least one way that someone could."

"How?"

"I would suggest that if we're going to sit here in the car, you at least turn on the fan."

Gerald did so.

"How could someone else get in if they didn't break in?"

"My *guess* is that someone else has a key."

"Stephens said that nobody else has a security key, other than the cleaning lady. Are you telling me you think she gave it to someone?"

"Gerald, you've really been married far too long. For Heaven's sake, think about it! That nosy, nervous old cat next door hears someone coming and going during the day when the husband's at work: She hears someone coming in not long after someone goes out in the evening, only she doesn't come to the obvious conclusion."

"Another man."

"What would be more natural than to give him a security key so he could come and go without being seen. And what could be more natural when she's had an upsetting quarrel with her husband than to call her lover for...solace."

"Who would have arrived less than an hour later."

"Yes. I'm disappointed in her. I would have thought..."

"What?"

"Nothing," said Ransom, embarrassed. "I think it's highly likely that someone else was here."

"I still think the obvious is more likely. They got into an argument and he killed her."

"And then left and came back forty-five minutes later?"

"Maybe he forgot something."

"Apparently he forgot to kill her," said Ransom lightly. "If you weren't behind the wheel I'd refer you to your notes. Remember that creaking busybody next door heard Mrs. Stephens let the person in."

"All right," said Gerald, growing more exasperated, "so they argued, he stormed out, kept getting worked up on his own, went back and killed her."

There was an angry silence.

"That is a perfectly plausible solution," said Ransom matter-of-factly.

Gerald did what in the movies is known as a slow take. He found his partner watching him with a sly smile and a raised eyebrow. Despite himself, Gerald erupted into laughter.

"That really is your most irritating tone of voice," he said, wiping a tear away from the corner of his right eye.

"It's taken years to cultivate."

Gerald took a deep breath, released it slowly, and relaxed his muscles.

"Really, why are you so sold on the idea of a lover?"

"Partially because of the seemingly odd comings and goings from their apartment, and partly because of what she told us in my office...or didn't tell us."

"What she told us in the office?" said Gerald, with the sinking feeling that he was again expected to play the role of Watson. "What she didn't tell us..."

"Yes?" said Ransom with a grin that Gerald would have found infuriating if he'd noticed it.

"*We* got the impression that she thought she'd done something wrong. That she'd 'sinned.' Something that would disturb her husband if he knew about it."

"Maybe a lover."

"Old mores die hard," said Ransom.

"But, that brings us back to the husband. If he found out about the lover, doesn't it give him a motive?"

"I think we need to look in other directions, at least for the time being."

Gerald pressed the gas pedal and pulled out onto the Drive.

"You know, there's another thing in Stephens's story that you've overlooked—I mean, that doesn't ring true," said Gerald.

"Hmmm?"

"That business about his wife's belief in fortune-telling. He said she didn't really believe in it. Well, it was obvious to the two of us that she believed in it. She believed in it enough to come and report it to the police—which doesn't exactly happen every day."

"He said, in fact," corrected Ransom wearily, "that her wholehearted belief in fortune-telling was a recent development."

"That's just what I don't buy! What would change her attitude from doing it 'for fun' to such an undying belief?"

"That's *dying* belief, in this case. And I think I have the answer right here."

He pulled the flier that he'd found on the table in the Stephenses' apartment out of his jacket pocket. "I think she met a fortune-teller who knew something."

"You mean someone who could actually see the future?"

"Oh, yes," said Ransom. Then he added with decision: "I want you to go back to the office. See if Robinson's gotten hold of the sister. I need to talk to her. And find out if there's been any word from the medical examiner's office."

"What are you going to do while I'm doing all the grunt work?"

Ransom pushed the lighter into the dashboard and pulled a cigar out of his pocket.

"I think it's time I had my fortune told."

FIVE

Melina

OHIO STREET west of Michigan Avenue is an area like many others in Chicago, where old and new architecture exist side by side, not in the least ashamed of their respective appearances in each other's presence. The 1890s brownstones have no sense of being dwarfed by their looming neighbors, but stand as diminutive reminders of a less complicated age, when artistry was worked in stone and meant to last. The towering glass structures, built a century later, feel themselves (if buildings can be said to feel anything) the natural outgrowth of a hundred years of progress, standing as proud emblems to a streamlined present and future.

In between two medium-sized modern buildings stood the structure that was a marvel of grace and beauty when it was built in the late nineteenth century. Formerly a luxury hotel, like many of its kind it had degenerated into a stopping place for roaches before being bought by a developer who had it gutted, filled it with spacious, airy offices, and refurbished the outside to its original splendor, the entrance replete with a curved concrete staircase with balustrades sporting stone lions, poor cousins to those that grace the Art Institute.

It was in this impressive throwback to a more elegant time that Melina was to be found. Ransom walked up the wide steps after being dropped off by Gerald, who continued on to headquarters to fulfill Ransom's requests.

Ransom passed through the first glass doors into a small vestibule, one wall of which had on it a large black directory with white lettering listing the occupants in alphabet-

ical order by last name. There were about fifty names, each
with a room number and button linked to a buzzer in each
office. For a moment Ransom feared he'd have to search
the whole list, since he didn't know the fortune-teller's last
name. He glanced at the *M*s and was relieved to find her
listed simply as Melina.

He pressed the white button, which vibrated against his
finger, noted the room number, and waited with his hand
on the knob of the inner door. After a moment, there was
a loud buzz, the lock unbolted, and he pulled open the door.

The walls and ceiling of the foyer, like the facade of the
building, appeared to have been restored to their original
splendor. But on closer look, Ransom realized that very
little had been done in the way of restoration. The work
seemed to be limited to a very heavy coat of white paint.
The floor and curved staircase were covered with a carpet
that was strictly industrial, thin but tough, and a sort of off-
rust color. To the right of the staircase was an old cage-
type elevator, which was fortunately waiting on the first
floor. He pulled open its door and smiled when he saw that
a square of the same dull carpeting graced its floor.

The elevator carried him upward at a leisurely pace, and
he watched each floor go by in turn. On every floor was a
row of doors, formerly hotel suites, now offices, and on
each door was a brass plate announcing the occupants. The
effect of the doors with their identical plaques was oddly
clinical, given the elaborate exterior of the building, and
gave the impression of a high-class zoo or elegant asylum.
It was as if the building had undergone open-heart surgery,
and its life-giving central core replaced by an artificial
pump.

The elevator stopped on the tenth floor and Ransom
stepped out, closing the gate behind him. The second door
on his right bore a plaque that said:

Melina
Reader—Adviser

The lettering was formal enough for a tax consultant. He knocked on the door. After a brief wait, it was opened by a beautiful, angular black woman who wore a tight-fitting blue jersey dress that showed her classic figure off to its best advantage. Her dress was adorned with a wide black belt that accentuated her tiny waist.

"Yes?" she said in a voice as deep as a coal shovel.

"Are you Melina?" said Ransom, at his most business-like.

"Yes."

"I'd like to consult with you."

Her rather small mouth twitched up at the corners, her eyes sparkled.

"Ah, yes. Come in."

The office was surprisingly small: one room, painted white (Ransom had thought, not too seriously, that it would be black), one window looking back into an incredibly clean alley, and a small bathroom whose door was on the wall to the right of the office entrance. The only furniture in the room was a desk with a wide top, a comfortably padded desk chair, and two chrome-legged chairs with black-padded seats facing the desk.

Melina gestured to one of these chairs, and Ransom sat. She took her place behind the desk. The appearance of the woman and the office was one of clearheaded profession-alism.

The woman herself was nothing like Ransom had expected. Despite Angela Stephens's disclaimers, Ransom had half expected to find Melina beturbaned and in flowing robes, all jangling bracelets and dangling earrings: sort of a modern-day Maria Ouspenskaya. There was nothing of the gypsy queen about Melina: Still less was she a voodoo priestess. Ransom thought, not without a sense of irony, that he might feel more comfortable if she were. Instead, Melina almost reeked of normalcy. Her jet black hair was straight and brushed back, her skin a clear, smooth umber, and her eyes large and set close together, in perfect pro-portion to her thin face. Ransom tried not to be disconcerted by the woman who for all intents and purposes could have been a corporate lawyer.

"So, you're interested in my services," she said as if she were offering to represent him in court.

"Yes, I am."

"Your name is?"

Ransom raised an eyebrow. "You mean you don't know?"

Melina smiled at him sweetly. "I'm not a mind reader."

"Touché," he said, returning her smile. "My name is Ransom."

"Just Ransom?"

"Yes. I'm known by my surname."

Melina's eyes twinkled. "And your Christian name?"

"Is of no consequence," said Ransom with a smile.

Melina intertwined her fingers and eyed the detective as if he were a subordinate about whom she had sincere doubts.

"Mr. Ransom, are you a believer?"

"In what?"

"In anything outside of your own realm of experience."

"I have a very wide range of experience."

She leaned back in her chair.

"You don't look like the usual type of client that comes to me."

"I should say you don't look the usual type of fortune-teller."

She made a deprecating noise in her throat.

"That makes it sound like I work in a traveling carnival."

"I'm so sorry. I didn't mean to offend."

"Let's say that I dislike sounding like something out of a werewolf movie. I do not wave my hands over a smoke-filled crystal ball. I read cards."

"Which is much more scientific."

"Touché to you." She was not to be shaken.

"I'm so disappointed," said Ransom, casually leaning

back in his chair, "you won't find any pentagrams in my palm."

There was a calculated pause. "Oh, I can't promise you that."

Ransom cleared his throat. "How do I differ from your usual clients?"

Melina spread her hands, which Ransom noticed had soft, slender fingers with long red nails, and raised her shoulders ever so slightly.

"You don't look anxious. Most of the people who come to me look very, very anxious."

"Most of them?"

"The rest look hungry. You don't look either."

"Hmmm."

"So what are you, Mr. Ransom?"

For a second he was taken aback. He had the uncomfortable feeling that she had seen right through him. He got a glimmer of why Angela had found her so plausible. He hoped that his face had not betrayed these thoughts.

"I'm just interested."

Melina's lips twitched upward again as if approving of his answer.

Ransom eyed the woman with cool appraisal. It was seldom in the course of an investigation that he came across a suspect whom he thought was a match for him. This, he believed, might just be one of those occasions. He felt that this woman, with her creamy brown skin and her liquid eyes, was a challenge to be met.

He wondered also at how readily the word "suspect" sprang to mind. What on earth did he suspect her of? Certainly not murder. But as much as he enjoyed the mental acrobatics in which he indulged when faced with an incongruous person or situation, he couldn't deny that he found them suspicious. Melina's impeccable professional manner didn't jibe with her chosen profession. It nettled the detective.

For her part, Melina didn't flinch under Ransom's scrutiny. With the poise of a living portrait, she reached into the upper left-hand drawer of her desk and pulled out a small, well-worn box containing a deck of tarot cards. Although she handled the box familiarly, it looked decidedly out of place in her hands. She seemed completely at ease. If anything, her smile reflected a good deal of amusement at the impression she made.

"Perhaps these will help me look the part."

"Are you playing a part?"

"No more than anyone else," she countered without hesitation. "I was simply using a figure of speech. Now. What would you like to know?"

Once again Ransom had the uncomfortable feeling that she had seen through him. He had to remind himself that he wasn't there in disguise.

"Don't you know?" he said.

"As I've told you, I'm not a psychic. I see I should clarify. There are many especially gifted people walking this earth. It is unusual for one person to possess more than one spiritual gift—just as it would be unusual to find a concert pianist who is also a virtuoso on the violin. When it comes to abilities of a more unearthly nature, I am gifted at reading cards, not reading minds."

"I see."

"Though," she said as an afterthought, "I'm sure there are people whose ability at mind reading is just as valid as mine with the cards."

"Of that I have no doubt," Ransom replied with a nod.

Melina slipped the cards out of their box and fingered them affectionately.

"So. I assume you want to know your future."

"I'm more interested in the past."

"Ah!" said Melina, her voice warm and deep. "You want to know how much I can see!" She held the cards out to him, her eyes never moving from his. "I need you to touch them...shuffle them if you like."

He glanced at the cards, reached out and took them.

"Oh, I'm not interested in my own past," he said, absently sliding cards off the top of the deck and sticking them haphazardly back in.

Melina sat back in her chair and crossed her arms. Her lips twitched down at the corners in a faint sneer. "God, I knew it! A policeman."

"A detective."

He reached into his pocket for his badge, but she stopped him.

"Don't bother. I believe you. You look like a policeman."

"Do I?"

"You have the look of a self-satisfied friz," she said with an indulgent smile. "And besides, you have visited me before."

For a fleeting moment Ransom thought she referred obliquely to some sort of past-life experience, then realized that she used the royal "you" to refer to the entire police department. Not for the first time he silently thanked his late mother for teaching him to think before he spoke, an admonition that had not only saved him much embarrassment but had ably assisted him in the everyday pursuit of his chosen profession.

"Have you been bothered by the police?" he asked lightly.

"Pragmatic minds allow of nothing they cannot touch."

Ransom smiled inwardly at the oxymoron. For the first time, he thought he just might be faced with an uneducated (or undereducated) woman who was merely a good actress.

"*Have* you had trouble with the police?"

Once again the indulgent smile played about her lips. He found her ability to put him off guard quite annoying.

"Oh, I wouldn't call it trouble. They stop by now and then to make sure I don't feel too secure—I assume when they have nothing better to do. They rattle my cage and then they go away."

The expression on her face assured Ransom that she lumped him into the category of cage-rattler.

"So why are you here?" she asked him finally.

"As I said, I'm interested in the past."

"You said..."

"Not my past."

"Whose, then?"

"Angela Stephens."

He spoke the name quickly and clearly, hoping to see a reaction. In this he was disappointed.

"Yes?" she said with no noticeable inflection.

"I understand that she's one of your clients." He purposely used the present tense.

"Yes."

He continued to absently shuffle the cards. "I would be very interested to know if anything out of the ordinary happened at your sessions with Mrs. Stephens."

Melina leaned in toward him, resting her arms on the desk and intertwining her fingers.

"Surely you understand that the sessions with my clients are confidential."

"You do not," he said, unable to contain a note of sarcasm, "claim to enjoy the privileges of the confessional in your profession."

"The question doesn't arise," she said with the smile that Ransom was beginning to find irritating. "I hardly think one would call on someone 'in my profession' to give evidence."

He tapped the cards on the table and laid them down.

"That all depends on your reputation. I have recently been reminded that even the police on occasion use the services of psychics."

"Psychics, not card readers," she corrected him calmly once again. After a pause, almost despite herself, she asked, "Did Mrs. Stephens send you to me?"

"I'm working on a case in which she's involved."

"Did she file some sort of complaint?"

"Oh, I wouldn't know whether Mrs. Stephens has any complaints about your services. I would think not. I would think she found your readings very accurate. Frighteningly accurate.''

She looked almost as if she would ask him another question, but instead she picked up the cards and began to fondle them, not taking her eyes off them.

''That is very flattering.''

''I was wondering just how one of your clients would have come to that conclusion.''

''How do you mean?''

''I mean, how did you prove yourself—how do you show your clients that you're the genuine article?''

''I read their fortunes. My readings are accurate.''

''About the future?''

''Of course.''

''But you also do readings of a client's past, don't you?''

''Occasionally.''

''Why would you do that?''

She began to lay out the cards on the desk, one card at a time, at what would be the points of a pentagram.

''Ah! I understand. Sometimes, when a client is skeptical, it helps to read the past. The accuracy of these readings will often cast any doubts aside.''

He watched as she laid a card in the center of the pentagram, then started to place a second card by each point.

''And you've done readings of Mrs. Stephens's past?''

She glanced up at him. ''When she first came to me, I saw that she was…the best word for it would be frivolous. Believing but not believing. Playing a game of having her fortune told.''

''But you don't play games,'' God, I'm enjoying myself, he thought.

''I am serious about my gifts.''

''So you did readings of her past.''

''Yes.''

''To convince her of your talents?''

''Yes.''

''And was she?''

''Was she what?''

"Convinced."

Melina smiled broadly this time. "She keeps coming back."

Ransom returned her smile. "The sure sign of a satisfied customer. I should say you were most convincing."

They eyed each other across the desk for a moment like dueling Cheshire cats. Melina was the first to break, beginning to lay a third set of cards on the points of the pentagram.

"So, what did you see in her past?"

"Things that will remain between my client and me."

"Did you see a lover?"

She placed the last card in the center of the star. "As I've said, I cannot reveal the intimate details of a client's life."

Ransom sighed and uncrossed his legs.

"Miss Melina, even a doctor can open his records when the patient is dead."

This, at last, received a reaction: Melina looked up at him and raised her right eyebrow.

"The woman is dead?" she said with an undisguised note of satisfaction that Ransom found distinctly distasteful.

"She was murdered."

Melina turned her palms up, spread her arms, and shrugged. "This should serve as positive proof of my powers."

So that was it. That was all the death of that beautiful woman meant to this creature: proof of a job well done. Maybe she would include it in her next brochure.

"You may rest assured that Angela Stephens is suitably convinced now."

Melina was unshaken.

"Which brings me back to my earlier question. What did you 'see' in her past?"

"That is still private," she answered with the same infuriating smile, which Ransom wanted more and more to wipe off her face. "And it would still be inadmissible in a court of law."

"Unless…" said Ransom carefully, "she verified the things you said."

"I do not require verification of my readings."

"But I do, Miss Melina, I do."

She pushed her chair back, got up, and walked over to the small window.

"Mr. Ransom, even if I could tell you that there was a man in her life—other than her husband—what good would it do you? The cards give images, not names."

Melina draped herself gracefully on the windowsill, turned, and looked at him.

"Which brings us to the present," said Ransom in a tone meant to imply he had won something. "Or should I say that brings us to the future."

"As you wish."

"Perhaps I should tell you that Mrs. Stephens came to see me before she died."

"She did?"

This was a real victory. Melina had registered surprise— and something more than surprise: something animal. That was it, Ransom thought—a startled animal who was doing all she could to not bark a question. He saved her the trouble.

"Yes. And she told me that you said she was going to be murdered."

"The cards said she would be murdered," she corrected, less calm.

"What exactly did the cards say?"

"Just that: that she would be murdered."

"But not by whom."

"As I said, the cards don't give names."

He looked at her for a moment, more in an attempt to make her uncomfortable than anything else.

"But I understood from Mrs. Stephens that the cards were a bit more forthcoming than they'd been in the past."

"What do you mean?"

"Well, the cards offered you a description of the murderer, didn't they?"

"Oh, that..." she said, returning to her place behind the desk.

"Handsome man, late thirties to mid-forties, dark hair graying at the temples."

Melina appeared to be regaining her composure without having lost it.

"That is the hanged man—I mean, the picture on the card of the hanged man."

"Surely that doesn't mean that every time the hanged man appears in a reading, it's a description of a murderer."

"Of course not," she said in something approaching testiness, "the meaning of each card depends on the position in which it falls in the individual reading, among other things."

"In other words, you call them like you see them."

"You could say that."

She turned over the middle of the three cards lying in the center of the pentagram she'd formed of the cards he'd shuffled. Ransom's eyes were immediately drawn to the center card. It was a leering skeleton, under which was printed the single word DEATH.

"Like this. It would appear there's death in your future," she said.

"There's death in everyone's future."

"Exactly. But without looking at the rest of the cards, I can't tell whose death or where or when it will happen."

"I see," said Ransom. He stood up abruptly. "I see."

She waved her hands over the cards.

"Don't you want me to do your reading? I'm running a special for policemen today: free of charge."

"No, thank you," he said, heading for the door, "I already know my future. It's the same as my past. But don't let me stop you. My future might be of interest to you."

He opened the door and started through it, then stopped as if he'd just had an idea.

"By the way, how much *do* you charge for a reading?"

"Fifty or a hundred dollars, depending on what is desired."

"Really?" said Ransom. He thought for a moment and added, "Do you ever get more money for your services?"

He let the door close behind him and left the building, feeling as if he had successfully won both the battle and the war: He had finally succeeded in wiping the smile off her face.

Ransom's step would not have been quite so spritely had he been able to watch the scene that continued in Melina's office, much like a tag line in a B-movie mystery. The fortune-teller's fear gave way to serious thought. After a few moments, the corners of her mouth turned upward into the smile that Ransom had found so objectionable.

She reached for the phone.

SIX

Interlude

AFTER LEAVING MELINA, Ransom stopped by headquarters just long enough to see if the sister had been found. She had not. Robinson reported that repeated calls to Eva Brinkley's apartment had yielded nothing more than an answering machine, and there was no proper etiquette for leaving a message of murder.

Robinson had finally managed to track down the manager of the aging twenty-unit Diversey Avenue apartment building in which Eva lived. Fortunately, the manager was one of the wiser breed that demands an application from each tenant before renting to them, and this application included the name and address of the tenant's employer: in Eva's case, the Hennesy Manufacturing Company on West Belmont.

Having returned to headquarters earlier, Gerald received this information and went to Hennesy's to find the sister. He returned from this errand just as Ransom arrived.

"It was no go," Gerald reported.

"How do you mean?" Why isn't she there?"

"Because she wasn't there. I talked to a Maria Cardiz," Gerald answered, referring to his notes for the name, "Eva's supervisor. She told me Eva took the day off."

Ransom raised as eyebrow. "An unscheduled day off?"

"According to Miss Cardiz, she asked for the day off earlier in the week."

"Did she give a reason?"

Gerald flipped his notebook shut with a sigh. "Miss Cardiz assured me that her employees are all allowed unexplained personal time."

"Meaning what?"

"Meaning she didn't find it any of her business—or mine."

"Am I to assume that Miss Cardiz was rather daunting?" said Ransom with a smile.

Gerald sighed again. "She was one of those plump women who look like they'll melt to the floor if they loosen their belts. Her hair's tied back in a bun so tight it looks like it's pulling the creases out of her face."

At this Ransom laughed out loud. "Gerald, my dear partner, we've been together too long."

"A scary thought."

"We'll have to hope little Eva hasn't gone away for the whole weekend. This is a very inopportune time for her to disappear."

"Suspicious."

"Perhaps. I greatly distrust people who are not readily at hand after a murder. They fall somewhere close behind people who are too close at hand when there's a murder."

"How did it go with the fortune-teller?"

"We had a very interesting conversation during which nothing was said directly."

Gerald rolled his eyes to the ceiling. He had learned to consider it a bad sign when Ransom became cryptic. "I suppose you'll get around to telling me what you're talking about."

Ransom rested both palms on his desk and leaned toward his partner. "Sleight of hand, Gerald. I feel that sleight of hand is being practiced on me, and I don't like it."

"What do you mean?"

"I don't know yet. Had Angela Stephens just been murdered one day, I would have agreed with you that it was a simple domestic homicide. But the situation is far too bizarre, for lack of a better word, for domestic crime. It's too complicated. Needlessly complicated, you would think. There are all of these silly details to deal with: the husband without a sound motive or alibi; the prodigal sister; the odd comings and goings at night; the phantom lover, if there is one.''

"And the fortune-teller," added Gerald.

Ransom sat back in his chair wearily, allowing his head to loll against its hard wooden back.

"And the fortune-teller. Where in the hell does she fit in?"

"Unless she's for real," said Gerald despite himself.

Ransom eyed him. "Oh, no, she's far too shrewd to be real. Never trust a woman with cards, my dear Gerald."

"So what do we do now?"

Ransom glanced through the doorway of his office at the tobacco-smeared clock on the squad-room wall. He jumped up from his chair.

"Oh, God, it's almost four o'clock. I've got to get out of here!"

"Wait! What do you want me to do?"

Ransom paused by his office door.

"Three things: Keep trying to get hold of the sister; also, see if you can get hold of the Stephenses' attorney. Stephens didn't say whether or not she left everything to him—I didn't ask him directly about that, and I don't think I'll bother. I'd rather have it from the horse's mouth."

Ransom started out the door, and Gerald called after him. "What's the third thing?"

"Let Stephens go," he said without looking back.

THE CAR CAME to a stop in front of Emily's house a bit more abruptly than Ransom had intended. His right hand caught the handle of the cardboard carrier as it tumbled forward, and a slightly guttural yelp escaped through the airholes. He righted the box and sat quietly for a moment, collecting his thoughts and going over the plan in his head, trying to convince himself once again that his plan would work despite the sinking feeling he had now that he'd arrived.

In the month since Fedora's death, Ransom had sensed in Emily the desire for feline companionship, coupled with a reluctance to replace her friend. It was to remedy this situation that Ransom had come to Emily's house early on this Friday evening. He believed he'd devised a way to supply her with a new companion without trampling on her tender sensibilities.

To do this, it was necessary to bypass Emily's sense of duty to her former pet and appeal to her innate compulsion to rescue the helpless. If Emily would not replace Fedora to fill her own desires, she could be counted on to take in a cat in need.

To this end, Ransom visited the local animal shelter and adopted the oldest, oddest cat he could find. He waded through a veritable sea of tabby kittens and young tiger cats until his eye was caught by a cage that he first took to be empty. On closer inspection, he found, half hidden under the newspaper that lined the cage, a six-year-old white female that pressed itself into the corner as if it were trying to melt through the wall. The only coloring on its snow white body was an almost perfect circle in the center of its head. Half of this circle was black, the other orange. It looked for all like a terrified, furry bellboy. When the cat realized it was being watched, it turned its head and looked at the detective with large, wet green eyes. She looked as if she were about to cry. A canny smile spread across Ransom's face. She was perfect.

Taking a deep breath, he took the cat from the box that had been provided by the shelter, removed its collar and tags, and tucked the animal under his arm. This was not an easy or pleasant task, as the cat was rather large, and with the heat of the day and fear of the situation her fur was unpleasantly damp and loose. As Ransom walked quickly up the walk to Emily's front door, fur cascaded off the profusely shedding animal and glued itself to Ransom's sweat-soaked, navy blue blazer. He rang the bell.

As they waited for Emily to answer the door, the cat looked up anxiously at Ransom's face, as if searching for a sign of character or intention. At the first creak of the door, the animal reared up its head and buried its face in Ransom's armpit.

"Jeremy!" exclaimed Emily, a smile brightening her wrinkled face. She was the only one who called Ransom by his full Christian name. "I didn't expect to see you again so soon, though you're always welcome."

"Oh, yes. Well, something came up, and I thought you might be able to assist me with it."

"A case?" said the old woman, raising her thinly penciled eyebrows.

"Missing person," said Ransom, pulling the cat into fuller view. "This little lady seems to have lost her way."

Emily and the cat caught each other's eyes and froze, much like any two animals coming upon one another unexpectedly. Emily looked down at the animal, her face a complete blank. But if Emily's expression was unreadable, the cat's face was an open book: It was love at first sight. The cat stretched her head forward and let out a sound something like that of a lost, starved orphan begging for food.

Emily slowly raised her head to look at Ransom, her eyes so filled with knowledge that he looked down at his shoes like a guilty child and shifted his weight.

"Come in."

"WHERE DID YOU say you found her?" said Emily with a twinkle in her eye.

"In the parking lot outside my building," said Ransom quickly.

"She obviously belongs to someone."

"What makes you think so?"

"My dear Jeremy, you're a detective! Look at her!"

Ransom looked down to the corner of the stove, from behind which the fat, fur-covered face stared up at him. The glowing green eyes blinked in the dark crevasse.

"I don't know what you mean."

"This animal is far too healthy to have been on its own for long. Somebody's been feeding it." Emily eyed Ransom impishly over the rim of her cup. "Perhaps I should take out an advertisement."

"No!" said Ransom more loudly than he'd intended. The startled cat disappeared completely behind the stove.

Emily's eyebrows rose until they touched the fringes of her gray hair. "No?" she said with mock bemusement.

"I made very thorough inquiries around the neighborhood and came up empty. I don't believe advertising would serve any useful purpose." He stopped and took a sip of his tea. "Besides, advertising is dangerous. If you advertise a cat in the paper, Satanists come to claim them and use them in their rites."

Emily blinked.

"At least, that's what I've heard."

Emily continued to gaze at him over her teacup in her most disconcerting, knowing way.

Ransom sighed and rested his elbows on the table, dropping his forehead in his hands. "Emily, I don't know why I try. I've said before we should have you on the force."

"You are not a plausible liar, Jeremy. Your love of the truth will always betray you." Emily lowered her blue china cup onto its saucer and folded her delicate hands. "Now, where did this lovely animal come from?"

His original plan foiled, Ransom decided to tell the truth, or something closely resembling it.

"Well, I just stopped into the animal shelter..." He glanced down at the animal, who had come just far enough out to perform the usual feline ablutions. With one white leg sticking straight in the air, it paused in a particularly private moment and glared accusingly up at Ransom. Ransom sighed. "...and I saw this thing there. I decided I should take it because it's...old...and it's difficult for them to find someone to take older cats." He concluded this with a note of defiance in his voice, which was not missed by Emily. After a pause, he added, "That was not a metaphor."

Emily's understanding gaze held Ransom until he shifted in his seat with uncharacteristic uneasiness. She then lowered her gaze to the cat, who had finished her toilette and sat on her haunches, her tail wrapped around her legs, staring anxiously upward at Emily like a criminal in the dock waiting for the verdict.

"Well," said Emily finally, "I suppose I should take care of her." Then with a note of tenderness in her voice, she added, "I wouldn't have been inclined to get another cat myself, but as long as she needs a home."

Ransom was relieved. He knew he hadn't fooled her, but he also knew that his real reason for supplying the cat would remain an unspoken understanding between then.

Emily smiled. "Jeremy, is something bothering you?"

Ransom raised his eyes to hers. "What makes you think that?"

"You seem preoccupied with something other than the wellbeing of our local feline population."

He ran his index finger idly around the rim of his cup.

"I'm working on a case that I'm finding...annoying, for lack of a better word."

"In what way?"

"I find myself, I suppose through sheer perversity of character, disliking the solution to a murder that's been handed to me on a platter."

"Oh, dear," said Emily, then added absently, "but then, of course, I suppose as with most things it's more satisfying to earn something."

Ransom searched her face for any indication of facetiousness, but as usual, Emily proved inscrutable.

"I'd like to think I'm not being deliberately stubborn."

"I've always known you to be quite levelheaded. It's hard to believe you could delude yourself in that manner."

Ransom absorbed this silently. "Maybe you could help me believe that."

"Why don't you tell me what it's all about."

Ransom related the facts of the case to Emily from the discovery of the body to the present, purposely saving the Melina aspect for later.

"Given the facts, Emily, at what conclusion would you arrive?"

Emily sat back in her chair and primly placed her hands in her lap.

"I should say that it seems obvious that the husband was the guilty party."

"So would I."

Her blue eyes twinkled at his. "But you don't believe it."

"No."

"Are you going to tell me why?"

Ransom's cheeks puckered, and the corners of his mouth curved upward coyly. "Mrs. Stephens told me that she was going to be murdered."

"Well!" said Emily, her face glowing with interest. She leaned toward him.

Ransom told Emily about Angela's visit to his office, and of the unusual story she'd told of her predicted murder. He left out the effect Angela had had on his libido. Emily's sparkling eyes grew wider as he spoke.

"So this was the supposedly intelligent young woman whose belief in fortune-telling you found so hard to accept."

"Umm-hummm."

Emily rubbed her hands together. "Well, it would appear her belief was justified."

"All too justified if you ask me," said Ransom, "and her belief in it was so strong that I got the impression— both Gerald and I did, really—that she saw her death as a foregone conclusion—that she really accepted the prediction, and she wasn't trying to get me to prevent her murder, but to avenge it."

Emily sat back in her chair again and made a sound that is commonly written as *tsk.*

"Good Heavens," she said breathily, "it must have been like being visited by the ghost of Hamlet's father, only she came to you before the fact."

"And she was a damn sight more attractive."

Emily raised her gray eyebrows slightly. "I daresay. And I imagine that like Hamlet, you feel you've been given a special charge to avenge the murder."

Ransom blushed to the roots of his close-cropped hair, which made it look not unlike crabgrass growing out of red clay. "It's strange you should mention Hamlet. When Mrs. Stephens was in my office she quoted him."

"Did she?" said Emily with admiration.

"There are more things in Heaven and earth, et cetera."

"Oh," said Emily with a thoughtful sigh, "that's certainly as may be, but I'm afraid I would be forced to side with Horatio in this case."

"Then you agree it looks fishy."

"My dear Jeremy, I think it looks a good deal more than fishy," said Emily simply. "And the suspects?"

"Suspect. Singular. There's only one so far."

He described the case against Frank Stephens and the subsequent interrogation of the suspect and the fortune-teller.

After a pause, she said, "It all makes the husband look rather dubious, doesn't it?"

Ransom let out an exasperated sigh. "So everyone tells me."

"But you don't believe he did it."

"No. I know he had the fight with his wife, and he has a damnably stupid alibi. But the rest of it doesn't make sense. Then there's the question of motive. I suspect, though I don't know, that Mrs. Stephens had a lover. If Mr. Stephens found out, he had a motive. I suppose people still murder for that sort of thing. Though I don't see why anyone would murder over a dalliance in this day and age."

"Then again, you're not in love," said Emily gently.

"No, I'm not," said Ransom, with barely masked embarrassment. "I'll have to press Stephens on the question of a lover."

"Couldn't he have had another motive?"

"You mean money? Stephens is tolerably well off on his own. I suppose he could just be greedy. Of course, we've yet to find out the terms of her will, so we don't know how he would benefit.''

"And that's all?"

"Love or greed, the two basic motives, or any of the shadings they allow.''

Emily clucked her tongue. "Jeremy, I'm amazed that with your love of Victorian literature you would say that. Where's your Dickens? Your Collins?''

"What do you mean?"

"There are other motives. Vengeance, for one. Revenge. Revenge is a motive that goes back just as far, if not farther, than money and greed.'' Her smile became more impish. "It even goes back farther than Mr. Dickens. Why, *Hamlet* is basically a revenge story, once you set aside all that pother about 'a young man who can't make up his mind.' And look at all the trouble it caused. I mean the revenge, not the play.''

Ransom couldn't help but laugh out loud at this as he took another sip of tea. Emily thought for a moment and then continued.

"And there are people who perform evil acts simply because they are evil people.''

Ransom turned to Emily, his forehead furrowed with surprise.

"Oh, yes,'' continued Emily, meeting his gaze, "I firmly believe that some people are simply evil. As has been said—though I can't remember by whom—some people do evil for evil's sake.''

Ransom considered this. In his earlier days on the force, before he had become something of a specialist in difficult cases, he had come into contact with what could most politely be termed the dregs of humanity. He had interrogated murderers who had slit throats for pennies; others who had killed out of profound sexual frustration (Would Emily have considered that love? he thought ruefully); and some who had killed those who had had the bad luck to be, in truth or in imagination, in the killers' way (these cases fell alternately into the love and money motive categories).

But that had been long ago, in the early days of his career. Over the course of time he had evolved into a specialist in crimes that stimulated the intellect rather than the stomach: His specialty was to solve the seemingly unsolvable, and most of these crimes had clear motives.

He realized, with a tinge of remorse, that as his specialty had narrowed, so had his thinking. Perhaps money and love—yes, and revenge—were the most common motives, but occasionally—very occasionally—in his work he came up against exactly the thing that Emily had said: evil for evil's sake. However, he was not ready to accept that this was such a case. Especially when there was a possibility of motive.

"Jeremy?" said Emily, a touch of concern in her voice.

Ransom cast an appraising eye at the old woman whom he'd learned to admire early on. "I agree," he said firmly, "there is the matter of evil. I will also admit that even in the absence of motive it would seem that Frank Stephens is the obvious suspect."

Emily considered this in a silence that hung heavily between them. This silence was broken by Emily discreetly clearing her throat and saying carefully. "So, what you're saying in essence is that you don't believe Mr. Stephens killed his wife because it so clearly appears he did."

"Not entirely," said Ransom, coloring slightly. "When you say it like that you sound exactly like Gerald."

"Detective White is a very pragmatic person. As am I."

"He'd be very proud to hear you say it."

Emily continued as if she hadn't been interrupted. "You, on the other hand, are intuitive. In you this is a gift."

Ransom looked questioningly at Emily, but would never had condescended to ask her to continue in this vein. Fortunately for him, she went on unprompted.

"Unbridled intuition can be dangerous. However, you are intuitive at the same time you are levelheaded." She paused and eyed him shrewdly. "I'm sure you know that."

He looked at her for a moment, his eyes narrowing, considering her words seriously. Emily had the unnerving ability to bring him up short.

"Emily, do you think I'm letting my..." The words "ego" and "pride" came to mind, but he couldn't bring himself to utter them. He began again. "Do you think I'm not allowing myself to accept the facts?"

She laughed melodically, her eyes sparkling and the gray fringes of hair that framed her forehead dancing. "Good Heavens, no! I would take your intuition over the facts any day!"

Emily adjusted the skirt of her dress. It was a new dress, a pale blue background printed all over with muted pink-and-yellow flowers. She settled herself down and folded her hands on the table, her back as straight as a schoolteacher's.

"I think there's another reason to disbelieve in Frank Stephens's guilt."

"Hmmm?"

"Well, the story you've told me raises several questions, as I'm sure you know. But if *Mr. Stephens* is the murderer..."

Ransom began to interrupt, but Emily stopped him with a raised hand.

"As I say, *if* Mr. Stephens is the murderer, it raises one question above all others."

"Besides why did he do it," said Ransom with a smile.

"That is correct," she said as if he had successfully completed a problem on the blackboard. "The question is not why did he do it, it is *why Melina?*"

A soft whirring sound, somewhat like a tiny motorboat puttering at regular intervals, became noticeable from the lower corner of the stove. The cat was lying serenely curled up like a large white croissant, its chin resting on its crossed forepaws. The as yet unnamed animal had apparently found a home where it felt secure.

"Why indeed," said Ransom at last. "It's the point I keep coming back to."

"You've said that you suspect Melina has been paid by someone. If Mr. Stephens planned to murder his wife, why on earth would he pay a fortune-teller to warn her about it ahead of time?"

"Vengeance?" he replied in a slightly mocking tone that made him feel almost immediately ashamed of himself.

Emily emitted a "hmmm" that echoed Ransom so closely it sounded like a family trait.

"I don't think you should discount the possibility of vengeance being involved. Have you considered the method of murder?"

"What do you mean?"

"Well, I've always considered strangulation a very personal means of murder. It's one thing to use a weapon, it's quite another to use one's hands." She let out a little shudder.

They fell silent for a moment. Emily gazed thoughtfully into her teacup, and her expression clouded over. Finally, she looked up at the detective.

"Jeremy," she said, her voice having taken on a tone so serious it made him sit up straighter in his chair, "I think you should tread very carefully in this case."

"Why do you say that?"

"If revenge really is involved...well, it's a very nasty business. And it has a way of spiraling out of control."

"I'll be careful."

"Remember," she said, placing her withered elderly hands on his, "in *Hamlet* the death of the king was only the beginning."

SEVEN

The Investigation Continues

RANSOM WOKE FROM a sleep that was neither dreamless nor restful. He had the curious sensation of having spent the night doing mathematical problems in which the sums didn't quite come out right. This left him with the hungover feeling that often comes with a restless night. He considered himself fortunate that this morning he could not remember his dreams.

He had a hearty breakfast of toast, brandy, and Excedrin, after which he felt steady enough to wash and shave. While shaving, he studied his face, particularly the area around the eyes. He had very blue eyes, the shade of a clear summer sky. He was well aware that his eyes were his best feature, and he had been able with a prolonged, piercing gaze to melt more than one hardened criminal into blubbering, blank confessions. At least he liked to think so. For the first time in weeks, as he searched his own reflection, he thought that he didn't look so bad, considering: considering that forty was three years away; considering his crow's feet were running to furrows; considering that one fairly luminous gray hair that stood like a beacon in the center of his chest.

He shook his head in an attempt to derail this train of thought and splashed cold water on his face, clearing his head and wiping away the last remnants of shaving cream.

Ransom arrived at area headquarters a little late (Why, he wondered, was one always late when one hasn't slept?) to find Gerald waiting for him.

"I've been on to the medical examiner this morning," said Gerald without preamble.

"And I suppose he was as helpful as usual."

Gerald smiled. "Oh, yes. He verified that Angela Stephens died of strangulation."

"And that sews up the case for us, doesn't it?" Oh, God, Ransom thought, I'm not going to be able to help being irritable all day. "Was there anything else?"

"The usual bruising and a broken rib. The ME was fairly certain that all signs of violence happened afterward, from the fall."

"All except for the ones on her neck," said Ransom, trying with all his might not to sound brittle.

He was unsuccessful. "Uh, yeah." Gerald was already aware that he would spend the day on eggshells.

"Sorry, Gerald, I didn't sleep well."

"It's all right."

Really, thought Ransom, it was beyond endurance for Gerald to be so steadfastly understanding, since Ransom didn't believe that his partner had ever experienced a sleepless night. Had Ransom not been so sure of his partner's intelligence, he would have sworn that Gerald slept the untroubled sleep of the terminally stupid. But he knew better.

Ransom often found Gerald to be the most irritatingly even-tempered person he'd ever met. Gerald never knew a wakeful night, and if he did awaken in the night, he had the steady breathing of his wife Sherry to lull him back to sleep. He had the obligatory two children and the house to weave into his blameless dreams. Gerald did not have women calling him a fool as he plunged into fathomless chasms. Really, thought Ransom, I should shoot myself through the head now and have it over!

"There is another thing," said Gerald, interrupting his partner's malignant reverie.

"Hmmm?"

"We found her."

"Who?"

"Eva Brinkley. The prodigal sister. She's on her way in here now."

"Ah, good. I'm always glad to widen the range of suspects."

Gerald shot him a wary glance. "A suspect?"

"And why not?"

"For one thing," said Gerald carefully, "you haven't met her yet. And I really don't think we need another suspect."

"I have an uncomfortable feeling that there's another 'and' on its way."

"And," said Gerald rather reluctantly, his pasty skin draining of the remainder of its blood, "I was on the phone this morning with the Stephenses' lawyers."

"You've been insufferably busy this morning," said Ransom, more sharply than he'd meant to. He dropped into the chair behind his desk, put his feet up on it, and pulled a cigar out of the drawer. He lit it without even a trace of remorse. "You'd better let me have the worst of it."

"Very short and sweet: no will."

Ransom's face hardened. "You're kidding."

"Nope. She left no will."

Ransom rose from his desk and went over to the window, his characteristic gesture when faced with information that doesn't jibe with his views. He gazed reflectively out at the view of building backs, low roofs, and alleys. Even from the rear Chicago was a beautiful city. He took a long drag from his cigar and exhaled the smoke, which spread out across the glass.

"Good God, you would think she'd have learned from her parents the importance of making a will! After seeing how carefully her parents provided for her and laid out responsibility for her sister, you would *think* she would have prepared!"

"Maybe that's why she didn't," said Gerald.

"I would have thought she was smarter than that!" He realized almost at once how he sounded and met Gerald's concerned gaze with a sheepish grin. "Gerald, you look positively maternal. I realize I must sound like the lead in a road company of *Laura*."

"It makes for a change."

Ransom turned back to the window. "She did strike you as intelligent, didn't she?"

"I'm not as quick at first impressions as you are. Maybe if she hadn't died, she would have proved you right."

Ransom emitted a sharp laugh. "Don't be silly, Gerald. If she hadn't died I never would have seen her again."

Ransom tapped a long ash from the end of his cigar on the windowsill. The clump of ash dropped, hitting the toe of his cheap black shoe and scattering on the floor. Since promising Emily to stop smoking, he'd removed the ashtray from his office. The result was an increasing amount of cigar remnants finding their way to the floor.

Gerald quietly settled down onto the couch. He knew well enough to recede into the background while his partner was lost in thought. He adjusted the legs of the wrinkled suit trousers, the same muddy tan pair he'd worn the day before. Though not even nine-thirty it was already over eighty degrees outside, and despite the chugging air conditioners in the windows, it seemed barely less than eighty indoors. And it was stuffy, besides. And getting stuffier as the air filled with smoke. Though Gerald was beginning to feel claustrophobic, he waited patiently, quietly tapping his right thumb against his knee.

"So," said Ransom, breaking the silence at last, "what happens?"

"Everything goes to suspect number one."

"Right," said Ransom as he came back behind the desk and resumed his chair. "Everything. Including her family business, which by rights should go to the sister. Did you find out what that amounts to?"

"Brinkley's is a small chain but by all accounts worth quite a bit."

Ransom puffed in silence.

"So what does that leave us with?"

Ransom tapped his cigar against the corner of his desktop, and more ash fell onto the floor. His eyes narrowed. "Too little and too much."

"What?"

"Information. We have a strong circumstantial case against the husband...." At this Gerald registered surprise, and Ransom shot him a glance. "I'm not blind, Gerald. We have a strong enough case against Frank Stephens to plant doubt about his innocence in a jury's mind, but not enough to convict him unless we come up with some definite physical evidence."

"Like what? Fingerprints?"

"I should hardly think a jury would be surprised to find that Stephens had left fingerprints on his wife. On the other hand, we have too much information. We have what amounts to an eyewitness account of the murder by the victim via a fortune-teller."

"Who you don't believe in."

Ransom faced his partner across the desk, his expression a mix of admiration and cunning. "Oh, I believe in her, Gerald, with all my heart and soul."

It was Gerald's turn to raise his eyebrow in genuine surprise.

"I believe that she was paid to say the things she said to Angela Stephens."

"You mean paid off?"

Ransom inclined his head slightly, indicating assent.

"By who? And for what possible reason?"

"I'm sure I don't know."

"It doesn't make sense," said Gerald, determined to hash out the point. "Why hire a fortune-teller? She wouldn't be any use as evidence; she'd be laughed out of court. And if the husband killed her, what reason would he have at all?"

Ransom suddenly froze in place. Slowly his features, creased with concentration, relaxed and smoothed. His eyes widened with revelation.

"My God, Gerald, I just had a terrible thought!"

"What?"

"You may be right!"

GERALD DIDN'T HAVE time to react, as further discussion was interrupted by the appearance in the office doorway of an apparition. Ransom was checked in the act of rising from his chair, looking as if he were seeing a ghost. This vision was enhanced by being seen through the hazy smoke of his recently extinguished cigar.

"Have you arrested the bastard?" said the woman with barely restrained fury.

It was the sound of her voice that wakened Ransom. He had known they were sisters, but he had not been forewarned of the striking resemblance between the two women. Eva Brinkley was a slightly younger and much more unpolished version of Angela Stephens. Eva had the physical characteristics of her sister, presumably family traits, but none of the refinement. She had Angela's ice blue eyes, but if Angela's were cool, Eva's were cold. Eva had the same perfectly oval face, without the softness and gentility that were so evident in her sister.

It was in Eva's face that Ransom could detect the most distinguishing differences. Though five years the younger, Eva bore the marks of the lifestyle she'd supposedly lived on her own. There were deep lines around her eyes and mouth, like cracks in asphalt. Her forehead retained three reddish lines from being held creased too long. If Angela's face had borne any marks at all, they were signs of character. In Eva they were signs of dissipation. In Ransom's eyes, she was the type of woman who would gain five years physically for every two she lived. Taken as a whole, Eva Brinkley was an ultimately disappointing version of her older sister.

"I asked you a question!"

"I'm sorry, Miss..." His voice trailed off, feigning ignorance of her identity.

"I'm Eva Brinkley. Angela Stephens's sister. Did you arrest the bastard?"

"Did you have a particular bastard in mind?"

Gerald glanced at his partner and saw the type of smile one would attribute to a malicious Mona Lisa. This could only mean that Ransom's snap assessment of Eva Brinkley had been unfavorable. Gerald had the sinking feeling that the day might go steadily downhill.

After an angry pause, Eva said, "Is that supposed to be funny?"

"Hardly," said Ransom, his smile disappearing. "The police take a dim view of hurling accusations."

Eva was unmoved. Ransom continued:

"Now, who did you expect us to arrest?"

"Her husband, of course! Frank Stephens!" She spat the name at him, her eyes burning with anger. "Even the police should be able to figure that one out!"

"We have spoken to Frank Stephens," said Ransom nonchalantly.

"Then why the hell isn't he in jail?"

"Because we do not have the evidence to hold him...at this time."

Eva laughed bitterly. "Evidence! What kind of evidence do you need, anyway? That junior G-man of yours who called me said Angela was strangled. What do you need? You need to find his goddamn hands around her throat before you can arrest him?"

"Miss Brinkley, I realize you've had a shock, but you must understand that in the absence of evidence, we have only probabilities, not proof. At the moment. And a jury will not convict on probabilities."

"Do you mean that he might get off scot-free?"

"No," said Ransom with feeling, "you may be sure that the murderer will not go free."

For the first time, Eva's expression changed. The anger seemed to subside a little and was replaced by something else. With what, Ransom was not exactly sure. There was no fear, but there was definitely a slight wariness.

"The murderer? You mean you don't *know* who killed my sister?"

"As I said, there are probabilities." He lowered himself back into his chair and continued with a casualness that Gerald found astonishing under the circumstances. "Some greater than others, but we haven't decided on one just yet.''

Eva took a step into the office, her eyes narrowed. ''What are you talking about?''

Ransom motioned for her to sit in the wooden, straight-backed chair that her sister had occupied two days earlier. Eva crossed the distance from door to chair with swagger instead of elegance and dropped gracelessly onto the chair. She crossed her denim-clad legs, and her right hand reached up and slid the heavy black purse off her shoulder and onto the floor in one swift, automatic gesture. The strap left an indentation on the shoulder of her salmon-colored, satin-esque blouse.

Ransom folded his hands and rested them on the desk, his eyes calmly boring into Eva's head.

''Despite what you may see on television, Miss Brinkley, the police do not generally go off half cocked. We investigate, we gather evidence, and if warranted—if you'll excuse the double meaning—we make an arrest.''

''Even if you *know?*'' Eva said, regaining some of her heat. ''Even if you *know* that he did it?''

Ransom was silent for a moment, then said quietly, ''Do you know that he did it?''

For a fraction of a second Eva looked startled. It was no more than the blink of an eye, but Ransom had registered it. She's not as good as she thinks she is, he thought.

''Of course he did it!'' she snapped with an odd lack of confidence.

''Why?''

''Why?'' She almost rose from her seat, but didn't. ''Why the hell do you think? Doesn't he get some of her money?''

''Miss Brinkley, your sister died intestate.''

This stopped her. ''What does that mean?''

''She didn't leave a will. It means that her husband will get everything.''

''Even...'' She stopped. If Eva was stung by this discovery, the only indication was a slight hesitation before she continued. "Well, doesn't that prove it? Isn't that the evidence you need?"

"A legacy falls under the heading of motive, not evidence. And as I was recently reminded, there are many other motives for murder than money."

Gerald sat on the couch, enthralled as he might have been at a particularly well played sporting event. His partner was in exceptionally rare form, and Gerald began to feel it would not be such a bad day after all.

Eva brushed the damp blond hair back from her eyes, in a gesture that seemed to mock her sister's similar action. "Who in the hell else would have a reason to kill my sister? She was a saint!"

"You didn't always think so."

This at last broke the sister's composure. She faltered. "I...I don't know what you mean."

"Wasn't there a break between you?"

"Who told you that? Him?"

"Is it true?"

"Yes!" She fairly yelled the word at him. "I didn't see her for a long time. Almost ten years. Not until about a year ago."

"Why?"

"Why what?"

Ransom could see in Eva's eyes something that burned from anger to hatred. He wasn't quite sure at whom it was directed.

"That's none of your goddamn business."

"Anything that affected your sister's life may have affected her death."

Ransom picked up a stray pencil and tapped the point on the desktop. Eva looked away from him and down to the floor as if she didn't wish to face the detective while revealing anything personal.

"If you have to know, I went through a...'rebellious period.'" She said the words as if she'd read them in a book. "I know you're supposed to rebel against your parents, but I didn't have that luxury. All I had was a sister who thought she was my mother—or acted like my mother.''

"She was, I believe, *left* that responsibility?"

Eva curled the right side of her mouth upward in an unbecoming manner and barely pried her teeth apart when she responded, "Oh, yes, Mommy and Daddy left me to her in their will, like property."

"Hmmm," said Ransom, his tone reflecting an understanding of both sides of the situation.

"The first chance I got, I got out."

"When you received your money from your parent's estate."

Eva's head snapped up and faced him. "You seem to know a lot."

"A tolerable amount," said Ransom with a sly smile. "Why don't you fill me in on the rest?"

"Why bother?"

"You never know what piece of information may help us in our work. What brought you back?"

Eva hesitated for a moment. "The same thing that always brings them back at the end of bad movies and cheap novels. I hit bottom. I ran out of money. I lived on the streets. I did a lot of things I'm not proud of. I realized my life was shit and so was I. I didn't have to worry about what hell would be like, because I was already there." She paused and batted the hair out of her eyes again. "Maybe I just woke up one too many times next to someone I didn't know. I used to screw men for a place to sleep. Sometimes. Just so for a night here and there I wouldn't end up sleeping between garbage cans in some alley God knows where. Whatever caused it, I decided that Angie—Angela—was right."

"About what?"

"About everything." she said warmly. Then, with a touch of self-mockery, she continued: "I guess I had one of those 'revelations' where you realize that everything somebody was doing for you was for your own good. Yeah, it sounds pretty goddamn corny to me, too, but that doesn't make it any less true. So I came back. And Angie welcomed me.''

''Just like that?''

''That's the kind of person she was. I don't expect you to believe that,'' said Eva, her eyes burning at him. ''She helped me find an apartment and paid the rent the first couple of months. Then she helped me find a job. She must've pulled a helluva lot of strings, because I don't exactly know how to do anything.''

''She was good to you,'' said Ransom, his voice expressionless.

''Better than I was to her.''

Tears suddenly welled up in Eva's eyes. Ransom could not help thinking that they'd appeared on cue.

''That's why it's so hard that she got killed now—right when we were getting to know each other again. Right when we were getting close.''

Ransom silently searched her face. Eva looked at him defiantly through her tears, making no move to wipe them away. After a moment, Ransom broke the silence.

''Tell me, how did Frank Stephens react to this reunion?''

Eva's face clouded over.

''Frank!'' she exclaimed bitterly. ''Frank is one of those people who label you for life when they meet you. As far as he's concerned, once he's got your number, that's all there is to it.''

Gerald stifled a laugh, and Ransom shot him a warning glance.

''He didn't believe you'd changed.''

''He doesn't believe anyone *can* change.'' She sat in stony silence for a moment, then sighed as if she were making a mammoth concession. ''I guess I couldn't expect him to. But he's wrong. I have changed. Angela knew it!''

Ransom stopped the intermittent tapping of his pencil. He pushed back his chair and rested his arms on the chair's. He looked hot, and damp, and alert.

"Miss Brinkley, when you returned, did you notice any change in your sister?"

"Change? Of course she changed! It'd been almost ten years since I'd seen her!"

"I don't mean physically. I mean...changed."

Eva looked at him blankly. "What do you mean?"

"Was she happier? Sadder? Anything out of the ordinary?"

There was a pause during which Eva's expression altered gradually from hostile to thoughtful. The deep creases appeared in her forehead, and it was easy to see why they left red lines. Ransom noticed with distaste that deep wet stains were spreading under the arms of her blouse, their center a dingy yellow.

"Well," she said finally, "Angela never was a laugh riot. She wasn't unhappy, but she didn't exactly show she was happy either, if you know what I mean."

Ransom inclined his head slightly.

"But when I came back she didn't seem as happy as she used to be. I don't think she was happy about her marriage."

Why, why, why, thought Ransom, smiling to himself, *does everyone insist on pointing at the husband?*

"Did she tell you that?"

"No. She wasn't the type who would tell you her personal problems." She stopped and then, with the air of someone hedging her bets, added, "Usually."

Ransom felt this might be designed to garner further inquiry. He decided to pass it for the moment. "But you still thought there was something wrong?"

She had been looking down at her shoes as if inspecting them for dirt and not finding it, even though she knew it was there. She looked up at Ransom pointedly. "I just didn't think she was happy. I can't explain why."

Ransom glanced down at the drawer that held his cigars. He would have dearly loved to light one up, sit back in his chair, and ponder the situation while this formidable young woman waited. He would have liked to smoke it slowly and silently, until Miss Eva Brinkley shrieked with impatience. But he refrained: not out of any sense of propriety, but because he thought it a shame to waste a cigar.

He straightened up in his chair, drawing it back to the desk. "Miss Brinkley, did your sister ever give you the impression—or tell you—that she was afraid?"

Eva looked at him with distrust. "Afraid of what?"

"Afraid for her life."

"Afraid for her life?" Her face contorted in a cross between incredulity and anger. After a brief pause, a touch of wariness seemed added to the mix. "Why would she be afraid?"

Ransom considered Eva coolly. He was sure something was there.

"I think I should tell you that your sister came to see me on Thursday morning. She told me she thought she was going to be murdered."

"She did? Well I—" Eva began quickly, then stopped, a mass of confusion. She looked like she was of two minds, not knowing how to proceed. Ransom said nothing to alleviate her discomfort. After a moment, her look cleared.

"I told her to," she said with determination.

"Did you, now?" said Ransom, bearing once again the look of an avenging Mona Lisa. "So you knew she was afraid."

Eva's face became a mask of petulance and disgust. "I knew she went to some goddamn fortune-teller that scared the shit out of her! But the whole thing was stupid! Who in the hell would believe one of those goddamn cranks! Angie must've been out of her mind."

Ransom leaned in toward her. "Then why did you tell her to go to the police?"

"Because!" Eva barked as she rose from her chair, pushing it back with force. She paced the length of the room once, stopping in front of Ransom's desk and glaring at him. "Because I thought she'd realize how stupid the whole thing was if she looked at it rationally. Like, I meant it as sort of a 'reality check'—that she'd see how silly the whole thing was if she talked to someone in the real world! For God's sake, I never thought she'd actually go to the police! I thought she'd see how stupid it was before it came to that!''

Ransom looked her in the eye for a moment, then said, ''I daresay you were right.''

Once again a shadow of wariness crossed Eva's features. ''About what?''

''We did think your sister's story about the fortune-teller was silly, didn't we, Gerald?''

Gerald nodded silently.

''We also thought that your sister believed in this prediction much more firmly than one would have expected. Isn't that right, Gerald?''

''That's right.''

Eva glanced at the two detectives in turn. ''And now?''

Ransom leaned farther across his desk toward her. ''I don't think it's silly anymore.''

Ransom was not sure what he thought the sister's reaction would be to this statement, but he certainly didn't expect the reaction he received. Eva looked almost relieved.

Eva resumed her seat, never removing her eyes from Ransom. He returned her steady gaze.

''Well what are you gonna do about it?'' she said, her right nostril twitching, giving her a faintly sneering look.

''I intend to find out who killed your sister.''

She peered at him through narrowed eyes. ''Are you the only one who doesn't know who did it?''

''In a murder investigation, many questions arise.''

Her wariness returned. ''Like what?''

''Miss Brinkley, since the discovery of your sister's body, we've been trying to locate you. Would you mind telling me where you've been?''

Eva knit her brows and appeared to once again be deciding on which course to follow. After a moment, her facial muscles relaxed.

''I've been with my boyfriend,'' she said matter-of-factly.

"All this time?" said Ransom with one raised eyebrow.

"Angela was the saint, not me." Almost at once she seemed to regret having said this. She tried to make amends. "You have to excuse me, it's not every day you find out your sister's dead."

"I understand," said Ransom, in a tone that implied that he understood more than she thought.

"My boyfriend works nights. He was off on Friday so I took the day off. I went over to his place on Thursday night and stayed with him till this morning."

"What does he do?"

"He's one of the headwaiters at La Gioconda."

"Hmmm," said Ransom, seemingly impressed.

"You know it?"

Ransom glanced down at his desk and then back to Eva, a grin lighting his lips. "It's a little out of my range."

"Anyway, he was off yesterday and he's working a double shift today, so he had to leave for work early. I came home. That's when that other detective called me about Angie."

"Might we have his name and address?"

There was a slight pause. Her expression darkened. "For what?"

"To check on your whereabouts, of course."

"You bastard!" she yelled, a fist coming down hard on his desk as she jumped from her chair. "You think I had something to do with this?"

His smile spread into its most infuriatingly engaging. "Miss Brinkley, I don't think anything. But the sergeant would have my head if I didn't double-check the whereabouts of all interested parties."

"I've got nothing to hide. Go ahead and ask him! He'll tell you just what I've told you! His name is Larry. Larry Parker." She noticed that Gerald White was writing down the name in his small notebook, and she barked the address at him. She then wheeled back around to Ransom. "Is there anything else you want, or can I go bury my sister?"

If she had thought this would shake Ransom, she was

mistaken. He said with all the simplicity at his command, "As soon as the autopsy's been done, she'll be released to her husband."

Eva's face turned white with anger, and she marched to the office door. She paused in the doorway and looked back at him, her eyes flashing as she spoke. "Well, it looks like Frank gets *everything* then, doesn't it!"

With this she crossed the threshold into the squad room, flinging the door closed behind her.

"How nice of her to close it for us," said Ransom, sliding his hand into the drawer and retrieving a cigar.

"What the hell was that all about?"

"That?" said Ransom, lighting the cigar and taking a satisfying puff. "Oh, I didn't like her."

"Why?" said Gerald with a surprising lack of caution. "Because she's not her sister?"

Ransom released a stream of smoke into the air. "No, because she had that look of a person who's perpetually up to something. I felt the irresistible urge to wipe that look off her face. I rather enjoyed myself."

"Jer, I don't usually question your judgment..."

"Umm-hmmm."

"...or deprive you of your fun, but for God's sake, the woman learned—not even an hour ago—that she lost her sister."

Ransom smiled at Gerald through the haze of cigar smoke. "Perhaps she didn't *lose* her."

Gerald was at a loss to understand this and knew better than to try. When his partner reached the point of spouting his enigmatic, Holmesian statements, there was no dealing with him. Though silently reminding himself that he still thought the husband guilty, Gerald knew that look in Ransom's eye could mean only one thing: He thought he was onto something. And Gerald also knew his partner's track record.

But he still found it annoying to be relegated to the role of Watson. If he hadn't so admired Ransom, he might have gone so far as to resent it.

It wasn't merely due to this admiration that Gerald so willingly accepted the role of sounding board; it was also due to his highly tuned sense of self-awareness. In many ways, Ransom's assessment of Gerald was on target. Gerald was a satisfied man. He had his wife and two daughters, all of whom he loved. He had no desire for the limelight, nor did he have an unquenchable desire to get ahead. He was happy where he was, and if his role was to be Watson, he was entirely satisfied to be the best possible of the breed. This was all with the knowledge that should his satisfaction ever wane, he would change his situation.

With all this in mind, Gerald once again acquiesced to the role that Ransom would continue to assign him.

"I suppose when this case is over you'll let me know what 'Maybe she didn't lose her' is supposed to mean. In the meantime, what do you want to do next?"

"Get on to the crime lab. I want to know everything they found in that apartment. Especially on the second floor. If she went over the balcony—which we know she did—there was somebody up there with her. I want to see if he left any trace."

"He?" said Gerald with a wry smile.

Ransom swiveled slowly back and forth in his chair, rocking tranquilly. "He, she, them. I want to know who was up there."

"And what are you going to do while I'm doing this telephone footwork?"

Ransom stopped rocking and looked at his partner.

"I'm going to finish my cigar."

IT WAS ALMOST eleven-thirty by the time the two detectives found themselves on their way to La Gioconda, after Ransom had smirkingly informed his partner that they should have an early lunch on Mr. Parker, Eva Brinkley's boyfriend *cum* alibi.

The steering wheel slid uncomfortably in Gerald's damp hands. He loosened the top button of his sweat-soaked collar and gave one strong pull at the knot in his tie.

"Are we actually going to eat?" said Gerald, with an unusual tinge of irritation.

"Maybe later. What did you get from the crime lab?"

"Do you know you smell like smoke?"

Ransom frowned. "Do I?"

"I think you've been smoking twice as much since you've given it up."

Ransom gave a surreptitious sniff to his sleeve. "I don't smell anything."

"Maybe it's just this damn humidity makes it cling to you more than usual."

Ransom's nose continued to twitch, first at one sleeve, then the other. "I really don't smell anything," he said, with a look of baffled concern.

"I'm not surprised."

Ransom raised an eyebrow. "Gerald, you seem positively peckish today."

"Sorry. It's the heat. It must be a hundred already—again."

"This is Chicago, Gerald."

"I know. I spend all winter wanting summer, and all summer wanting winter. Go figure."

"You are a true Chicagoan. So what did you hear from the crime lab?"

Gerald turned off of State Street and onto Chicago Avenue, heading west.

"There really wasn't much in the way of material evidence. Their maid does as good a job on the furniture as she does on the floors, but her usual day is Tuesday, so she hasn't been there for a week. There was the usual panoply of fingerprints in the living room and kitchen—"

"Panoply?" said Ransom.

Gerald continued, ignoring him. "—presumably the family and guests. But the second floor was a different story. Both in various locations in the bedroom—nightstand, dresser, etc.—and on the balcony railing, there were four different sets of prints. One is the victim, one the husband, the third is the maid."

"How do they know the maid's fingerprints? She hasn't been printed, has she?"

"Logical assumption. The apartment has a utility room off the kitchen where brooms, cleaning supplies, and so on are stored. They dusted them and found only one person's."

"Umm-hmmm," said Ransom. He had just taken a drag from his cigar and glanced self-consciously at his partner. He turned his head and released the smoke out of the window. "A logical assumption: the maid. We can check that further later on if necessary."

"Yes. So. On the second floor there were four sets of prints: victim, husband, maid, and one set unidentified." Gerald paused, glanced at his partner out of the corner of his eye, and wiped a sleeve across his forehead before continuing. "So I suppose you want to assume—"

"We can assume that the fourth set may be her lover."

"Or anyone else," said Gerald as dryly as he could while drenched with sweat.

"Well, let's find out who the unidentified prints belong to."

"Already taken care of—I told them to send the prints to identification."

"Good."

At this point they reached La Gioconda. The restaurant was located on Superior Street just west of Orleans, in the warehouse district of River North, which had been converted into a popular strip of art galleries and trendy eateries. The art galleries had come first, as many different patrons of the arts with a lot of love but little money had taken over the low-rent warehouses and converted them into some of the finest and most respected art galleries in the city. As often happened with gentrification, the value of the area had risen to the point where some of those who had been responsible for the change found they could no longer afford to stay there. The area was in a state of flux, losing some of its founding galleries and gaining some less respectable but more viable in their stead.

The restaurants had come next. Once it became known that wealthy people were spending their evenings in the newly formed gallery district, some of the smarter restaurateurs moved in to cater, at premium prices, to those people who would require more sustenance than the meager wine and cheese offered at gallery openings. Thus more of the warehouses were emptied of their crates and dust and rats, and filled with fine wines and expensive appetizers.

La Gioconda was just such a place. Ransom suspected that its trendiness would last for no more than two years, at which point it would revert to a storage facility, most probably for restaurant fixtures. But one could never tell. In Chicago it was not unknown for today's trendy eatery to become tomorrow's institution. For the time being, La Gioconda was the rage. On weekdays it was besieged with businessmen and -women who would go out of their way to eat in the most crowded and inconvenient location, so long as it was the place to be. On Friday and Saturday nights, when the galleries scheduled their openings, the wealthy might have an hour or more wait for a table, and no amount of bribery could shorten this process. Eleven-thirty on a Saturday morning might be the only time during the week that the restaurant was approachable.

As they pulled into the tiny parking lot adjacent to the building, a young Indian in black pants, white shirt, and red jacket ran up to the driver's window and spouted anxiously, "Get out! I park for you! I park for you!"

"That's all right," said Gerald, scanning the lot for an open space.

The Indian's face contorted. "You can't park! Valet parking only! I have to park car!"

Gerald wearily flashed his badge at the young man. "No, you don't."

The young man looked startled and stepped back from the car as if afraid he was about to be clapped in handcuffs and whisked away to some vaguely imagined concentration camp.

"There," said Ransom, pointing to an empty space.

Gerald nodded and slid the car into the spot on the far side of the lot. They got out of the car and walked to the huge red doors of the restaurant. The valet seemed to have vanished, but they were greeted by a doorman who sported a red uniform that seemed impervious to sweat and who had a huge smile plastered across his face. He swung the door open for them.

"La Gioconda," Gerald said as he recoiled slightly from the icy blast of the conditioned air that slapped his face. "That's Italian, isn't it?"

"It means 'The Laughing Lady,'" said Ransom, "It's owned by a woman named Melissa Trewitt, who came here two years ago from Boston. Supposedly she's using a divorce settlement to fulfill her lifelong dream of operating a restaurant in a former rat's nest."

"Where do you learn stuff like that?"

"I read the paper, Gerald."

"You don't have children."

If Gerald had any idea of the internal convolution his partner was experiencing of late concerning his age and status in life, he would never have spoken these words. As it was, Gerald, who was incapable of malice, had merely tossed this off as a statement of fact. It was due to the fact that he preceded Ransom through the door that he missed the momentary hesitation in Ransom's step and the pained shadow that quickly crossed his face. They hadn't gone two more steps before Ransom had recovered.

They passed through a white archway into the main dining room, which was brightly lit and bustling with activity. The room was huge and airy despite the fact that it contained almost fifty tables, most of which were full. The floor was covered with a deep-pile tan carpet, light enough not to weigh down the overall brightness of the room, but dark enough to cover a multitude of sins. The walls were not white but very close to it, and each table was covered with a long white cloth of what appeared to be above-average material. In the center of each table was a small vase with a bouquet of white and pink carnations, fresh each day. The room was alive with a scurrying staff, who were clad in the obligatory white shirts, black pants and ties, and black jackets whose left lapels sported carnations. It gave one the feeling of having one's whims catered to by a group of highly efficient, pleasant, hyperactive penguins. Ransom thought with a rueful smile that with the addition of some pastel chalk dust he would feel he'd entered *Mary Poppins*.

Gliding amongst the tables was no less than the personage of Melissa Trewitt herself, clad in her trademark black evening gown though it was not yet even noon. Her skin, including that of the ample cleavage visible due to her plunging neckline, was fashionably pale as death. Her long tawny hair was pulled back on each side of her head with gold clips, and her thin lips were painted a deep red that made it look as if she'd bitten down a trifle too hard on them and had drawn blood.

Melissa Trewitt firmly believed that the hallmark of a good restaurateur was omnipresence. She prided herself on the fact that her patrons were aware of her presence, assuring them that the owner was presumably at their disposal should anything be needed. "Presumably" was the operative word. She felt it her duty to preside, not participate. To this end, she contrived to appear completely unapproachable, a task at which she proved successful, since after two years of business she was only approached by the staff if it was unavoidable, and only by patrons with a death wish.

But Melissa Trewitt didn't have to worry about trouble. There was never a problem at La Gioconda. This was primarily due to the fact that she could sense trouble the way a panther can sense fear, and quash it before it happened. She could freeze-dry a full-grown angry accountant at twenty paces with a mere glance.

At first sight of Ransom, Melissa Trewitt saw trouble. As she approached the detectives from across the room, Ransom could feel all the moisture evaporate from his body.

"What?" she demanded in a tone designed to relieve them of their testicles.

"Good morning," said Ransom with infuriating geniality.

"What do you want?"

"Couldn't we just want lunch?"

Melissa Trewitt folded her sleek, pale arms beneath her ample breasts and set her jaw. Ransom smiled at her.

"I am Detective Ransom, this is Detective White."

"Dicks! I knew it!"

Ransom glanced at Gerald. "I seem to be awash in prescient women of late."

Melissa curled her lips. "If you've finished with the dime-store dialogue, maybe you'll tell me what the hell you want."

"Might we have a word with you?" said Ransom, his equanimity unshaken.

"We might, if I wasn't busy running a restaurant at the moment."

Ransom flashed his most engaging smile, which he somehow managed to infuse with a tinge of menace.

"Perhaps you could take a moment out of your busy schedule to have a word with us?"

They stared at each other in stony silence. Melissa Trewitt didn't move. She didn't even blink. Finally, Ransom leaned in toward her conspiratorially.

"I'm sure your good patrons will be able to chew without your assistance for, say, five minutes?"

Melissa seemed to calculate just how long a pause would throw the detective off balance, then with a sigh marched off to the right and through a door.

Ransom looked at Gerald. "I like her."

They followed her through the door and found themselves in a spacious office whose decor was a match for the restaurant itself. The desk, chairs, and long sofa were substantial without appearing heavy, and the whole room was bathed in the noonday light that streamed in through the skylights that made up half the ceiling space.

Melissa Trewitt was draped across the plush leather desk chair, looking much like a fine piece of clothing that had been tossed carelessly on the furniture. She had already somehow managed to smoke her way through half a Benson & Hedges 100 in the few seconds it had taken them to follow her.

"I would offer you a seat, but I want to be finished with you by the time I finish this." She waved her cigarette at them, then stuck it between her thin lips and took a long, deliberate drag from it.

"We only need a moment of your time," said Ransom, wielding politeness like a sword. "Actually, we're interested in one of your employees."

She snapped her head around to face him, her eyes flashing. "You mean this isn't even about me?"

Ransom's right eyebrow raised involuntarily. It was quite unusual to find someone who was upset at not being the center of attention in a police investigation.

"No," he said slowly, "the name of one of your headwaiters was mentioned in relation to a case we're working on."

Melissa's expression was a mix of irritation and interest, though she attempted to feign otherwise. Her response was a puff of smoke.

Ransom continued. "So we'd like to ask you a couple of questions, then we'd like to speak to him if it's convenient—or even if it's not."

"It's not convenient," she said with resigned irritation, "but I assume it's unavoidable."

"I'm glad you see it my way," said Ransom with a note of triumph designed to further rankle the woman before him.

Melissa hit her cigarette against the glass ashtray on her desk. "Get on with it! Who do you want to know about?"

"You have a man working for you named Larry Parker."

"Ah, Larry!" said Melissa with a knowledgeable smile. "What has he done?"

"So far as we know, nothing."

"You said his name came up in a case."

"Only indirectly."

"How does he figure in? As a suspect."

"No, he appears more in the nature of an alibi."

Melissa's eyes narrowed, and she spread her left palm flat on the desktop. "Then what the hell do you want to talk to me about?"

"Well, in a case of this nature—where an alibi is important—we like to make sure that someone who can provide an alibi is...let's say reliable."

"Are we talking about a murder?"

"You leapt to that one awfully fast."

Melissa inhaled the cigarette deeply, blew the smoke into the air, and stubbed the remainder of the cigarette out in the ashtray with a rapid pecking motion. She looked like she was killing an insect.

"So what do you want to know?" she said as she leaned back in her chair.

"Is he reliable?"

Melissa folded her arms. "I wouldn't let him near a cash register."

There was a pause. "And is that your entire assessment of him?"

"I wouldn't let him near my daughter, either."

Ransom looked at the restaurant owner with something bordering on distaste. "Do you have a daughter, Miss Trewitt?"

Her face colored. "It was a figure of speech."

"Miss Trewitt, I was under the impression that Larry Parker was in a position of some importance in your restaurant."

"Ha!" she barked. "A headwaiter? In my place the headwaiter is just the asshole who bosses the busboys around and seats people. They're no big deal."

"Aren't they left in charge when you're not here?"

"I'm always here."

"If you don't trust him and he's not important, why do you keep him on?"

Melissa Trewitt's face hardened. As she spoke, she tapped an index finger against the desk as punctuation. "You know what kind of restaurant this is? We do not cater to pig-people here. We cater to what is laughingly known as 'society' in this city. The wealthy. Those who have made it and those who are on their way. Those who will pay twenty dollars for an appetizer to prove they're important." She shrugged. "In other words, pig-people with money."

"And?"

"Larry is good-looking. He has a good face and a good ass, both of which are appealing to half of the women who eat here and three-fourths of the men. Handsome waiters make people think they're being served handsomely. And Larry is charming. Pig-people of all varieties need to be charmed, and Larry seems to be good at charming them. Especially the ones with money. They get charmed. They spend more. That's what I want."

Ransom gazed at the woman, assessing both her and her information. He was certain that whatever else she might be, Melissa Trewitt was straightforward. And he was sure her judgment could be trusted.

"I see," he said at last. "And now if we could have a word with him?"

Melissa stood up abruptly and walked to the door.

"I'd appreciate it if you could make it short. I'm not overstaffed," she said acidly.

She opened the door a crack, then stopped and looked at the detectives over her shoulder.

"This person he's supposed to alibi, is it a woman?"

"Yes."

She smiled knowingly and left the room with a toss of her head.

Gerald turned to Ransom and let out a long, high whistle.

"Hmmm. An interesting woman and an interesting exit. I wonder whatever made her choose the name."

"Melissa?" said Gerald, confused.

"La Gioconda." said Ransom. "The Laughing Lady."

"I don't know," said Gerald nonchalantly. "I can only imagine her laughing if someone fell on a knife, as long as it didn't happen on her property."

Ransom raised both eyebrows to the center of his forehead. "Gerald, you will forever be a source of amazement to me."

After a moment the door opened and in walked a strikingly handsome man in his early thirties, whose dark complexion was testimony to many well-timed afternoons at Oak Street Beach. His face was chiseled into perfectly proportioned angles, visible through the tan skin stretched tightly across bone. His eyes were small rims of olive green with huge pupils. His long dark hair was slicked back and tied in a ponytail and was prematurely gray at the temples in a way that on an older and less angular man would have looked merely dignified. On Larry Parker it looked rakish to the point of eroticism. Melissa Trewitt's assessment was more than accurate.

He was a model of self-assurance, tall and erect, and on him the restaurant's 'uniform' took on the appearance of evening clothes. In fact, everything about him seemed heightened. Taken as a whole, Larry Parker had the air of a man who got by not by the seat of his pants but by their zipper.

My God, thought Ransom, is every man I come across in this case going to look better than me? He had the uncomfortable feeling that it was going to be hard to hide his dislike of the headwaiter.

"You wanted to see me?" said Parker with a smile that transformed his face into a pool into which anyone was welcome to dive.

"You're Larry Parker?"

"Yes."

Ransom gestured to him to sit in one of the chairs that fronted the desk, but Larry preferred to remain standing for the moment, apparently implying that although he would like to help in any way, his time was limited. Gerald

seemed to fade back against the office door, quietly extract-
ing his tiny notebook and pencil from the pocket of his
jacket.

"We would like to have a few words with you."

"About?"

"Didn't Miss Trewitt tell you who we were?"

"No," he said, the broad smile still lighting his face,
"she just told me there was somebody in here who wanted
to see me."

"Ah. Well, I'm Detective Ransom, this is Detective
White."

Parker looked slightly confused and glanced back over
his shoulder.

"I'm sorry, I didn't see you," he said.

Gerald inclined his head slightly.

"Invisibility is one of Detective White's peculiarities."

"I see," said Parker genially. "Well, since you're detectives I bet this is going to take some time, so I'll sit.
This is about Eva, isn't it?"

"Yes," said Ransom, raising an eyebrow. "Then you
have heard what happened?"

"Eva called me here at work before she left for the police station. Too bad about her sister, isn't it?" The con-
viviality with which he said this seemed highly incongruous.

"We think it's a tragedy. If you'll excuse my saying so,
having been told about it, I'm rather surprised you haven't
gone to be with her."

"Well, yeah, that's what you should do, I guess," Larry
replied in a cheerful, businesslike manner, "but I'm like
everybody else. This place makes a fortune, I do not. If
I'm not here, I don't get paid. And I can't afford to not get
paid. Boring but true."

"Yes, but I would have thought in the present circumstances one usually made sacrifices."

"That's true," said Larry, knitting his brows together in
concern. "But, well, I don't really know Eva that well."

"Really? I thought you'd known her for some time."

"No, not really. About a year. Maybe a little less. I feel sorry for her. I mean, you would for anybody who lost her sister. And maybe I'll try to see her after work. But"—he gave a slight shrug—"you know, what can I do? If I knew her better or if I knew her sister, I'd have gone right over."

"Then you'd never met Angela Stephens?"

Parker shook his head. "I'm afraid we aren't at the point yet where I'd be brought home to meet the family."

Ransom considered Larry Parker silently. After a pause the detective spoke with a note of mild bewilderment in his voice. "And yet, she turned to you in a crisis."

"What can I say?" Parker replied with his same winning smile and the slight shrug that seemed to tip the weight of the world off his shoulders. "Sometimes women, you know, decide they're in love faster than men. And…" His voice trailed off with measured uncertainty. "Well, maybe I shouldn't say this."

"Please," said Ransom genially.

"Well, I don't know how well you know Eva—or, if you know anything about her at all—it's just that I don't think Eva has many people to turn to."

"Hmmm. Well, I'm afraid that's going to make our reason for coming a bit awkward," said Ransom in a tone that suggested he would like nothing more than to make it as awkward as possible.

"Why?"

Ransom came around to the front of the desk and sat on its left corner facing Parker. He towered over the head-waiter, leaving half a foot of space between them.

"I'm assuming that Miss Brinkley told you the circumstances surrounding her sister's death?"

"She said the husband killed her."

"Aha. In a case of murder it's a matter of routine for us to check on the whereabouts of all interested parties at the time the murder was committed."

It was Parker's turn to raise his eyebrows. "You mean Eva's a suspect?"

"No, I mean just what I said: She's an interested party."

"You're not sure about the husband?"

Larry Parker looked up at Ransom as he said this. Ransom realized as he looked down at him that Parker's pupils were much larger than the amount of light in the room warranted. He doubted that they had come by this condition naturally.

"Only in my mind, Mr. Parker. I have doubts, but they should be easy enough to dispel."

"How can I help you?" said Parker agreeably.

"That's what's so awkward," said Ransom with mock embarrassment. He glanced at Gerald's impassive face and thought he detected the hint of a smile. "You say that you don't know Miss Brinkley all that well, but you see, you are her alibi. She told us that she spent the last day and a half with you."

"That she did," Parker replied candidly. "It was by way of getting to know each other better."

"Hmmm. I should say that by now you'd know each other pretty well."

"Some ways better than others," Parker replied after a brief hesitation, the corners of his mouth twisting up in what could best be described as a gentlemanly leer.

"And how did the two of you spend the past day and a half?"

Larry's face took on a boyish bashfulness Ransom felt sure was calculated to win the hearts of all within sight.

"Well, mister…you know, that's kind of personal."

Ransom raised a questioning eyebrow that without a word made it clear that Parker was expected to continue, discretion being out of place in a murder investigation. Ransom had long since mastered the art of speaking with his eyebrows.

Parker continued with an ingratiating smile and a shrug. "All right, on Thursday night, after work, we had an 'intimate dinner' at my place and then an intimate night, if you know what I mean. We're both healthy, you know. Yesterday we spent wandering around. We had lunch at Water Tower Place. Umm…let me see…we went back to my place for a while in the afternoon—late. We went out to dinner and saw a movie at McClurg Court. Then we went home and did more of the same. I had to leave for work this morning before nine-thirty—I do a double shift on Saturdays—and she went back to her apartment when I left for work. That's the *Reader's Digest* condensed version.''

Ransom gravely considered Larry Parker for a moment. It was a plausible story, delivered plausibly. But then again, it would be hard to imagine this man being anything but a picture of composure.

"And she was never out of your sight?'' said Ransom finally.

"Well, sure she was. I didn't go to the bathroom with her, for Christ's sake!'' He paused for a moment, during which Ransom's expression didn't change. Parker continued somewhat more pointedly. "She certainly wasn't out of my sight long enough to run off and kill her sister, if that's what you mean! And besides—'' He stopped abruptly.

"Besides?'' said Ransom, his eyes sparkling with interest.

Parker hesitated, apparently aware that he had gone further than he'd meant to. But he realized there was no going back. "From what she tells me there wouldn't exactly be a reason for her to kill her sister.''

"Oh, really?'' said Ransom, cocking his head to one side.

Parker's smile diminished, but his glow remained. "Well, Eva told me a little about her break with her family. I can't imagine she'd be expecting anything…I mean, that she'd think her sister would leave her anything.''

"Did she ever speculate on the subject?''

"I mean if she thought about it at all.''

"But she never said anything to you to lead you to believe she was thinking about her sister in terms of a legacy.''

Parker gave the detective a patronizing glance. "Look, I

don't know what your experience with women is, but when you're...when you're...you know..." He appeared to rack his brain for a proper expression. "...in some 'romantic situation' they don't usually talk about an inheritance."

Ransom's face hardened. He was sure if one more person mentioned his age or experience with women he would blow their brains out. He firmly believed this hair-trigger response to be one of the dangers of inadequate gun control laws. Though delivered in an offhand manner, Parker's words had stung, and Ransom wasn't about to let him get away with it.

"For not being very close to her, you seem to spend an awful lot of time in romantic situations."

Parker leaned back in his chair with exaggerated casualness. "Just between you and me, Eva's hot. She's real *hot*."

"Indeed?"

"She knows what she likes, and she's not afraid to tell you—not like some women."

Ransom paused for a moment, then said, "You surprise me, Mr. Parker. You strike me as the type of man who would want more than that."

"We like a lot of the same things."

"How convenient for you."

Gerald emitted a quiet sigh and rolled his eyes up into his head: something he was wont to do when his partner began sparring in this fashion.

"And exactly what desires do you share other than the corporeal?"

"Huh?"

"Physical."

"Oh. The same as everybody else," said Parker lightly. "Food, warmth, companionship, some fun. Enough money to get it."

"Hmmm." Ransom eyed Parker piercingly, then continued, carefully choosing his words. "I'd think you'd make enough money in a restaurant like this to have all those things." He hesitated, then added shrewdly, "Unless, of course, you develop any expensive habits."

To the casual observer, Larry Parker's expression didn't change. But even though the smile remained, the glow became a frozen glaze. The large black pupils, staring a moment before, became vacant, and a vein over the right eyebrow pulsed sporadically. Ransom felt the same sense of achievement he'd experienced at the close of his interview with Melina. However, although Parker's veneer had been penetrated, it hadn't cracked. For the time being Ransom would have to be satisfied with knowing that he'd rattled the waiter.

"I think that will be all, Mr. Parker," said Ransom genially, "for now."

Larry Parker rose from his seat, his face reanimating. He smoothed back the hair on both sides of his head simultaneously, his smile reflecting a sense of having happily completed a difficult task. If he'd been shaken a moment before, no evidence remained.

"Thank you," he said simply. With that, he turned and walked out of the office, nearly colliding with the ever-invisible Gerald, who stepped out of the way of the door just in time.

"I HAD MUCH MORE success with Melina, our not-so-mysterious fortune-teller, you know."

"Really?" said Gerald as he turned the keys in the ignition.

"When I left her, she wasn't smiling."

"Parker was."

"It's much harder to wipe a chemically-induced smile off someone's face."

"Cocaine, I'd say."

"You'd be right. He's a bit too bright and too thin to be real."

"But then again," said Gerald, "I thought he was pretty straightforward."

"Really?" Ransom pulled a cigar from the pack in his

pocket and stuck it between his teeth. "He struck me as the type of man who uses honesty as a weapon."

"What does that mean?"

Ransom lit the cigar with several short puffs, then with a glance at Gerald blew the smoke out the window with exaggerated courtesy.

"It means that some people use honesty to hide the truth. They are perfectly frank about things that don't matter in order to hide the things that do. You know that as well as I do. On the surface he was fairly straightforward about his relationship and about the time he's spent with Eva Brinkley. But what does that leave us with? It leaves us with a pair of lovers who will alibi each other. Nothing else."

"So you don't believe him?"

"I wouldn't believe anyone on drugs. And it's a rather expensive habit," he added as an afterthought.

"So he's a user," said Gerald, growing more exasperated by the moment. "So are a million other people. That doesn't give us anything."

Ransom rested the base of his nose between his index fingers, a wisp of smoke trailing from the cigar that dangled off to the side. He appeared wholly absorbed in intense thought. After a moment, he said, "I like Larry Parker as a suspect. He's simply too slick. Too straightforward and blameless. Too everything, for my taste. All in all I'd say Mr. Parker is so slick you'd think he was born with a greasy spoon in his mouth."

"He's a suspect twice removed. He's the lover of a woman who isn't even a suspect. That leaves us with less than nothing. No real connection."

"No real connection..." said Ransom reflectively, "...all these disaffected, disassociated people. God. We have a husband estranged from his wife for reasons even he doesn't understand. We have a sister who disappears for almost ten years without a word. The sister has a lover whose interest in her seems primarily carnal. You look at all these people and have to wonder what the hell it's all about. You have to wonder if anyone ever really connects—if they ever really know anyone else, or care about them.''

Gerald looked at his partner, his concern apparent. After a moment, he said with a slight shrug, ''I'm pretty fond of my Sherry.''

''You and Sherry are an anomaly in my experience.''

''You spend too much time with murderers.''

''You say that as if it were possible to spend 'enough' time with murderers.''

''No, just that they're not the norm.''

After a long contemplative silence, Ransom dismissed the subject with a puff of smoke.

''That being said, why don't we leave off examining me and return to examining the case at hand.''

Gerald laughed loudly. ''I finally figured out why you smoke! It's not for enjoyment at all, is it? It's for punctuation!''

Ransom smiled despite himself and said, ''The case, Gerald.''

Gerald ran through the suspects one by one, almost like a student recounting his lessons. ''All right, in the list of disconnected people connected with this case, we've already mentioned Larry Parker, who's the furthest removed. We know of no connection or motive. Next comes Eva Brinkley, the nearest relation besides the husband, at least in the past year since her relationship with her sister is on the mend. The problem with her is she has nothing to gain and everything to lose.''

''We don't know that she knew that.''

''But it's a fair assumption.'' said Gerald quickly. ''It would be very odd if Angela Stephens had altered her will in Eva's favor after such a short time.''

''If she'd had one.''

''If she'd had one. Still, Eva Brinkley stood to lose everything by her sister's death, including the business left by her parents.''

Ransom gazed out the windshield. ''Unless she can rely

on the kindness of Frank Stephens, which I sincerely doubt."

Gerald's usually impassive, pasty face flushed with annoyance. "Are you going to let me finish?"

Ransom made a gesture of acquiescence.

"Okay," Gerald continued in a slightly less heated tone, "that leaves us with the husband. He has a weak alibi and two good motives: His wife may have been having an affair and he gets all her money—and before you say it, I know he doesn't exactly need the money."

Ransom smiled at his partner and said smugly, "Very good, Gerald."

The two detectives looked at each other for a moment. Under Ransom's steady gaze, Gerald began to realize he'd neglected something. After a moment, it came to him.

"Oh, yeah, the fortune-teller!"

"Ah!" said Ransom. "The wild card."

Gerald grimaced. "The most disconnected person of all. If you're right, and she's a fake and was a paid guest star in this mess, then—"

"Then we can make several assumptions about her. We can assume she was hired by someone who knew Angela well. Melina was supplied with several intimate details concerning Angela Stephens's past, which she used to build up Angela's confidence in her powers. She was also provided with information concerning Angela's present, and a guilty secret which her husband presumably didn't know. It is possible, though, that the husband *did* know. We can also assume that all of this was simply a buildup to the *real* objective, and that was to get Angela Stephens to believe Melina's prediction of the future."

"But I still don't see the point in it," said Gerald, shaking his head.

"I can only see one reason for the whole Melina episode," said Ransom. He paused long enough to take a long drag from the cigar and release a stream of smoke through the open car window. "To frighten her. To terrorize her.

To make her suffer. For what? For something we have to discover.''

"All of which brings us back to the husband.''

"Oh, no, my dear Gerald. All of which brings us back to Melina.''

EIGHT

The Fool

RANSOM KNEW THAT further questioning of the fortune-teller would not take place the minute he and Gerald rounded the corner and saw the flashing blue lights. Two squad cars were just pulling away from the curb, while two more stood outside the converted hotel, along with a couple of unmarked cars Ransom recognized.

Melina's office was a flurry of activity. The evidence technicians were already at work, and the occupants of neighboring offices being sought.

Detective Mary O'Brien stood in the doorway of Melina's office. O'Brien was in her early thirties and the picture of a fresh-faced colleen. She had soft white skin with a fair sprinkling of freckles and long, wavy brown hair that always looked tousled but never out of place. Though still young, she successfully contrived to assume the air of a world-weary, seasoned barmaid, with more than her share of good humor. When she saw Ransom and Gerald getting off the elevator, her face broke into a welcoming smile.

"Due to unforeseen circumstances, Melina was unavailable," said O'Brien, leaning against the doorjamb and crossing her slender, milky white arms. "I seem to remember the offer of a beer about...three months ago. I'm still awfully thirsty."

"It hasn't been in the cards," said Ransom with a slight shrug. "I take it your presence here means she's dead."

"As a doornail," she said with a nod toward the office.

Ransom started to enter the office, but Mary O'Brien slid her hand up the opposite side of the doorway to block his way.

"So what brings you to my little patch of ground?" she said with a friendly sparkle in her eyes. The emphasis she put on the word "my" was not lost on Ransom.

"Curiosity?" he said lightly.

"I would think a man like you would be afraid to know the future."

He shook his head. "Only because I'm sure it's dull as dishwater. I just wanted to have a little chat with her."

"I've heard about your little chats," said O'Brien, still barring the door. "People have come away from them with little stripes burned into their skin."

"They're never more than lightly singed."

Ransom thought that under normal circumstances, he'd enjoy a little swordplay, verbal or otherwise, with the lady detective. She could, with a slight raise of her shoulder or turn of her ankle, ooze the sexuality of a country peasant. It was all the more alluring that she didn't seem aware she was doing it. But at the moment there were more important matters at hand. He glanced meaningfully at the arm that blocked his way.

"Are we feeling a bit aggressive today?"

She pushed herself out of the doorway. "You should see me when I'm off duty," she said with a toss of her head that rivaled Scarlett O'Hara. Ransom half expected her to say "fiddle-dee-dee."

"How did she die?"

"She was shot," said O'Brien, leading the two detectives into the office.

"In the middle of the day?"

"In the middle of the office. One shot. Right through the heart." O'Brien smiled. "You would think she would have seen it coming."

Ransom winced.

"I'm sorry. I've been dying to say that. But you know how it is. A woman in charge—I'm not allowed the same privileges as you boys."

The body of the murdered woman lay sprawled halfway over the back of her chair, as if the force of the bullet had driven her back. Her mouth was slightly open, a thin trickle of blood running out of the right corner like virulent sleeping drool. Though her eyes were open, her face seemed closed and impassive.

Melina's once lithe, elegant body was marred by the prominent hole in the center of her chest, her blue dress stained in varying shades of red, brown, and black. She looked like a serene, deformed doll. Ransom stared down at the fortune-teller, the ensuing respectful silence marred only by the slight smirk that played about his lips.

"This was obviously done in the last hour or so. I don't suppose anyone heard the shot."

"The boys are still checking the tenants of the other offices, but it's Saturday, you know, and hardly anyone else is in today."

"Umm-hmmm."

"And of the ones that are here, we've gotten the usual 'car backfiring' stories."

"Of course," he said vaguely, his brow furrowed. He seemed to be memorizing the dead woman's face.

O'Brien looked down at the body. "Still, I suppose you can hardly blame people. Nobody really expects to hear a gun go off, do they?"

"Not before lunch," said Ransom. "Still, this seems to be an awfully noisy way of killing somebody in the middle of the day."

"Would you prefer she were stabbed?"

Ransom smiled. "It was just an observation."

Mary O'Brien eyed Ransom with interest. Like everyone else in the department, she was aware of Ransom's reputation, and given that, what his presence might mean. Gerald remained close to the doorway, a position advantageous in more ways than one: He could see everything and avoid coming between two sparring detectives.

"So, Ransom," O'Brien began cautiously, "what exactly is your interest in this woman?"

"Oh, any detective should be interested in Miss Melina."

"How so?"

"She has—I should say had—an amazing talent for predicting murders."

"Did she now?" said O'Brien as she flipped her hair back with her right hand.

"Oh, yes. She predicted a murder I'm investigating, and she predicted her own."

O'Brien raised an interested and incredibly attractive eyebrow at this.

"To be specific, she read my fortune and told me there was a death in my future. Well, here I am."

"But you're alive and she's not."

"She didn't specify *whose* death would be in my future. She did, however, predict a death."

"Well, then, it seems she was good at what she did, wouldn't you say?"

"I'd say if she'd been for real we could have used her," he replied, curling his upper lip. "Someone who can see crimes before or after they're committed would come in handy."

"You don't believe she was on the level, then?"

"We think..." Gerald started injudiciously, but was stopped by a narrow-eyed glance from Ransom.

Ransom sighed. "To the perpetual chagrin of Gerald, no, I don't. I would in principle alone be skeptical of someone who claimed to predict the future." He gestured nonchalantly at the corpse. "I am much more skeptical of someone who knows the intimate details of murders before they happen, straight down to a detailed description of the killer."

"In other words," said O'Brien mischievously, "she knew too much."

Ransom nodded toward the body. "I should say that was obvious."

"Well," said O'Brien after a pause during which she and Ransom eyed each other appraisingly, "she's real enough now, don't you think?"

"Real as the grave," he replied somberly. "Who found the body?"

"Ah! Her twelve o'clock appointment. Mrs. Lucille Cander. She's in the empty office next door. You want to talk to her?"

"If you don't mind," said Ransom with surprising deference.

With a slight shrug and a nod of assent, O'Brien led the way to the next office, followed closely by Ransom. Gerald, as usual, brought up the rear.

"I questioned her, of course. She got here at five to twelve for her appointment—she's a regular—every Saturday, same time."

Ransom said something that sounded like "hmph."

O'Brien nodded. "Like a regular appointment with a therapist from Mars, don't you think? Anyway, Mrs. Cander arrived at eleven fifty-five, the office door was open, she went in, saw the body, and screamed."

"Was she the one who called the police?"

O'Brien paused with her hand on the knob of the office door directly to the left of Melina's and grinned in unsuppressed amusement. She spoke quietly. "Mrs. Cander is what I would call one of those 'wet women.' You'll see what I mean. I don't think she was capable of movement after her discovery. Someone working a couple of floors down heard her scream, came up, saw what had happened, and called the police. When we got here we found—I don't want to sound unkind—blubbering. I'm sorry, it's the only word I can think of to describe it. That's pretty much been her state ever since. We've been waiting for her to calm down enough to go home."

She pressed her ear to the door, through which came barely audible intermittent noises that could best be described as low gurgles. "Uh-huh. Sounds like we're getting there."

She twisted the knob and quietly opened the door. There on a hard wooden chair by a hard wooden desk sat Lucille Cander. She looked everything one would expect a woman named Lucille to be: somewhere in the muddy stages of middle age, a little plump, a little washed out, and wearing a little too much makeup in an attempt to hide these flaws. Ransom repressed a smile. O'Brien's description of her as a wet woman was highly accurate. Mrs. Cander's face was puffy from crying, and her eyes were red. They seemed in danger of bubbling over at any moment. She held a blue embroidered handkerchief directly beneath her eyes with both hands. Her tears left ugly streaks on her face, and a couple of large drops hung tenuously from her chin, as if undecided about whether or not to take their final leap. Taking in the entire picture, Ransom thought Mrs. Cander looked as if she'd just been told her son was being drummed out of military school.

"Now then," said O'Brien as brightly as an officious nurse, "are you feeling better?" There was just a touch of irony in her tone.

Lucille Cander's soft, plump hands twisted the lace-trimmed handkerchief stained with deep red lipstick and wet with tears and other bodily fluids that Ransom thought it better to ignore. "Yes, thank you," she said with such exaggerated forlornness that Ransom felt inclined to strike her. "I'm better now. It's the shock, you know."

"Don't worry about it," said O'Brien not unkindly. "Anyone would be shocked under the circumstances."

"Oh, it's not that!" said Mrs. Cander breathily. She held the handkerchief cupped over her nose as if trying to avoid a bad odor. "It's not just finding a body. It's that it was Melina. My Melina, of all people!"

"Your Melina?" said Ransom curiously.

Mrs. Cander looked at him blankly, then looked back at O'Brien questioningly.

"This is Detective Ransom, Mrs. Cander." O'Brien explained. Then, with a wicked smile at Ransom, continued. "He's working with me on this case. He'd like to ask you a few questions."

Gerald coughed.

Without removing the handkerchief, Mrs. Cander turned on Ransom two large, wet, doelike eyes. They seemed to be an uneven mix of drama and distress, as if she were caught in oncoming headlights and didn't know whether to run or take a bow.

Mary O'Brien also watched the detective with interest, wondering what more he thought he could get from this doughy woman.

"Mrs. Cander," he said gently, "Melina was more than just a fortune-teller, wasn't she?"

Mrs. Cander nodded vigorously. "You must have consulted her!" Her voice took on a faraway tone. "She was very gifted."

Ransom sat on the edge of the desk and leaned toward her. "I mean to you."

"Oh, yes!" she said quietly. "Melina was a friend. A confidante. A person to whom I could turn to unburden myself in times of need."

"A confidante," said Ransom, impressed.

"I mean in the spiritual sense." Every word she uttered seemed to drip from her. "How else could you express it when someone is able to read your thoughts? Your very soul?"

Ransom glanced at Gerald, then back at the woman.

"You found Miss Melina's predictions to be accurate?"

"Oh, yes!" she said excitedly. "Yes!"

Lucille Cander recounted a fair litany of predictions that had been made by Melina: each one in the vague terms of a daily horoscope that would apply to anyone. But Mrs. Cander was convinced. Examples of Melina's expertise cascaded from her like water down a slide. Each example as bland and predictable as the next: She'd receive an unexpected call, and she did. She'd meet a dark, handsome stranger, and she did.

"Why, Melina even told me I'd come into some money, and I did," she said breathily. "My husband died."

"Oh, I'm sorry," said Ransom.

Mrs. Cander shrugged. "I really didn't like him very much. But don't you see, Melina was right! My husband didn't have very much money while alive, but he was heavily insured."

Ransom raised an eyebrow. "But Melina didn't predict your husband's death?"

"No. She could see the money very clearly, but the source was a question mark. The future can be like that, you know. Some things are clear, some fuzzy."

"That's the way I feel about the present," said Ransom. He considered the woman for a moment, then pressed forward. "Did she ever warn you of things that might happen in the future? Things you might want to avoid?"

Mrs. Cander shook her head, her eyes telling Ransom that he didn't understand. "Of course not. In the two years I've known her, she never once told me of something bad. That's what was so wonderful about her!" Tears welled up in her big, round eyes, and fully expecting a renewed bout of blubbering (by this time he'd accepted Mary O'Brien's term), Ransom decided to close the interview.

"Thank you, Mrs. Cander. You've been a great help."

"You must"—her words were interrupted by a gulping sob—"you must find the person who did this!"

"We'll do what we can," Ransom replied.

He rose as Mary O'Brien opened the office door. Gerald slipped through the doorway first.

"I'll send someone up in a few minutes to take you home, Mrs. Cander," said O'Brien, following Gerald.

"But..." She stopped Ransom with her watery eyes. "But what am I going to do now? How will I know what the future will bring?"

"The way the rest of us do," said Ransom as gently as he could, "when it happens."

In the hallway, Mary O'Brien cornered Ransom. "May I ask what you hoped to accomplish with that line of questioning?"

Gerald smiled. He'd been asking that ever since he'd been partnered with Ransom and had never received an answer that was anything less than infuriating.

"Merely to confirm a theory," said Ransom simply, but his smile was, indeed, irritating.

"And what does that mean?" said O'Brien.

Thank God, thought Gerald, it's not just me.

"It means, Miss O'Brien, that you were right: Melina knew too much. And I'm a step closer to knowing it, too."

"I'd be careful if I were you," she said with a smile, and jerked her thumb in the direction of Melina's office. "You've seen what happens when you know too much."

"I think I'll be all right," said Ransom offhandedly. "I don't tell people what *I* know in advance. And besides, I have my trusty Gerald to protect me."

O'Brien shifted her weight and rested her open right palm on her hip. Her skin glistened. "You will let me know when you solve my case, won't you?"

Once again the possessive wasn't lost on him. But at least she didn't sound as if she were going to cause trouble. That was what he admired most in Mary O'Brien: the equilibrium that allowed her to roll with the punches while maintaining her humor. It didn't matter to her who solved a crime as long as it was solved.

"You'll be the first," he replied.

"Then maybe you'll buy me that beer you owe me."

"Mary," he said with a smile, "when this case is over, I'll not only buy you a beer, I'll wrap a dinner around it."

IGNORING THE ELEVATOR, Ransom took the stairs two at a time. Gerald scrambled down the steps after him.

"What the hell are we in such a hurry for?" Gerald called at Ransom's retreating back.

"Do you have Eva Brinkley's phone number with you?" said Ransom over his shoulder as he continued down the stairs.

"Of course."

"There's a pay phone in the lobby. Call and see if she's there. If she is, tell her we'll be there to talk to her within the hour. If she's not—that's even better!"

"What?"

"I'll wait outside!"

When Gerald came out of the building, he found Ransom

sitting in the sizzling car, reflectively adding a green haze
of cigar smoke to the soot and grit of the hot summer city
air. Gerald shook his head in disgust. He wasn't sure he'd
be able to withstand Ransom and the heat at the same time.
He gritted his teeth and climbed into the cloud-filled car.
As he stuck the key into the ignition, Ransom put a hand
out to stop him.

"Was she there?"

"Yes. She didn't sound happy, but she said she'd be
there."

"Let's look at what we have."

"Why, why, why," said Gerald with sweaty irritation,
"do you always have to do this in a stationary car! It must
be a hundred and twenty degrees in here!"

Ransom eyed his partner impatiently. He curled his lip.
"You drive, I'll talk!"

Gerald started the car.

"Where to?"

"Frank Stephens," said Ransom curtly. His impatience
was purely logistical. There were many points he felt the
need to mull over aloud, and it was less than a mile to the
Stephenses' apartment.

"That dripping woman has given us some very important
information."

"Finding the body so soon helps," Gerald said, steering
the car onto Chicago Avenue and heading east. "So you
think that either Stephens or Brinkley killed her. So you
didn't really want me to make an appointment with her,
you just wanted to know if she was home."

Ransom grinned. "Oh, I want to talk to her again, all
right. But you're partly right. We don't know exactly when
Melina was killed, but it was within the last hour or so—
that's when the 'car backfiring' business happened, according to the locals. Eva Brinkley lives on Addison, less than
five miles away. She could easily have made it home by
now, even on a bus or the El. Stephens is, of course, within
walking distance."

"For that matter," Gerald added, "La Gioconda is less

than a mile from Melina's office. Larry Parker might have been able to do it on a short break from work."

"Nice relaxing break from routine," said Ransom, exhaling a long stream of smoke out the window. "This leaves us with a proximity problem. The only three people we know of connected with the Angela Stephens case were close enough to commit this murder. So far as we know. We'll be sure of all three of them once we've seen Stephens."

"But—" Gerald began.

"Surely you're not going to suggest that these two murders are not connected."

"No, I wasn't," said Gerald, and decided against pursuing what he actually was going to say.

"Anyway, finding the body so quickly wasn't exactly what I was talking about when I said Mrs. Cander had given us very important information."

He stopped. After a moment, Gerald gritted his teeth and said, "What, then?"

"The character of Melina herself. I've told you I think the fortune-teller is the key to this business. Mrs. Cander has fitted the key in the lock, and it's left for us to turn it."

Gerald turned the car onto Michigan Avenue and headed north onto inner Lake Shore Drive. "The point, Ransom."

"The point is that Melina told Mrs. Cander only good things: the vague, idiotic things that someone of her type would believe applied only to her. Fortune for money. She said what she thought her audience wanted to hear, what she was paid to say. It stands to reason that the same was true of what she told Angela Stephens. She was paid to say them. But not by the victim. I would think that would be enough to prove to you that Melina was involved."

With much relish, Gerald turned to his partner. "No, her death was enough to prove that to me."

"Touché, Gerald," said Ransom with an odd smile. "We can only hope that Melina remains consistent in her prophecies."

"What do you mean?"

Ransom stared ahead through the windshield, considering, as he answered. "The first card was death. The second, the fool. The third was the hanged man: meaning, in this case, that the murderer would be apprehended—or so she said. With the first two prophecies taken care of, we can only hope Melina was right about the third." Ransom took a deep, determined drag from his cigar and blew the smoke out the window somewhat contemptuously.

"Wait a minute," said Gerald, "I can see that the death card was Mrs. Stephens and the last card remains to be seen, but who was the fool?"

"Melina," Ransom answered simply.

"Why?"

Ransom turned to his partner, his eyes sharp and penetrating. "Because she thought she could get away with it."

As THEY PULLED INTO the semicircular driveway of the Stephenses' apartment building, the detectives were met once again by Walter, the tall, lanky doorman, who wore the same uniform and the same toothy grin.

"I was wondering when you'd get here," said Walter as Ransom stepped from the car.

Ransom frowned. "What do you mean?"

Walter's teeth sparkled in the sun. "I see Mr. Stephens come back, I figure you won't be far behind!"

Ransom stopped in the process of closing the car door and looked at Walter. "Come back? When did you see Mr. Stephens come back?"

Walter looked apprehensive for a moment, his grin wavering. "Late yesterday. I see him come back, I figure you got to release him!"

"Oh," said Ransom with an odd sense of relief.

"Yeah. So I see you drive up again, I figure you got more on him, right?"

"Not exactly..." said Ransom slowly. Gerald had climbed out of the steaming car and waited for them by the steps to the front door.

Ransom put a hand on Walter's shoulder and spoke to him conspiratorially.

"Walter…has Mr. Stephens been out of his apartment?"

Walter's smile waned, and he pulled his head back, his eyes darting questions. "You mean since last night? I wouldn't know 'bout that."

"No, I mean this morning, say in the past couple of hours. Have you seen him coming or going?"

"Well, not through the front door, but…"

"But then there's that damnable back door," said Ransom, his hand dropping to his side from Walter's shoulder.

"They thought of puttin' one of them cameras inside there—in the lobby—but there's a lotta old ladies in this building don't want me sitting behind a desk in the air-conditioning buzzing them in. They want me jumping up and pulling the door open so's they don't twist their little white wrists on it."

Ransom looked up into the face of the youngish black man and was met once again with the broad, tooth-filled grin. Ransom was reminded of how much could be hidden behind a smile.

THEIR KNOCK WAS met by stony silence. Ransom thought, not for the first time, how a building never seemed so much silent as listening. This feeling was accentuated by knowing that the very feline Mrs. Percy was next door hanging on their every sound.

Gerald knocked on the door again. After a long interval, during which both detectives began to fear the husband wasn't home, they heard a very faint voice say "come in." It was so faint, in fact, that it sounded as if it had been spoken through despair rather than through the door.

Ransom turned the doorknob and quietly pushed open the door.

"Mr. Stephens?" He could feel his voice echo in the long entrance hallway.

"Yes." The word sounded almost inaudibly from the living room.

The detectives followed the sound into the room as if following the song of the sirens. The summer sun had passed behind the Lake Shore high-rise, leaving the vista viewed through the windows facing the lake blindingly bright, while the living room incongruously dark. Frank Stephens sat fading into the elegant couch. He was clad only in a light purple silk robe tied loosely at the waist with a pale yellow sash. He looked as if all power had been drained from his body by an unseen force. He didn't look as if he'd just returned from killing an errant fortune-teller. In fact, he looked as if he hadn't left the apartment for years.

Ransom suddenly felt ridiculous, but knew he had to ask the question. "Mr. Stephens, have you been out of your apartment this morning?"

Stephens's eyes, which seemed to have sunken perceptibly into his skull during the past twenty-four hours, stared vacantly at the wall behind the detectives.

"I don't have anywhere to go," he said. His voice sounded vacant and hollow, as if it called to them from beyond the grave.

"Mr. Stephens…"

"My wife is gone…" he continued, unhearing.

"You've been here all morning?"

"The president of the bank called me this morning. He told me he thought it would be best if I took a leave of absence for the time being. Until this business is over. Until this is cleared up…that's what he said. But it will never really be cleared up." He stopped speaking, his body unnaturally still. "I have nowhere to go."

Gerald glanced at Ransom, wondering for a moment if he would press the point.

"So you did not leave your apartment."

"No." Stephens exhaled the word.

Ransom pulled from his inner pocket the flier that seemed to have become part of his jacket. It was damp with sweat and had become limp. He stepped forward and held it in front of Frank Stephens's eyes, which seemed to stare through it.

"Mr. Stephens, I showed this to you yesterday. Now I ask you again: Have you ever seen it before?"

Stephens didn't answer. Ransom said to him gently. "Please look at it."

Stephens's eyes twitched slightly, but didn't seem to move otherwise.

"I haven't seen it before."

"But it was found on a table in your home."

"I haven't seen it before."

"And you never heard of the woman advertised in it? Melina, the fortune-teller?"

"No."

"You're sure?"

"My wife...my wife...would be able to answer that for you...." Stephens's voice faltered and faded in and out like a badly tuned radio. "But...of course...she can't...my wife saw a lot of those people...I never knew their names...I doubt if she did."

"All right," said Ransom. He slipped the flier back into his pocket. His face became clouded and serious. He hooked his thumbs in his trouser pockets and considered Frank Stephens. After a long moment, he spoke quietly, but his words cut through the silence like tiny daggers.

"Mr. Stephens, did you know your wife was having an affair?"

Gerald's mouth fell slightly open, and he turned two hard, disapproving eyes upon his partner. He then looked back at Stephens. This was one of those rare moments when Gerald was of two minds and was not exactly happy with his work.

Stephens didn't move or even flinch. Tears welled up in his eyes involuntarily and ran down his face. He looked almost like one of the weeping icons to which pilgrimages are mounted.

"No," said Stephens with a faint gasp that made it sound as if the last nail was being driven into his heart.

"You never suspected?"

"No," he replied. He blinked, and tears caught his lashes and hung from them like dew.

Ransom looked at Gerald and gestured to the door. They started out, but Ransom paused in the doorway and looked back at Frank Stephens. The streaming tears made dark purple blotches on the immaculate robe.

"We *will* find out who did this, Mr. Stephens."

It was a promise.

"WAS THAT NECESSARY?" said Gerald hotly as they climbed back into the car.

"What do you mean?"

"We don't even *know*—for sure—that Angela Stephens was having an affair. We don't know it for a fact. How could you drop that bomb like that?"

"You know as well as I do," said Ransom defensively, "that fading Victorian hero routine is the easiest thing in the world to sham. I wanted to see if I could snap him out of it." He stopped and pulled out a cigar, giving himself some time to calm down. When he had lit it and taken a puff, which he exhaled with a sigh, he continued. "And to tell you the truth, I really wanted to know if he knew."

"God, Jer!"

Ransom stiffened imperceptibly and turned narrowed eyes upon his partner. "We are trying to find a murderer, Gerald—someone, I may add, who murdered two people. And if memory serves, that was *your* chief suspect we were just interrogating. Interrogating, Gerald, not attending a dinner party. The rules for proper manners are different."

There was a simmering silence between them that lasted only a moment before Ransom added with less rancor, "And besides, you *know* it was necessary."

"Yeah, I know it," said Gerald as he angrily shifted the car into drive and peeled out of the driveway, "but I don't like it." His anger became one with the heat, then broke like a fever: quickly but with a long way to go before being the same.

"Well, maybe I was wrong about him," Gerald said, in a tone that divided his disgust equally between himself and his partner.

Northbound Lake Shore Drive was clogged with traffic due to the road construction that seemed to shift from place to place on the Drive but was a constant presence. But even with the traffic, it took barely half an hour to reach Belmont, the exit they took to reach Addison. In that time, Gerald's anger had dissipated but not disappeared, and Ransom had finished his cigar.

Gerald's dilemma was perhaps a bit more difficult than Ransom's. Ransom was right: Stephens was Gerald's favorite suspect, and the attitude Stephens had presented on their last interview would have been the easiest dodge to maintain. And Gerald couldn't get past the fact, much to his chagrin that he had entertained the idea that Stephens was, indeed, putting on an act. (At least that much is to my credit, he thought.) Until Ransom had dropped his bomb. It seemed that in trying to wake Stephens out of his daze, he had woken Gerald up instead. The indignation he'd felt in Stephens's apartment had given way to a profound doubt about the husband's guilt.

It was in this frame of mind that Gerald steered the car onto Addison Street. Eva Brinkley's apartment was located three blocks west of the lake in a building of sickly yellow brick. The building consisted of a block of shops in varying degrees of dilapidation, above which were two floors of cheap, dark apartments.

The detectives located the entrance to the apartments between a used bookstore and a resale clothing store. Ransom wondered if it were possible to buy anything new in this area. The entrance was an old wooden door with peeling varnish around its grime-encrusted lattice windows. They stepped through the door into a tiny, dirty vestibule. Old newspapers, undelivered or undeliverable mail, and sales circulars littered the floor. They had to close the door behind them in order to read the double row of rusty mailboxes on which were taped the names of each tenant. They located the Brinkley box, which was marked 3C, and Ransom pressed the cheap plastic doorbell at its base.

"It had to be the third floor," said Ransom over his shoulder.

A loud, angry buzz sounded from the vicinity of the lock on the inner door. Gerald awkwardly pulled the door open with his right hand while he and Ransom pressed themselves out of the way against the left wall of the vestibule. They headed up the stairs, which were covered with a dingy maroon carpet. Radios and television sets blared from behind some of the doors. At least one loud marital squabble, presumably involving money (or lack of it), emanated from a hallway overhead. Ransom once again marveled at the concept of apartment living, where it was possible through the advent of drywall to know the intimate details of the lives of people you'd never seen.

"Far cry from Lake Shore Drive," Ransom mused, puffing his way up the stairs.

"But so close," said Gerald. "Chicago's funny that way. You can live cheap by the lake as long as you don't have to look at it."

"I wasn't talking proximity, Gerald, I was talking about socioeconomics."

"I know that," said Gerald with a sigh, rolling his eyes behind Ransom's back.

"I just meant there is a marked difference of lifestyle between Angela Stephens and her sister."

Gerald shrugged. "Well, when you run away from money, you run away from money."

"Very well put."

They reached the first landing and rounded a newel rubbed raw of varnish by years of use and neglect, then continued up the second flight.

"This isn't so bad," said Gerald. "I lived in a place like this up in Rogers Park when I was just out of the academy."

"That would have been before Sherry."

Gerald smiled. "Way before. You've met Sherry. Could you see her living in a place like this?"

Ransom thought better than to comment on this. "You're lucky you made detective before you met her."

"Luck had nothing to do with it. I think the police gods just wanted to pair you up with somebody who wouldn't want to blow your brains out."

Ransom cocked an amused eyebrow at his partner. "Do you ever feel like that?"

Gerald smiled. "That's another one of those impulses I never act on."

"You know, Gerald, these past few days have been a real eye-opener to me. You seem to be seething with hidden hostilities."

Their banter was broken by a shout from above.

"What the hell do you want from me?" Eva Brinkley bellowed from the doorway of her apartment.

The detectives heard her voice just as their heads cleared the second landing. When Ransom spied the woman's face, he once again had the unpleasant sensation of her being a distorted version of her sister. But with her face contorted with anger, the image was further marred in a way that made him feel as if Angela were disintegrating before his eyes. He tried to recall Angela's beautiful, troubled face, tempered with serenity, as it had appeared in his office. He was almost successful.

"We have a few more questions we'd like to ask you," said Ransom as he and Gerald stepped onto the landing.

"Well, make it fast!" snapped Eva. She flung the door back with a bang that Ransom was sure would leave a dent in the wall and marched into her cramped studio apartment, an unspoken, ungracious invitation for the detectives to follow her.

It was, indeed, a far cry from Lake Shore Drive. A settling crack spanned the right wall from floor to ceiling like a thin, black, angry bolt of lightning. Soiled Kmart curtains hung limp from flaking mock-brass rods like spiritless ghosts.

Eva yanked an unfiltered Camel cigarette from its pack, shoved it into her mouth, and lit it with a light blue Bic lighter whose flame was so low it barely did the job. A glance at the cracked amber ashtray on a small end table showed Ransom the remains of at least a dozen others.

"Well?" she demanded, her eyes flaring at them.

"There are some things we'd like to know about your sister," Ransom replied calmly.

"Christ! Is there no end to this?"

"If we want to solve your sister's murder, we need to know more about her."

"If you really wanted to solve it, you'd arrest Frank Stephens and fry his ass." She inhaled the cigarette as if she intended to suck out its life in one breath.

"We can't arrest on suspicions, Miss Brinkley," said Ransom tolerantly, "even obvious ones. Now, in order for us to proceed, we need to know more about your sister and her frame of mind."

Eva looked confused and angry. "You're not going to start saying she killed herself, are you?"

Ransom closed his eyes for a moment and sighed. "No, Miss Brinkley. I can't possibly conceive of her strangling herself."

"Well," said Eva, with a laugh like the bark of a mid-sized dog, "there's a point in your favor."

Ransom maintained his composure with some effort. "Do you want us to find your sister's murderer?"

Eva glared in Ransom's general direction for a moment, then breathed a flat "yes."

"Then we need your help. We need to know what was going on in her life."

Eva stood for a moment blankly staring at the floor as if trying to remember something that was just out of reach— something she knew was sad. A thin trail of smoke streamed from the cigarette she held between two fingers, her arms crossed below her breasts. A wisp of ash dropped from the cigarette onto her skirt.

"You're asking the wrong person."

"But you're her sister," Ransom protested gently.

"I was away a long time."

"And you spent the past year catching up. What did you talk about in all that time?"

"Everything. Lots of things. Our past. Our parents. The past before I left, at least. As far as the recent past goes, she mostly wanted to hear about *my* life. She wasn't that open about hers."

Each phrase escaped her like verbal prisoners of war.

"Didn't she talk about herself at all?"

"She wasn't the type," Eva answered irritably. "She was the type who's more interested in other people than she was in herself."

"She *never* talked about her friends—the people she knew?"

Eva paused for a moment. Just long enough of a moment to make it clear to Ransom that she wasn't telling all. "Not really."

"Didn't she have any friends?"

Eva stood framed in the window, backlit by the bright afternoon sun. The curtains stirred behind her like shrouds in a hot breeze. When Eva spoke, her voice was harsh and cynical.

"My sister was one of those women who went out with the sixties: a professional wife. Her job was to be Frank's wife: to appear at dinners and other crap like that; entertain the other professional wives of Frank's bosses, and every now and then the wives of his staff. My sister was smart, and she was better than all that. She wasted herself."

"Hmmm. Your sister seemed quite charming to me. It's difficult to believe she had no friends."

"I don't think her 'job' left her time for friends. All she had was acquaintances."

"But she had *some*."

Eva sighed heavily as if making a major concession. "Yes, I'm sure she had *some* friends."

"Did you know any of them?"

She gestured around the room with her cigarette, marking

it with wisps of smoke. "We're not exactly in the same crowd."

"This isn't so bad," said Ransom lightly.

"It ain't Lake Shore Drive, either," Eva replied bitterly. Ransom and Gerald exchanged glances.

"It's a dump," she continued. "You know it and I know it."

"Some people don't require as much as others," said Ransom.

Eva's lips curled maliciously. "Some people just don't get as much as others."

She turned her back to the two detectives and stared out the window so purposefully she seemed to pierce the heat with her eyes. Ransom considered her in silence. She wore a blue denim skirt that just about reached her knees. It was topped by a light blue shirt of indeterminate fabric through which he could see her sharp shoulder blades and tense, taut muscles. Her tendons were tight enough to strum.

"So," said Ransom after allowing Eva a suitably dramatic pause, "you didn't know any of her friends."

"No."

"And she never spoke of anyone?"

Eva slowly turned a quizzical look at Ransom. With her arms crossed, the smoke from her cigarette appeared to be rising from her left breast.

"What's this all about? Why all these questions about her friends? Are you trying to find somebody else that might've wanted to kill her? If that's your game, I can save you a lot of time: There wasn't anybody. Nobody! Nobody but that goddamn Frank Stephens who you can't see for the goddamn trees would want to kill my sister. She was a saint."

Ransom looked Eva in the eye for a moment.

"As I've said before, you didn't always think so."

Eva stiffened perceptibly, her eyes flashing at him. She looked as if she might let fly at him, verbally if not otherwise. But after a moment, she turned her gaze resignedly to the floor.

If I saw that on the stage, thought Ransom, I would be convinced that she was an angry woman who couldn't argue with the truth.

"Well," said Eva at last, "it's true. I didn't always think she was a saint. She tried to be my mother. She did things I didn't like for my own good. I didn't think she was a saint then. But I was younger then. I didn't know what was good for me myself. But I'm older now."

"But that's just my point," said Ransom with a genial shrug. "If *you* didn't think she was a saint at one time, there might be others. That's why I wondered about her friends."

"I told you I don't know of any!" she said impatiently.

"What I'd really like to know," said Ransom, "is if she had a *special* friend. Surely in a year's time she would have told you about that."

"Special?"

"Yes."

Eva eyed him quizzically for a moment. Then her lips spread into a smile.

"You want to know if she had a lover!"

"Yes," said Ransom simply.

Eva stared at him a moment. Then she laughed. It was a dry, throaty laugh that embodied a lifetime of bitterness and disappointments, tinged with something Ransom felt bordered on cruelty. Her shoulders shook and looked as if their blades might slice through her blouse. She hugged herself.

"Is that so hard to believe? She married a man who's never thought beyond his own skin. Is it so hard to believe that she looked for something somewhere else?"

Ransom's expression remained unchanged. He found it difficult to set aside the feeling that every move Eva Brinkley made was overly dramatic, incautiously calculated to produce an effect. Though he admitted to himself that he'd never actually seen her do it, he had the impression that she was surreptitiously glancing toward him from the corner of her eye to check his reaction. He mentally castigated himself for maintaining his negative impression of her in the face of the facts. He had, after all, only feelings to go by—there was absolutely no proof or even basis for a suspicion that Eva had in any way participated in the death of her sister, and more often than not, the suspects in a murder case acted suspiciously as a matter of form—but at the same time he would not discount these feelings. He counted himself a sensitive in the true sense of the term. He waited her out.

Eva sucked greedily at the cigarette, then imprudently allowed herself to laugh again and was soon caught in a fit of coughing.

"I'm sorry," she said, looking far from it as she wiped a tear from the corner of her eye. "It's not really funny, it's the shock. I was just wondering what Mommy and Daddy would have thought of the idea of Angela having an affair. Would they have been shocked? Or would they refuse to believe it? Yeah, that's probably what they'd do."

Suddenly, her expression changed from amusement to fear. She apparently realized she'd committed an indiscretion.

"If I sound bitter, I am. But I'm not really as bitter as I sound. It's just hard to understand how two sisters like Angela and me, with the same upbringing and the same parents, can turn out so different. I'm not mad at my family. I'm mad at the gods who turn out one sister who turns everything to gold, and one who ruins everything she comes in contact with. That's the way it is, you know. I don't think it's anybody's fault. It's not that she was better than me, it's just the way things worked out. It's taken me a lifetime to realize that nobody's to blame for the way things turn out, it's just the gods or the Fates or whatever the hell you call it. But that's the way it was in our family. Everything goes right—I mean, everything went right for Angela—everything goes wrong for me. It's hard to be the one the gods keep screwing."

Ransom allowed a moment for this to sink in. Then he said softly, "You still haven't answered my question."

Eva looked confused. "Which one?"

"Did your sister have a lover?"

"Yes," she said finally.

"Aaaah!" said Ransom with a satisfied smile. "At last we make progress. Did she ever tell you who it was?"

"Of course not!"

"But she did go so far as to tell you she had a lover?"

"Only because she felt so guilty about it. As if anybody cares."

"Surely it would matter to someone."

Eva stared fixedly at Ransom for a moment. She looked at once wary and curious. She took one last angry drag from her cigarette, then crushed out the remainder in the amber ashtray with one fierce stab.

"I don't know what you mean by that," she said, watching the last wisp of smoke rise from the ashtray.

"Her husband, of course," said Ransom simply.

Eva's face brightened. "Well, there you are! That's what I've been trying to tell you! He was the only one with a reason to kill my sister. And now you know there was a reason other than money: jealousy. What the hell more do you want?"

"Proof," Ransom answered simply.

"Proof!" she yelled. "Proof! What would be proof? What would you accept as proof? You're not going to arrest that bastard until I bring you a picture of him murdering my sister, are you?"

"That would make things considerably easier."

Once again Eva stiffened. She cocked her head deliberately, looking down her shanty-aristocratic nose at him as if he were emitting toxic waste.

"You really are a bastard, you know that?"

He spread his palms and shrugged. "I'm just a skeptic."

Eva made a sound something like "feh" and lit another cigarette with angry angular motions.

"Miss Brinkley, as I've said to the point of delirium, we have no proof. Suspicions are not proof. Not even motives are proof. And quite frankly, we don't really even have motives."

"But I just told you—" she began.

"Frank Stephens does not to our knowledge need money. He has quite enough of his own."

"But that's not the only—" she began again, but he didn't let her finish.

"Before you confirmed it, we already had our suspicions—*suspicions*—about your sister having a lover. And that *could* be a motive for murder, but we don't even know that Frank Stephens *knew* about this affair."

Eva looked startled for a split second. Ransom thought, not without a sense of accomplishment, that it was the second genuine, uncalculated reaction he'd been able to draw from her, the first being the momentary wariness she'd displayed earlier. There was to be a third. The startled look on her face gave way to a genuine look of triumph.

"Oh, he might not have known, but he was going to."

Ransom cocked an eyebrow. "How?"

Her smile grew uglier, embodying a lifetime of frustrated desires. She inhaled deeply from the cigarette, its hot, glowing tip accentuating the heat and grit of the room. She added the smoke to the general oppression.

"Because Angela was going to tell him!"

A FAINT RATTLE, like a pea being tossed about inside a cylinder, had developed inside the old air conditioner that hung in the window of Ransom's office. He didn't think it boded well. He'd given it a sound smack with the flat of his hand as he and Gerald entered the room, the only result being a momentary wheeze before the rattling resumed. Fortunately, the old machine still managed to pump cold air into the dusty office. Unfortunately, it was no match for the heat, humidity, and general grime of a Chicago summer.

Gerald had gone home for the day, and Ransom would soon follow. But first he felt like relaxing in his ancient but comfortable wooden desk chair, its hinges creaking with every move, with his hands clasped behind his head and his feet up on the desk. One or two more scuff marks wouldn't make a difference. Huge metal fans mounted on floor stands stirred the stale air of the squad room beyond his door, providing a soft, relaxing background to his thoughts.

He closed his eyes and replayed the scene he'd played with Eva Brinkley. He couldn't seem to help thinking of it as a scene and feeling as if he'd been an actor forced to improvise his part in a play where the other characters had memorized their lines. In his mind's eye, he once again watched every gesture and considered every inflection of the murdered woman's sister. "Calculated" was the word that repeated itself in his head. Calculated with two exceptions: a brief moment of wariness when he'd said that Angela Stephens's affair would matter to someone. It was a curious reaction, since he was sure that it was obvious he'd been referring to Frank Stephens. Why, then, the sudden look of wariness on the face of the sister? Then there was the fact that she'd seemed startled when he'd said that Frank Stephens didn't know that her sister was having an affair. But why? Why wary at one point and startled at another? It was the question he kept asking himself. It was the same question he'd asked Gerald in the car.

"It explains the argument," said Gerald as he swung the car out onto Lake Shore Drive. Cars sped past them at an average of ten miles per hour over the limit.

"It explains a great many things," said Ransom irritably. "Too many."

"If she decided to tell her husband about the affair," continued Gerald, "I would expect an argument to follow. And it brings us back to a crime of passion type thing. I could imagine him killing his wife in a fit of rage."

"Really, Gerald?" said Ransom with a twinkle. "I can't imagine Frank Stephens managing a fit of rage. I think his scope is limited to a fit of testiness."

Gerald sighed. "I'll give you that. But you know what they say—"

Ransom stopped him short. "Yes, I do, and I'll thank

you not to repeat it. Now, there's another thing I have a problem with: the idea that Angela Stephens would actually tell her husband about the affair.''

"Guilt makes people do funny things. We both know that. And we both noticed how guilty she seemed about her 'secret.'''

Ransom turned his most incredulous look upon his partner. "Yes, but still, believing that she was going to be murdered and given a description of the murderer that generally fit her husband, would she then turn around and *give* him a reason to kill her? The mind boggles, Gerald.''

Gerald shrugged. "Unless she was a fatalist.''

"I think," said Ransom after a pause, "that we need to remember that we only have Eva Brinkley's word that Angela was going to confess to her husband. I don't like it.''

"Miss Brinkley is really…something," said Gerald.

"Not at all the type I'd like to meet in the proverbial dark alley," said Ransom somewhat absently.

"I don't know about that, but I sure wouldn't want to be on her bad side." Gerald pressed the brake as they became enmeshed in the crawling rush-hour traffic. As the car ground to a halt, he received a backlash of cigar smoke that had gathered in the backseat of the car.

Ransom, his most recent cigar stuck nonchalantly between two fingers of his right hand, rested his elbow on the open car window and his head on his palm. He looked almost as if a lopsided chimney lurched from his temple.

"She's sure angry," Gerald continued, "but I'm not sure who all that anger is directed at. She made no secret of the fact that she hates Frank Stephens, and that didn't start with her sister's murder. She's always hated him. But…there doesn't seem to be a rational reason for it. You would think it was because he stole Angela's affections from her—that would be the classic reason, I guess—but it doesn't really wash. She wasn't exactly on great terms with Angela when Frank and Angela married. It seems to me there's something more to this anger. You'd think she was mad at the world.''

Ransom glanced at him.

"As my mother used to say," Gerald added a little sheepishly.

"That's very well reasoned, Gerald. There's more to her anger. I think it's obvious that Eva's real problem with Frank Stephens is what he stands for."

"Which is?"

"Everything she's not." Ransom took a puff of his cigar and blew the smoke out the window. Since the car was at a standstill, the smoke managed to travel around its frame and blow directly into Gerald's face on a hot breeze through the window on the driver's side. Gerald winced. He couldn't win.

Ransom continued. "Frank Stephens is one of the 'haves' of this world, while Eva Brinkley is a perennial 'have-not.'"

"Of course," said Gerald carefully, "the same applies to Angela Stephens."

"Oh, yes, only more so," Ransom agreed placidly. "Despite having the same advantages as her sister, Eva has managed to come to nothing."

"Like she said herself," Gerald reminded him, "she's the one who was dealt the bad hand by whatever."

"Hmmm."

The car inched forward, a waffling motion appearing in the air directly in front of them as the hot air met the scorching asphalt.

Gerald glanced at his partner. "She was honest about being bitter."

Ransom sighed. "It's as I said before, some people use honesty as a weapon."

"But for what?"

"Consider this: She is not an adept enough actress to hide the fact that she's bitter. And she's self-aware enough to *know* that she couldn't completely pull off an act like that. If she thinks she's a suspect, she might think it puts her in a better light if she admits to being bitter at the outset. That way we go away thinking about how honest she is instead of how bitter she is.''

Gerald stared at the stopped traffic before him and fought the urge to blow the car horn in frustration. He settled for wiping his damp palms on his trouser legs.

"And do we think she's a suspect?"

Ransom smiled at him. "With so few players to choose from, I think we have to."

At this point in Ransom's ruminations, the landscape took on a more ethereal quality, and his and Gerald's voices both faded away on ripples of heat. The cigar fell from between Ransom's fingers onto the steaming pavement below, igniting it in a flash. Everything—all the other cars, the street, the buildings, the entire city—burned away in an instant and faded into a pale blue. Ransom sat alone and untroubled in the car, which at once began to melt away into a liquid metal of indeterminate temperature. Ransom slowly slid down into the murky silver liquid. As he disappeared beneath the surface, he heard a woman's voice—a voice he thought he recognized—cry "fool!"

Ransom woke with a start to find Sergeant Newman standing in his office doorway. Newman's gray-and-black hair was damp from humidity and sweat. The frayed collar of his blue shirt was unbuttoned and his tie hung loosely about his neck. His old navy blue blazer was draped casually over his right arm. He looked ready to leave.

"Am I keeping you up?"

"It's been a long day, Mike," said Ransom.

"So I heard. I saw White on his way out."

Ransom smiled. "Has Gerald been indiscreet?"

"He said he had nothing to tell me. I wondered if you did."

"Nothing for publication."

"Then how about the unpublished version?"

Ransom gazed out the window at the steamy streets without answering. There was little he disliked more than having to answer to anyone, but with a firm understanding of the chain of command in the police force, he accepted Sergeant Newman as a necessary evil. Not that he disliked Newman. He didn't. But he had remained a detective instead of climbing up further through the police ranks for two reasons: First, he sincerely enjoyed homicide detection. He enjoyed solving the human puzzles that came his way. Secondly, his superiors were generally good enough to leave him on his own. The fact that Newman was here now—that the sergeant had sought him out—meant that he was worried for some reason. Or merely that he was trying to gently assert his authority. Ransom couldn't decide which. One thing he was sure of: He was in no mood for a speech about manpower shortages and the need to dispatch a case as soon as possible.

But Newman began with neither. He came into the cluttered office and sat down on the hard chair across the desk from Ransom. It was the same chair that Angela Stephens had occupied not three days earlier. If there was any irony to be seen in this, Ransom chose to ignore it.

"I've always liked this office," said Newman conversationally as he pushed his damp hair back off his forehead. "It reminds me of my early days on the force."

"Surely you didn't come here to discuss the decor," said Ransom wearily.

"No, I just came to find out how you're doing."

"In what respect?"

"In general. How's it going?"

"World-weary," Ransom replied. It was worse than he thought. Newman was in his friendly, concerned mode. Ransom could feel himself emotionally withdrawing. If there was anything he disliked more than answering to anyone professionally, it was answering to someone personally.

This was one of the reasons he found himself so comfortable with Emily. She seemed to understand and respect the lone hand he played in life. In one of those strange contradictions that so often occur in this world, Emily's understanding of his need to stand alone served to make him feel closer to her, deepening their relationship with a sense of communication that is usually restricted to plant life. Emily understood Ransom and therefore was not apt to trample over him in an attempt to communicate.

It was not so with others. Someone like Newman would like as not stumble over Ransom's ego. Ransom resented the intrusion on the rare occasion that it happened and at the same time felt an irritating sense of gratitude toward the sergeant.

Surprisingly, on this occasion Newman seemed to be aware that he was nearing a border and proceeded with a touch more formality.

"Well, it's been two days since you asked me for the Stephens case...."

"It was yesterday morning," said Ransom, correcting him matter-of-factly.

"Yeah. I haven't asked for any sort of report...before now. But I thought you should bring me up to speed."

"In what way?" said Ransom. He really was tired, and he was sure he would prefer that Newman just ask him to report.

"What's happening with the Stephens case, Ransom?" said Newman, his temper finally giving way a little.

Ransom smiled. That was better.

"Gerald was telling you the truth, as he always does. There is nothing to report."

"After two days?" said Newman incredulously. He thought it just possible that Ransom was toying with him. "I don't buy it. I know you. You must have something."

Ransom shrugged. "I have nothing but suspicions. That's all. I'm afraid, Mike, that I may have been wrong about this case."

This caused Newman to raise both of his slightly bushy, graying eyebrows. He'd never heard Ransom even come close to admitting he'd been wrong before. He didn't think that this was an idea Ransom would ever wittingly entertain.

"How do you mean?"

Ransom spoke more to himself than to his sergeant, as

if he were voicing thoughts that had been nagging at him for some time.

"I'm afraid that this case may turn out to be ordinary in the worst possible way. This may be one of those murders where the guilty party is obvious, but we are never able to prove it."

Newman's temper gave way a little more. "Ransom, you stormed into my office yesterday morning and demanded this case! You told me a cock-and-bull story about this woman coming to your office with a prediction about her own murder. Then she gets herself killed. You told me all this at the top of your lungs because you were sure this wasn't an ordinary case. After listening to you it struck me as pretty damned weird, too! And now you're going to sit on your ass and tell me the case is ordinary?"

Ransom smiled. "Only in resolution, not in particulars."

"And on top of that, you sit there at the same time and tell me that the guilty party is obvious."

Retaining the smile, Ransom shrugged. "Of course: the husband."

Newman barked, "But you don't believe he did it."

Ransom said nothing. He allowed his gaze to wander back out the window. He pulled a cigar out of his shirt pocket, unwrapped it, and stuck the end between his teeth. He slowly crumpled the cellophane and tossed it into the stained, drab green receptacle beside his desk.

"Are you going to tell me why the husband didn't do it?"

Ransom flicked on the flame of his lighter and with a few rapid puffs breathed glowing life into the tip of his cigar.

"The fortune-teller remains the wild card in this scenario—if you'll excuse the pun," said Ransom, releasing a satisfying stream of smoke into the stale office air. "I think she was hired by someone to say the things she said to Angela Stephens. That being the case, I can't see why Frank Stephens would have hired her."

Ransom took another drag from the cigar, then exhaled the smoke as he eased casually back into his chair.

"For that matter, I can't see why anyone else would want to hire her, either."

Newman's damp, gray-streaked hair had fallen back across his forehead unnoticed. He stared at the detective with an expression that occasionally caused his subordinates to doubt his intelligence. After a moment, a deep angry red flowed into his features.

"You mean that's all you've got?" he said, his voice rising with incredulity. "You think he's innocent because you can't fit some bum-fuck fortune-teller into your case?"

Ransom shrugged, a gesture that served to further ignite the sergeant.

"For Pete's sake, Ransom, what does the fortune-teller matter anyway? What if she did predict the murder? It could have been a coincidence! It could've just been an unlucky guess. The fortune-teller might not have anything to do with it at all!"

"That could be true were it not for one thing."

Newman stopped in his tirade. Ransom turned his most engaging smile on his superior. "The fortune-teller's been murdered, too!"

Newman's chair almost toppled over backward as he leapt to his feet.

"What?!" he bellowed. "Why the hell didn't you tell me that to begin with?"

Ransom shrugged again. "I was giving you the information in the order I received it."

"And just what the hell do you intend to do now, if you don't mind telling me!"

Ransom sat up straight, leaned in, and eyed the sergeant shrewdly. He took a short puff on his cigar and blew the smoke out. "I intend to find out who killed Angela Stephens."

He paused for effect and sat back in his chair. His gaze returned to the window. The sun was lower, but it would still be sunlight for hours, and it would be hot forever, or at least it felt that way. He finished his report to Sergeant Newman without looking at him, almost as if speaking to himself.

"The future appears to be a dead end. I think we'll need to look into the past."

NINE

The Investigation Ends

"I THOUGHT IT would be nice to have some lemonade out here, before it gets too hot."

It was already too hot for Ransom, but he didn't say anything. It was thankfully not quite as hot as yesterday, but it was also only ten-thirty in the morning and already warm enough to promise another sweltering day. Ransom considered their cool, poised hostess. He thought that perhaps people with money were insulated against everything, including the weather. And Gladys Stephens had money. The Winnetka home she shared with her husband looked to Ransom as if it had been built in the middle of a golf course on which there was an incongruous abundance of trees. The lawn and trees and shrubs were manicured to perfection.

Mrs. Stephens had met Ransom and Gerald at the front steps of the sprawling ranch house and led them around to the back on a trail of neatly sanded stepping stones between which grass was allowed to grow thick and green. Ransom felt not unlike a lowly gardener, allowed the perimeter of the house, but not the inside. Had he been able to read the mind of Gladys Stephens, he would have found that it held not a bit of condescension or class consciousness toward the detectives, but something quite different. To Mrs. Stephens, the interior of her house stood in pristine elegance, built over years of care and diligence. It was a fortress against the cares and worries of the world: a refuge to which the family could return for nurturing, peace, and solace, protected. It was for this reason she was reluctant to bring the detectives into the house, but chose instead to meet them outside: It was a vain hope that her home would remain untainted by this travesty. It may touch her family, but not her house.

The path led onto a patio at the back of the house. At the end of the patio was what looked to Ransom like an Olympic-size pool whose clear blue water shimmered invitingly in the sun. A white metal drinktrolley, preset with a large, sweating pitcher of lemonade and several glasses, sat amidst a scattering of matching deck chairs.

The detectives sat in the chairs indicated, and Gladys proceeded to pour them each a tumblerful of fresh lemonade, which she then handed out with the composure of a perfect hostess entertaining valued clients instead of the mother of a suspect in a murder case about to be questioned by the police. Ransom was pleased—not so much pleased as relieved—to see her hand tremble ever so slightly as she replaced the pitcher on the trolley. It was good to know that despite appearance, the woman was affected by the situation. Her life wasn't completely insular.

"Frank Senior has gone on to church," she said, offering an explanation to an unasked question. "He hasn't missed a Sunday in years, so I told him to go ahead, since you said on the phone you wanted to talk to me."

"Yes."

"He wanted to go today very badly, to church. It's funny how you fall back on the old ways for solace in times of crisis. Not that we're fair-weather churchgoers, you understand. As I said, we go every Sunday. But these things tend to become rote. Then one day something happens and you find out how much the things you take for granted actually mean."

She stopped, took a sip of her lemonade, and looked out over the lawn. She had the look of a woman who didn't often speak randomly or freely. She seemed like a lost child who was speaking to keep back the dark. But she wasn't a child. She was an enormously handsome woman in her late fifties or early sixties. She'd let her hair go gray when its time had come, but had not let her figure go along with it.

She wore a pale yellow dress, cinched at the waist to accentuate her fine figure. The color would have brightened her aquamarine eyes, had they not been so dulled by distress. Oddly enough, it was her shoes in particular that caught Ransom's eye—they were dyed to match her dress, and were both fashionable and comfortable: the kind, as they say, that only money can buy. She crossed one shapely ankle over the other and absently tugged her skirt over her knee.

"Back when we were younger," she said, "I mean, back when our children were growing up, there used to be two services every Sunday morning, one at nine o'clock and one at eleven. But over the years, attendance fell off and it got to the point where there weren't enough people to warrant two services, so they dropped to one and decided to hold it at ten-thirty." She smiled sheepishly, as if painfully aware of chattering. "I guess they were splitting the difference. It's sad, though."

She stopped once again, and the air fairly tingled with her desperation to go on speaking: to keep her mind and her mouth busy and the detectives' questions at bay for as long as possible. But though her mind raced she could not manage to capture a solitary thought and put it into words. Her eyes widened, staring straight ahead of her in the general direction of the pool. She exhaled twice without perceptibly inhaling, as if she were an irregularly deflating balloon.

"This has been the worst few days of my life," she said to nobody in particular. Then she turned to Ransom. "It's all right that Frank Senior left, isn't it? Detective White said on the phone that it would be all right. You didn't give us much notice."

Ransom smiled compassionately. "It's quite all right. I'm sure you can tell us the things we'd like to know."

Gladys Stephens uncrossed her ankles and continued to stare across the pool, as if a solution might lie in that direction. There was a curious sense of embarrassment in her silence. After a pause that seemed interminable to her, she looked up sheepishly into Ransom's eyes.

"I'm lying, Detective Ransom. I'm sure if you're anything like the detectives in novels, you could tell that right away."

Ransom raised an eyebrow at Mrs. Stephens, a gesture that could have been taken for many things. Those who knew him would have recognized it as agreement. "In what way were you lying, Mrs. Stephens?"

"About my husband," she said, her cheeks turning a faint red that was not caused by the heat. "We are a church-going family, but that's not why he went when he heard you were coming."

She paused for a moment. When she continued, the embarrassment in her smile belied her words.

"I have no illusions about my husband, Mr. Ransom. He can go head-to-head with the world's greediest corporate lawyers without batting an eye, but when it comes to the emotions…when it comes to his personal life…"

Her voice trailed off, and she straightened her skirt again. Both of the detectives could sense the pain beneath Gladys Stephens's well-preserved exterior: years of having to deal with life's emotional and personal upheavals on her own.

She continued her explanation in a more matter-of-fact tone: "My husband has a tendency to disengage himself when things become emotionally…complicated."

"I understand," Ransom replied simply.

Gladys took two deep breaths, letting each out slowly. Some, but not all, of her tension was expelled in the effort. Her composure partly regained, Gladys said, "So, Mr. Ransom, what can I do for you?"

"We are at the point in our investigation of your daughter-in-law's murder where we thought it would be helpful to get some background information on the parties involved. What better person than you?"

"Me? Aren't you afraid I'd be biased?"

Ransom smiled gently. "We can take that into account. Anyone would be coming from some kind of bias. What we need is someone who knows the people involved and can supply some information about their pasts.''

Gladys considered this thoughtfully, her eyes fixed on Ransom's face. After a moment, she said, ''Before I answer any questions I should tell you that I don't believe for a moment that my son killed his wife.''

''Indeed,'' said Ransom. ''What makes you so certain?''

''I suppose any mother would say that about her son, but I'm not just saying it, it's true.''

''But how do you know?'' Gerald said, uncharacteristically reminding them that he was there.

Unlike most people who forgot Gerald White's presence, Gladys was much too good a hostess to be startled by a sudden question from a new quarter. She took a sip of her lemonade and replaced her glass on the trolley. She folded her neat, slender hands in her lap.

''Why am I so sure my son is innocent?'' she repeated with a look in her eyes that implied knowledge that was not purely factual. ''It was Frank Junior who called to tell us what had happened. He was trying to be brave, but I could tell from his voice that he was already withdrawing into himself. It is a trait which my husband has passed on to my son despite all my efforts to the contrary. In a situation of this sort, he retreats.'' She turned to Ransom, her eyebrows raising slightly as if she were about to test his powers of observation. ''Didn't he seem withdrawn to you?''

''He seemed as if he were in shock,'' said Ransom, ''which I consider a natural reaction given the situation.''

''Hmmm,'' she said doubtfully, her eyes wandering back to the pool, ''I wonder. I'm worried about him.''

''Also a perfectly natural reaction,'' said Ransom kindly.

''I suppose...but after a lifetime of watching him shut down in times of trouble I'd be hard pressed to admit that his reaction is the same as anyone else's. You don't know him like I do. Retreat is a way of life for him.''

''I was under the impression that your son was a very successful banker. You don't get ahead by retreating.''

"I'm talking about the emotional, not the practical. Emotionally he is so much like his father. If there were trouble between Frank Junior and Angela, he would withdraw—he would ignore it—he would retreat into himself. Basically, he would pretend there was no problem at all. That's not the mark of a man who would resort to murder."

Ransom eyed the woman for a moment, then leaned forward and said, "Mrs. Stephens, it is difficult to predict how anyone will act in any situation. Sometimes the people you know the best can surprise you at the most inopportune times."

"There are no surprises in my life, Mr. Ransom," she replied, her voice hollow and lost. She almost sounded disappointed. But she rallied and added, "My son couldn't kill anyone. He's just not capable of it."

She lifted her glass from the trolley but did not drink from it. Instead she clasped it between both hands, much as her son had done with his coffee cup while being interrogated, and rested her wrists in her lap. The house, sealed tight to contain the cool central air, seemed to hum behind them in the silence. Ransom glanced at Gerald as if to warn him not to be surprised. He then looked back to the troubled woman.

"Mrs. Stephens, your son has not yet been arrested, and there is a reason for that: At this point we wouldn't be able to prove that he murdered his wife."

A flicker of life returned to the woman's eyes, but Ransom was quick to quell any false hopes.

"I am not saying that he's innocent, or that he won't be arrested in the near future. What I'm saying is that I have doubts."

"*You* have doubts?" she said, absently turning the glass in her hands.

"Yes," said Ransom, sitting back in his chair, "and so we were hoping that you could give us a little background to help clear things up."

Unlike her son, Gladys Stephens did not continue to require something to hold on to. She replaced the glass on the trolley, folded her hands, and faced Ransom.

"What would you like to know?"

"What did you think of your daughter-in-law?"

Mrs. Stephens's left eyebrow raised slightly, a smile softening her features. She didn't seem to be looking directly at Ransom but rather over his shoulder at a picture of Angela Stephens somewhere in the past.

"She was a capable girl. Lovely. She had poise and grace and all of those things that the natural order seems to be breeding out of women these days." Mrs. Stephens's smile turned from amusement to chagrin. She inclined her head toward Ransom, then continued. "I know that sounds old-fashioned, but that's not the way I mean it. I believe wholeheartedly in equality for women and our country's need for the ERA. Unfortunately, a lot of the change that's occurred in my lifetime has been at the expense of finer things. I don't just mean for women. Men have lost their refinement, too."

She sighed heavily, and all remnants of her smile faded away. "Angela had those things—qualities that have gone out of style. Maybe that's why she had to die. Maybe she just didn't belong in this world."

Ransom raised an eyebrow at this. It was uncomfortably close to what had been in his mind when he viewed the murdered woman's body.

"I don't know why I said that," Mrs. Stephens continued wearily, "except that I'm well into my sixties now, and I'm tired of seeing lovely things pass away."

Ransom let that thought hang in silence for a moment before he continued.

"Is there anything else you can tell us about her?" said Ransom, trying to turn the conversation from reverie to fact.

Gladys Stephens smiled again as memories flitted through her mind.

"She felt things," she said at last.

Ransom furrowed his brow. "How do you mean?"

"Often people who possess poise can be aloof or distant. Perhaps for fear they couldn't become emotional and maintain their poise at the same time. But Angela was neither aloof nor unfeeling. What is that passage in the Bible? 'Rejoice with those who rejoice and mourn with those who mourn,' or something to that effect. Angela had that ability. Empathy, I suppose you call it. It's a gift. I remember one afternoon sitting in the kitchen with her having coffee, and we got to talking about families, and I told her about my sister—I had a sister when I was little, just a year younger than myself, to whom I was quite close. When I was twelve, we lost her to polio."

"I'm sorry," said Ransom gently.

Mrs. Stephens gave a slight shrug, but her face remained clouded. "It was a long time ago. But that's the point. When I told Angela about my sister, she cried. She had quite a rare amount of empathy for a woman with poise."

Gerald took a sip of lemonade and cautiously eyed his partner. Ransom's expression was thoughtful, and in a strange way, gratified. It was as if finally someone had shared his brief impression of Angela Stephens. His view of her had obviously differed from that of her husband and her sister. Though Frank Stephens had referred to her as an angel, he had in some incomprehensible way allowed that angel to slip away from him in the last year of her life. He viewed her now through a shroud of guilt and confusion: much of which, Gerald thought, really could be attributed to shock. Eva was easier. Eva's view of Angela was tempered with anger and resentment, though it wasn't quite clear at whom these feelings were directed.

Gerald was aware that Ransom, on the other hand, had formed the immediate impression of Angela Stephens as a woman possessed of grace and elegance, with the minor flaw of believing in fortune-tellers. The ironic thing was that this flaw, which might have remained an amusing foible in Angela had she lived, had somehow become fatal.

Ransom unconsciously reached toward his pocket for a

cigar, then remembered where he was and sat back in the uncomfortable metal chair.

"You make her sound like something of an angel," said Ransom casually, harking back to the words of Frank Stephens.

Without turning her head, Gladys Stephens considered him out of the corner of her eye. Something in his tone had struck her.

"Did you ever meet my daughter-in-law?" she asked.

Ransom was not one to fidget or blush, but it was possible for him to be embarrassed.

"I met her once," he said, "quite recently."

Mrs. Stephens's eyebrows raised a quarter of an inch.

"Well, if you met her then you know what I mean about poise. But I don't think I'd go so far as to call her an angel."

"Really?" said Ransom, his interest stimulated. "Why is that?"

Mrs. Stephens brushed at her skirt, as if she could whisk away the water stains left by her lemonade glass. "No reason. I would be hard pressed to call anyone an angel. But if you *are* pressing me, I would say she was as close to one as you would find in this life."

"With reservations."

She slewed around in her chair to face him. "Only that she was flawed like anyone else."

"In what way?"

Mrs. Stephens smiled at him with a mixture of weariness and exasperation.

"I really couldn't say." She turned back to the pool, gave the hem of her dress a slight tug at the knee, and then rested her arms on the arms of her chair. She was the picture of a woman who through a lifetime of practice could retain her composure in the face of anything.

Ransom glanced at Gerald, who seemed to be engaged in memorizing the landscape. Ransom smiled to himself and turned back to the woman.

"Mrs. Stephens, I know this is a difficult time for you,

and I have no wish to make it any worse than necessary, but I can't help pointing out that you sound unsure on the matter of Angela's faults.''

She didn't move.

''Perhaps we can approach this in a different way. Tell me about their marriage.''

Without turning her head, she said, ''What do you want to know?''

''Were they happy?''

''When they first married, they were very happy. Frank was already on his way at the bank, and Angela...''

''Yes?''

''Angela decided to stay at home.''

Ransom raised an eyebrow. ''Was that a problem?''

''No, no,'' said Mrs. Stephens with a slow shake of her head. ''At first I was surprised, because she'd worked so hard for her degree, but I think staying home was what she wanted in the end. She'd had a lot of responsibility when she was growing up and I think she was ready...ready to be taken care of herself.''

''Hmmm,'' said Ransom, turning this over in his mind. It made sense of something that had seemed out of step about Angela Stephens. Perhaps Mrs. Stephens had, in her simple way, solved *that* mystery. ''And then?''

''And then they settled into everyday life the same as everybody else. No better or worse.''

''But happy?''

She glanced at him. ''Oh, yes, I would say they were happy.''

''All right, they were happy when they were married and thereafter. What about recently?''

It was the brief movement of her hand that gave her away. It could have been a slight tremor or spasm, but whatever it was, he knew he struck a nerve.

''Recently?'' she said colorlessly. ''Recently I wouldn't know about.''

Ransom's impassive expression disguised his increased

interest. "You live fairly close to your son and daughter-in-law. Don't you usually keep in contact?"

The woman covered her mouth with her hand, and her eyes brimmed with tears. She rose from her chair without a sound and walked a few steps away from the detectives toward the pool. It was such a sudden and unexpected movement that for a second Ransom tensed, thinking she might fling herself into the water. But she stopped a few feet from the pool with her back toward them. Ransom couldn't help noting that even in the heat and the strain, her dress was unwrinkled.

"I knew something was wrong," she said suddenly, a quiver in her voice. "I knew something was wrong because we've always been close. Angela and Frank were here once or twice a week for dinner or just to visit. But in the past few months they tapered off. We haven't seen them at all in the past six weeks—so I knew something was wrong. It was just as it always was with Frank Senior and Frank Junior—something is wrong so they just disappear. He didn't want to face us. I told my husband I thought something was wrong, but he just ignored it. I didn't know how bad it was."

Several things came to Ransom's mind at once, not the least of which was the idea that there may have been more trouble in Frank and Angela Stephens's marriage than anyone involved was willing to admit. At the same time, he found it understandable that people would be much more willing to believe in the surface projected by the couple than to accept their reality, if surface and reality actually differed. But what struck Ransom most about Gladys Stephens, and perhaps about the rest of the Stephens family, was that all the money in the world had not saved them from emotional bankruptcy.

Mrs. Stephens stifled a sob that welled up in her throat. She controlled herself with effort.

"Whatever may have been going on between Frank Junior and Angela, I never would have believed it would come to this," she said without emotion.

Gerald looked at his partner with considerable surprise, but Ransom did not return the look—he was staring thoughtfully at the woman's back.

"Mrs. Stephens, you sound as if you really think your son killed his wife."

She turned to face Ransom and attempted to brush away her tears with trembling hands. The gesture was futile, as her reddened eyes continued to brim over. She looked neither worried nor afraid. If anything, she looked tired.

"No," she said heavily, "I don't believe he did it, or ever could. All I meant was that when something like this happens—when some tragedy happens—you can't help feeling that someone should have seen it coming."

Ransom glanced at Gerald, then turned back to the grieving mother.

"Someone did."

THE TEMPERATURE in the car was at least twenty degrees higher than in the open air. The sun was high and hot and beat down on the roof like an overzealous karate expert.

Ransom loosened the sweat-stained knot of his blue-and-red-striped tie. He undid his collar button and took a deep breath. It was like breathing in a steam room.

The remainder of their interview with Gladys Stephens had proven both enlightening and frustrating. The only person besides Frank and Angela about whom Ransom really wanted more information was Eva Brinkley. When asked about Eva, Mrs. Stephens had simply laughed and said, "Trouble. The girl was always trouble." When asked to elaborate, Mrs. Stephens was much less forthcoming. She had known Eva's earlier history only second- or thirdhand through Frank and Angela. Due to the increasing estrangement between parents and son, Mrs. Stephens knew nothing of Eva in the present other than the fact that she had returned.

Like her son, Mrs. Stephens found it difficult to believe that Eva could have changed over the course of time, but she had no firsthand knowledge.

Ransom pulled a cigar out of the pocket of his damp navy blue blazer, put it in his mouth, and pushed the lighter into the dashboard.

They had driven for about twenty minutes in hot, smoky silence when Ransom said, "You know, the one thing I find amazing about Gladys and Frank Stephens is their attitude toward Eva."

"What's so surprising?" said Gerald, his face glistening with sweat. Ransom had often marveled at the fact that while others tanned or burned in the sun, Gerald's skin seemed to grow pastier.

"It's the same with a lot of troubled kids," Gerald continued. "They're screwups when they're young and nobody will ever let them forget it."

"Gerald, you will always be a consummate literalist."

"I don't know what you mean," said Gerald with marked irritation, "but you know I'm right. People *do* change. Even if not exactly change, they mellow with age."

"Like a fine wine?" Ransom interjected with a puff of cigar smoke and one of his more annoying smiles.

"People do change!" said Gerald with emphasis. "The hardest thing is to get people who know you to let you change."

Ransom turned to his partner with a raised eyebrow. "Gerald, any more protesting and I'll begin to think you have a past."

Gerald made an exasperated noise that sounded suspiciously close to "Oh, shit!" and slapped his hand on the steering wheel. After a slight pause, his exasperation wavered and he dissolved into laughter.

"Maybe someday I'll tell you about it."

Ransom smiled and said, "The story of your stormy youth will no doubt be worth waiting for. As for the present, I meant that you were taking me too literally when I said I was amazed at their attitudes toward Eva. What surprises me is that both Frank and Gladys are convinced that Eva Brinkley is nothing but trouble, but neither of them connect the two."

Gerald furrowed his brow. "The two what?"

Ransom looked at Gerald as if astounded by his obtuseness. "The return of Eva and the death of Angela."

They had finally arrived at Lake Shore Drive, and Gerald was relieved that the midday traffic was lighter and he could drive just fast enough to stir a hot breeze through the car.

As Gerald accelerated, he said, "Maybe there *is* no connection."

"Perhaps," said Ransom, "but 'trouble'—they keep referring to her as trouble. And she seems to be the only real, solid trouble we can find in this case."

"In the past," Gerald couldn't help adding.

"But in the present," Ransom explained patiently, "she appears to be a very angry young woman with a boyfriend who uses drugs. That sounds like trouble to me."

"That may be true but there is one big problem with Eva as a suspect."

"What's that?"

"Timing," said Gerald. "Even if she had a reason to kill her sister, why wait a year? Why come back and wait a year to kill her? Why come back at all?"

Ransom looked at his partner thoughtfully. "That, my dear Gerald, is a very good question."

As the detectives turned onto Cedar Street, Ransom reflected on how this job came with certain conveniences that others envied. In this case, namely the privilege to double-park without being ticketed (one of his favorites). This was a privilege that definitely came in handy on the near north side of Chicago where parking spaces are at a premium. The Cedar Street area in particular, given its close proximity to Lake Michigan and downtown Chicago, is one of those areas where parking spaces are so scarce that car owners move their cars only if they have no intention of returning.

Gerald pulled up as close as possible to the cars parked in front of Lynn Francis's building on the south side of the street. Ransom could barely get out of the passenger side of the car, and he was sure that at least two of the parked cars would be unable to get out either. But he shrugged it off, sure that nobody would be trying to move the cars anyway.

Lynn Francis was in the enviable position of having procured one of the few front apartments in a converted brownstone on Cedar Street. She had managed to get it five years earlier when she was the personal assistant to a prominent Chicago businessman, who preferred to remain nameless in every aspect of his life. Lynn had been the one to run interference for him, and she commanded a salary in the upper five figures for her trouble.

But that was long ago. In recent days, her friends would tell each other that she had come down in the world, having given up her lucrative position in a businessman's office for a far less lucrative career in businessmen's homes. But Lynn didn't care. Not many of her friends remained, anyway, so if they were saying anything about her, she didn't have to hear it.

Lynn Francis was enviable in a more important way: She was an extremely satisfied and contented person. She didn't care what people thought: she was happy. Or as happy as was possible. She was as satisfied giving an expert polishing to her present employers' brass and silver as she had been juggling her former bosses' schedules. But the one thing that becoming "charwoman to the rich and famous" (as one of her friends had christened her) had given her that she could get nowhere else was the flexibility of scheduling that she so badly wanted. In fact, freedom of movement meant more to her than anything. It gave her one other thing that Ransom would have envied above all things: Sundays off.

After forty minutes in the steaming car under the midday sun, Ransom felt he could fairly swim to the door of the brownstone's garden apartment. This particular apartment had earned its name: The exterior was obviously tended by the loving hands of a gardener who cared about design,

symmetry, and color. Shrubbery that had once grown halfway up the apartment's picture window had been cut back,
then finally uprooted in its entirety to allow in the maxi-
mum amount of sun. A semicircle of petunias with varie-
gated leaves grew bright and healthy beneath the window.
Inside were two windowboxes planted with various kinds
of bright flowers, the names of which Ransom didn't know.

The detectives walked down four stone steps to a round
flagstone patio surrounded by a low circular stone wall.
Ransom felt as if he were descending into a fishpond. The
patio was spotted at regular intervals with semicircles of
flowers, color-coordinated and set close to the wall out of
harm's way. The front door to Lynn Francis's apartment
was partly shaded by an iron staircase that led up to another
apartment.

The door was painted red and had a curved top to fit
snugly into the archwaylike doorway. An octagonal window was set at eye level in the door and was covered with
a wide iron grid.

Gerald stepped up to the door and rang the bell. It struck
him for the briefest moment that he was beginning to feel
like Ransom's valet. It seemed he was always ringing doorbells for him. He made a mental note to let Ransom ring
the next doorbell they came upon.

Through the iron grid they saw a lace curtain stir, and
suddenly two large, very brown eyes peered out at them.
The eyes were surrounded by deeply embedded laugh lines.
Her eyes were not laughing now, but neither were they
displeased. If eyes were truly the windows of the soul, then
Lynn Francis was an open, questioning, playful woman.
She opened the door to them, her face breaking into a wide
smile.

Ransom thought he had rarely seen a fresher young
woman. The laugh lines were the only indication that she
was into her thirties. She wore no makeup other than a pale
red lipstick. Her complexion was dark and creamy, and her
shoulder-length, tawny hair was highlighted by the sun. Her

deep, rich brown eyes were flecked with gold. They sparkled as she greeted them.

"You're the cops, I take it."

Ransom returned the smile. He liked her. "I'm Detective Ransom, this is Detective White."

Sweat flew off Gerald's forehead as he nodded in her direction.

"Come on in!" said Lynn, dodging the wet missiles and flinging the door wide.

The detectives followed her into the bright living room. It was a beautiful room, with a polished parquet floor covered by a large, multicolored, oval-braided rug. The furniture all looked as if it had been recently delivered from Crate & Barrel, though the cushions on the chairs and sofa seemed lived in enough to be comfortable. They were covered with a rough fabric in warm tans and browns, and Ransom half wondered if they'd been chosen to offset her eyes. The walls were painted Navajo white and were adorned with watercolors of fields and farms, purchased at local art fairs. Every flat surface in the room seemed to be home to some form of vegetation, each housed in decorative pots, collected from the same fairs as the paintings.

"Have a seat," Lynn called over her shoulder as she breezed through the living room to a door that Ransom assumed led to a bedroom. "I'll be with you in a moment."

Her vitality seemed to permeate the room even without her presence. The detectives glanced at each other, the same thought apparently crossing both their minds. They looked around the room a little more, wandering a bit like first-time visitors to an art museum. They heard the murmur of voices in the next room. Gerald was the first to take a seat: a solid oak chair with oatmeal tweed slipcovers, located in a corner by the living-room window. It was obviously meant for quiet moments of reading or looking at the garden. He settled in comfortably and slid his little notebook and pencil out of his pocket.

Ransom remained standing a few moments longer. His attention was taken by a large watercolor of a farmhouse at sunset that hung on the broad west wall of the room. He could see why Lynn had found this particular painting appealing. With a few lines and limited use of color, it reminded one that there was a simpler life to be had if only one chose: an existence outside the crime and concrete that crowded Ransom's life. He couldn't look at the painting without an inward sigh.

The voices in the other room stopped, leaving behind an unidentifiable, low hissing sound: something like a machine breathing. After a moment, Lynn came smiling back into the room. Her crisp white blouse and knee-length brown skirt rustled as she walked. She didn't look at all surprised or disconcerted to find Ransom still standing. If anything, she looked complimented that he was so taken by the painting. She gestured him to the far side of the couch and seated herself on the opposite end. She glanced over the back of the couch at Gerald and said, "Detective White, you don't have to sit way over there. I won't be offended if you take notes in front of me."

Coloring slightly, Gerald looked up from his notebook, which suddenly seemed quite obtrusive.

"Gerald is enjoying the garden," said Ransom with a twinkle in his eye. "I assure you he'll be much more comfortable over there."

"Ah well." She shrugged. "As long as he's comfortable, I'm happy."

Ransom surveyed Lynn thoughtfully. Though she gave every impression of being a highly comfortable person, the kind to whom strangers would naturally gravitate for directions or help, Ransom sensed something puckish behind those sparkling eyes. He was sure that she liked people in general, but he thought she would probably enjoy sticking playful little pins in them just the same. In response to his scrutiny, Lynn innocently beamed an ingratiating smile at him, inviting him to begin the interview.

Ransom thought of many ways he could begin: pleasantries, such as admiring the room, or the flowers, or the paintings. Somehow, all the possibilities that came to mind struck him as particularly idiotic under the gently probing gaze of Lynn Francis. Her large, steady eyes seemed to compel one, in the nicest possible way, to get to the point.

Ransom cleared his throat. "I understand you work for the Stephenses."

"I'm the maid," she said with a broad smile that showed the absence of her embarrassment while accentuating his.

Ransom eyed her shrewdly and continued. "Quite so. You have heard about Mrs. Stephens's murder."

"Oh, yes, I read the papers."

"We're interested in getting some background on Mr. and Mrs. Stephens."

"Ah," said Lynn with an unmistakable note of disdain in her voice, "so I'm to be Rose, the underhouse parlormaid, and give you all the below-stairs tittle-tattle about my employers?"

Ransom replied haltingly, "I'm not sure I'd put it quite like that."

She glanced down at her immaculate brushed suede shoes and sighed. "Well, whatever way you put it, I'm not sure I like the idea of talking about my employers. I feel that when someone pays for a maid they're not just paying her to clean, they're paying her to mind her own business and keep her mouth shut. That's especially true for someone who's involved in the intimate details of someone's day-to-day life, in a position of trust. It would be a breach of that trust to run around gossiping about what I found in the Stephenses' laundry."

Ransom fought an uncanny desire to ask her if she *had* found anything interesting in the Stephenses' laundry. Instead, he offered her the type of smile he reserved for delivering unpleasant news in a pleasant fashion. Many found it peculiarly menacing; for Lynn Francis, he modified it with a special lilt that conveyed his own chagrin at having to press the point.

"I'm sure you must realize that in a murder investigation there is no privacy...for anyone."

Lynn's expression didn't change, but she couldn't hide

the quick glance at the door that she'd left slightly ajar, and through which the rhythmic hiss could still be heard. Her glance returned to Ransom. She seemed to size him up in barely a moment. Whatever her assessment of him was, it didn't register on her face.

"I suppose you're right," she said at last, relaxing perceptibly. "But I still don't like it."

"Understood."

The spritely smile reappeared. "Actually, I'm surprised your investigations have brought you all the way down to my level."

Oh, how she enjoys trying to embarrass people, thought Ransom. Then he said, "How so?"

"Well, I would have thought this was an open-and-shut case."

"Hmmm?"

"Popular fiction favors the husband in matters like this." The gold flecks in her eyes twinkled.

Ransom drew himself up and sighed. "With all due respect to popular fiction, reality favors facts."

This seemed to strike an approving chord in Lynn. It was as if Ransom had passed an invisible litmus test. Her smile faded and was replaced by seriousness. "Well, all right. I'm sure it looks bad for Mr. Stephens, but I would hate to think he'd done this."

As always when Ransom's interest was engaged, his eyes became more intensely blue. "Why do you believe things look bad for him?"

"Well because…," she began without thinking, then stopped.

"Yes?"

Lynn looked aggravated with herself. "For just the reason I said before. They always think it's the husband, don't they?"

"'They' don't always jump to popular conclusions," said Ransom a bit frostily. Then he softened. "It's just unfortunate that often popular opinion turns out to be right."

"There!" said Lynn triumphantly.

"But you wouldn't like that in this case, would you?"
She looked at him quizzically. "What do you mean?"

"You wouldn't like Frank Stephens to be found a murderer."

Lynn looked surprised for a moment, then let out with a loud, throaty, and highly infectious laugh. "I'm sorry, Mr. Ransom, but if Mr. Stephens murdered his wife, then yes, I do want him found out. No matter how I might feel about someone, I wouldn't want a murderer to be roaming around free."

"And how do you feel about him?"

"Oh, dear," said Lynn, quieting down but still amused, "I have a feeling I'm about to be called 'the other woman.' If that's where you're heading, you're on a very wrong track. You can't even imagine!"

Ransom gazed at her, his face immobile. After a moment, he said, "You haven't really answered my question, though, have you?"

"You didn't ask me the right question. You shouldn't ask how I feel about Mr. Stephens, you should ask what I think of him."

"All right," said Ransom with a shrug, "why don't you answer that one?"

She rested her left arm on the back of the couch, her fingers intertwined. She appeared to be recalling her impressions of the man and putting them in order.

She took a deep breath and spoke, alternately examining her hands and looking into Ransom's eyes.

"I've worked for the Stephenses for about two years now—maybe a little less. I suppose my impressions would be as accurate as anyone else's." She glanced up at Ransom. "Maybe a little more. I try to be fair, and I think I'm a pretty good judge of character."

"Yes?"

She looked back at her hands.

"I think that Mr. Stephens is a kind man. He's been kind to me, but a little...aloof wouldn't be the right word. 'Vacant' might be better. This sort of thing is a little hard to judge from my standpoint, because I clean for a fair number of wealthy people, and they tend to keep the help at a distance.''

Once again, she apostrophized "the help" with a merry note in her voice, as if the joke was ultimately on her employers.

"But all in all I would say he was the type of person who comes in and out of your life, and you always think 'What a nice person he is,' but no matter how many times you see him, you don't think you know him any better than you did the first time."

"That seems to be a pretty in-depth assessment."

"Like I said, I was there about two years. I would *have* to form some kind of opinion. I'd say Frank Stephens is both kind and patient. I'd say he needed to be."

"Why do you say that?"

"Because…'' Her face darkened as if she were troubled by a passing cloud. "Well, I would hate to sound as if I were speaking ill of the dead, because I really would object to that. I'm sure she was very troubled, and I don't believe anyone can really understand anyone else's motives."

"Mrs. Stephens, you mean?"

Lynn nodded. "She was all right when I started working for them."

"What happened?"

She shrugged. "She changed. That's all. She changed."

"In what way?"

Lynn sighed thoughtfully and brushed back a strand of hair that had fallen into her eyes. "It's hard to say. I didn't know her that well to begin with, remember. But she did change."

"If she changed enough for you to notice, wasn't there anything specific?"

Lynn furrowed her brow and thought for a moment.

"She became distant. She had been friendly and she became distant. At first I thought I'd done something wrong, but after a while I realized it wasn't *that* kind of distance."

"What kind was it?"

"Hmmm…absentminded…preoccupied. That sort of thing. Do you know what I mean?"

Ransom nodded, and Lynn took this as a cue to proceed. "But after a while it got worse—"

"After a while? How long ago do you mean?"

"A few months," Lynn replied with a shrug. "She began to look more than distant, she looked lost. I half thought of asking if there was anything I could do for her, but I didn't think it would help."

Ransom mentally pictured Angela Stephens as she'd looked in his office. Lost was a good word for her expression. Lost and resigned to be lost.

"Did you have any idea what the cause of this change was?"

"Well, of course!" she said brightly. She appeared to have had an attack of scruples in midsentence and came as close to blushing as Ransom would ever see her.

Ransom raised an eyebrow and smiled knowingly, "And the reason for the change was…?"

"It was a man, of course."

"A man," Ransom repeated flatly.

"Yes, a man. It was the same old boring story, the type you'd have thought someone like her would've been smarter than to get involved in."

"How did you know? Did you see them together?"

The right corner of Lynn's mouth curled upward. "I was only there two days a week. If she couldn't work her love life around me, then she was worse off than I thought she was."

Ransom could not repress a smile. "Then how *did* you know?"

"Well, I'm not sure I would have if she hadn't been so…acted so guilty about the whole thing. I mean, there were the *usual* signs—mostly that she seemed—well, not cold, but not attracted to her husband—in that sort of guilty fashion that women in that position get. Now, the times I've seen her with her husband she didn't really seem to be all there, you know what I mean? She seemed to be sleepwalking when her husband was around. Then there were the phone calls. She got lots and lots of phone calls in the 'I've-told-you-not-to-call-me-here' vein.''

"She didn't actually say that?"

"No, but it was in her voice whenever she picked up the receiver and heard the voice of whoever it was. You know, her voice got quiet all of a sudden, and there were guilty looks in my direction if I happened to be in the room. And of course, I was sent into another room to do something unnecessary, presumably to get me out of the room."

"It could have been her husband. Some people are reluctant to speak to their loved ones in front of—"

"The maid?" Lynn said with a wicked smile.

Ransom smiled back indulgently. "I was going to say in front of strangers."

"Actually, that's who I thought it was for the longest time. Her husband. But one day he came home while she was on the phone with…whoever. I'm afraid that was the dead giveaway, because she was on the phone on the little table by the entrance to the living room, and she was so surprised when her husband walked in the door that she turned red as a beet and fumbled the receiver back onto its cradle without even saying good-bye."

"Do you think Mr. Stephens knew what was going on?"

"Unless he was an idiot, which he isn't. She looked guilty as sin and explained it away by saying she'd been making another appointment with her 'seer'—that's what she called it—and she didn't want him to know…because she knew how he felt about that sort of thing."

"Maybe that's all it was."

Lynn shook her head slowly, ruefully. "Not unless she was in love with her fortune-teller. The little I caught of their conversations was…well, let's just say it wasn't exactly professional."

Ransom sat contemplatively for a moment, silently digesting this.

"Do you think Mr. Stephens bought her story?"

"Like I said, he's not an idiot." She paused for a moment, and her eyes wandered vacantly over Ransom's shoulder. "And I don't think she could have carried it off."

She stopped for a moment and stared down into her lap as if putting her thoughts in order. She looked, if anything, disgusted, although it would have been difficult to discover the source of this feeling. With a sudden and firm resolve, she looked up at Ransom.

"It all sounds more...tawdry than I want it to sound."

"Indeed?"

"I don't mean to make it sound as if Mrs. Stephens was just any other love-starved female who was carrying on on the side. She was something different."

"In what way?"

Lynn's eyes hardened, and she shook her head, as if she found it difficult to put her thoughts into words. "She was...an innocent, if that doesn't sound too stupid. I think she was a throwback to a different age, where people weren't—like they are today. I mean, money may buy a lot of things in this world, but I don't think it buys blinders. It wasn't the money that made her different or set her apart, it was something more profound. She was...untouched."

This was spoken with a degree of affection that went beyond that of an employee for her employer. It struck a chord in Ransom that once again coincided with his own impressions of Angela Stephens: that perhaps she simply didn't belong in this world. Ransom envied the fact that Lynn Francis had the opportunity for something of a relationship with Angela Stephens. Though at the same time, he wondered just how deep Lynn's affection for her employer had run.

"You must realize how odd that sounds," said Ransom after a pause, "Referring to a woman who was maintaining a husband and a lover as 'untouched.'"

Lynn smiled ruefully. "Then you don't understand what I mean. And I don't know that I could ever explain it. Let's just say I believe that if Angela Stephens became involved with another man, it must have been...out of the ordinary."

"What do you mean?"

"Just that...I don't believe she'd ever go out looking for someone. It must have just happened to her."

She looked over the back of the couch at Gerald. "Did you get all that?"

Gerald finished the note he was writing and looked up, unshaken. "Oh, yes, every word," he replied simply.

Ransom uncrossed his legs and stood. Gerald followed suit.

"Well, I don't think we need take up any more of your time."

For the first time, Lynn's self-assurance seemed to fail her. She fumbled as she rose and stammered slightly as she addressed Ransom.

"Uh...Mr. Ransom, could I ask you to do me a favor?"

"Of course," said Ransom, interested in her discomfiture.

Lynn recovered herself a little and looked Ransom squarely in the eye. But she still looked as if a moment that she had been dreading had finally arrived.

"Would you mind stopping in and saying hello to my lover?"

Ransom glanced at Gerald, who had joined them.

"It would only take a minute. She's been sick for a long time, and we hardly ever get visitors."

"Well, we—"

"I wouldn't ask, but she really doesn't get to see many people, and she got pretty excited when I told her that a detective was coming here." There was a brief, breathless pause. "I told her I didn't think you'd have time."

All of this was spoken fairly matter-of-factly, but Ransom could detect a note of desperation beneath the surface. It was at that moment that Ransom realized that the confidence Lynn Francis projected was not entirely natural. It was through sheer force of will that she maintained her composure. This demonstrated a great deal of inner strength to Ransom, but not the kind he'd originally thought she possessed. Somehow he thought her brand of strength was the more admirable, because since it required effort it was not without frailty. Ransom felt that if he begged off without meeting her lover, that strength would suffer a loss. Not outwardly. But something within her would crumble, and nobody would ever know about it.

"We'd be glad to meet her."

Though she didn't visibly change, Ransom could sense Lynn's relief. She smiled her thanks at him and led the way into the bedroom without any further explanation.

Neither Ransom nor Gerald were prepared for the world that awaited them through the door. The contrast between bedroom and living room could not have been more pronounced. Light pink and blue were much in evidence, and white lace trim was everywhere: on the curtains, the shams, even on the shades of the twin lamps on either side of the bed.

An emaciated young woman lay in the bed, covered with a fluffy, shiny pink comforter. She was fair-haired, and her complexion, which had been light, was now running to sallow. The gauntness made it difficult to place her age. She looked to be in her fifties, but her eyes told Ransom that she was probably at least fifteen years younger.

She was propped up in bed with a pile of pink-and-blue satin pillows, and the bed itself was raised high off the floor. She looked like an aging child floating on a pink cloud. Gerald felt vaguely that he'd entered Wonderland; Ransom felt that whoever had invented pastels should be shot.

The Alice in Wonderland impression was accentuated by the fact that the woman in the bed appeared to be inhaling from an enormous hookah, but she was not exhaling smoke. She didn't seem to be exhaling at all. She looked up at Ransom with eyes so bright they belied the condition of her body.

"So you're the dick?" she said between breaths.

"I beg your pardon?" said Ransom, surprised.

"The dick!" said the woman with an attempt at a wicked

grin. "The detective. Don't they always call you 'dicks' in the books?"

"No," said Ransom, "they only call us that in real life."

The woman laughed and coughed hoarsely. Lynn came to her side and laid a caring hand on her shoulder.

"Mr. Ransom, this is my friend, Maggie Walker."

"And this is my partner, Gerald White."

Gerald smiled sheepishly and nodded to Maggie.

"May I?" said Ransom, indicating the foot of the bed.

"Be my guest."

Ransom sat on one corner of the bed and felt himself slide a little on the satin duvet cover.

"Ms. Francis tells me you've been sick."

"A real detective could tell that just by looking at me."

"Touché."

She pushed the plastic nozzle away from her mouth. "I have to breathe this crap to try to keep from getting pneumonia. Not that it exactly matters. One thing or another will get me eventually."

Ransom could feel a sudden tension between the two women. Lynn's hand tightened involuntarily on Maggie's shoulder. Maggie softened, reached up, and patted Lynn's hand.

"But we do what we can," said Maggie with a shrug.

Lynn released her and wheeled the breathing apparatus away from the bed into a corner of the room.

"So," said Maggie as brightly as she could, "was Lynn able to help you?"

Ransom glanced at Lynn Francis as she returned to the side of her frail lover. She looked down at Maggie with a mixture of pain and caring.

"She gave me the most important piece of information I've had yet."

"Which was?" said Maggie, obviously proud of her friend.

"That Mr. Stephens isn't an idiot."

A smile radiated from Maggie's dry lips. "That clears everything up for you, does it?"

"Umm-hmmm."

Maggie laughed again, which brought on a brief bout of coughing.

"I'm glad, anyhow. From the little that Lynn's told me about Mr. Stephens, he seems a decent guy."

Ransom glanced at Lynn and then back to Maggie.

"So your friend was telling us."

"Of course," continued Maggie, "I suppose you can never tell. There's a lot of people who are mild-mannered on the outside but turn into lunatics when they're angry. I suppose you've seen a lot of that sort of thing in your work."

"I see my fair share."

"Like me. Before I contracted this...illness I was the most mild-mannered woman...I don't think I was ever even out of sorts."

"I wouldn't go that far," said Lynn with a loving smile.

"It's a lot harder—" she began energetically, then suddenly broke off, her face a mass of confusion. It wasn't that she couldn't find the words, but that she didn't know whether or not to say them. She turned her anxious eyes on Lynn, who smiled assurance down at her. Maggie calmed perceptibly, took a breath, and looked into Ransom's cool, steady blue eyes.

"It's harder to deal with that anger when there's nobody to be angry at. You think a lot about things like that when you're dying. When I got my diagnosis, I racked my brain to try to figure out who gave it to me, or how I'd gotten it. I was angry at everyone. I hated everybody I'd ever known."

Lynn's hand tightened again on Maggie's shoulder, but Maggie didn't relent.

"Yes, everyone. I found out what it means to be 'mad at the world'...when I ran out of them I blamed myself, and that was worse. In the end, I realized something even worse, and it made me the maddest of all."

During this Ransom had unconsciously reached out and

taken Maggie's hands in his. Her hands were cold and skeletal.

"What was that?"

Maggie sighed heavily and looked down at the pink comforter. She smiled sadly.

"That nobody was to blame, not even me. That nobody was responsible for my getting this disease. That like most of the good or bad things in life, it just happened."

"And your anger?"

She wearily lay back against the bevy of satin pillows.

"Life is too short, Mr. Ransom."

THEY APPROACHED the door to the Stephenses' apartment in the same silence that they had spent during the short trip there, each wrapped in his own reverie, neither particularly wanting to break the silence.

It had been a long day, with the continued heat and long drive to the far north suburbs and back to the near north side. Both detectives were hot and tired. But their journeys into the Stephenses' past had been fruitful: They'd found out from Frank Stephens's mother that he and Angela had been having marital trouble, and they now seemed to have confirmation that Frank had known about Angela's affair. That was the most important fact: Frank Stephens knew.

The only time they had spoken during the drive to the Lake Shore apartment was when Gerald asked, "You said earlier, when we were talking about why Frank Stephens would have hired the fortune-teller, that you were afraid I might be right about him. What did you mean?"

Ransom replied with disgust at his own ineptitude, "You said it yourself, Gerald: She'd be laughed out of court. He may have calculated that the presence of the fortune-teller in this business would make the case against him look ridiculous, whatever other evidence there might be against him. If that's true, then he's a damn sight more clever than I gave him credit for!"

Ransom still didn't like it. He knew that people still kill with much less motivation than infidelity, but he somehow

liked to think that those of Angela and Frank Stephens's
social class were above such sordid and mundane matters.
Even as this thought crossed his mind, he castigated himself. Nobody, no matter what his station in life, was above
human passions or human frailty. If his decade on the police force had taught him anything, it should have been that.

Gerald's thoughts were much less complicated than those
of his partner: He'd been right about Frank Stephens. Ransom's theories had taken them to hell and back—well, at
least to Winnetka and back, which amounted to the same
thing in Gerald's mind—but the outcome had been the
same. He'd been right: Frank Stephens was guilty. At least
their wanderings had netted them some results. They'd
found the proof that Ransom had insisted upon. It was circumstantial evidence at best, but it was damning enough
for an arrest. They might not get a conviction without a
confession, but past experience had proven that if there was
a confession to be wrung from a suspect, Ransom would
be able to do it.

Gerald would have been much more confident in his triumph were it not for the fact that he could remember vividly their last visit to this apartment, when he'd honestly
begun to doubt Frank Stephens's guilt. He tried to excuse
this slight deviation from his beliefs with the idea that it
wasn't the first time he'd been influenced, against his better
judgment, by Ransom's convictions. But Gerald still had
the nagging thought that in every previous instance, Ransom had been right. Gerald had a very unattractive impulse
to gloat.

Remembering his firm resolve to stop ringing doorbells
for his partner, Gerald arrived at the door and stopped. Ransom paused for a moment and glanced at his unmoving
partner. An absolutely infuriating, knowing smile spread
across Ransom's face, and when Gerald saw it from the
corner of his eye, he thought it would have been much less
irritating to go on ringing the damn doorbells.

Ransom reached up and rapped on the door; it fell open

at his touch, which both detectives considered to be a very bad sign.

Ransom pushed the door open and called Stephens's name into the stale silence of the apartment. There was no answer. They started into the apartment cautiously, and once past the door they were assaulted by something that smelled like a fetid public toilet. It was an aroma familiar to the detectives, and they knew what it meant. They hurried into the living room and saw on the floor to the left of the doorway a pool of human excrement, spreading like a foul marker across the very place where Angela Stephens's body had lain. The detectives stopped, and slowly, in unison, their eyes traveled up to the balcony overlooking the living room.

Frank Stephens hung from the balcony railing, the long, elegant sash from his silk robe coiled around his neck. His head hung forward and slightly to the left. The robe hung open and moved slightly, eerily, in an apparent draft.

"Oh, God," said Gerald softly.

His jaw firmly set, his eyes steady, Ransom gazed up at the dead man. Quietly, he said, "It is a far, far better rest I go to than ever I have known."

Gerald clucked his tongue and added, "The hanged man."

TEN

Another Interlude

THE DISCOVERY OF Frank Stephens's lifeless body sent Ransom into an emotional tailspin the likes of which he'd never known. The remainder of the afternoon found him moody and sullen. When spoken to by the evidence technicians, he was irritable to his highest degree; when spoken to by Gerald, his responses were dull and hollow. When spoken to by Sergeant Newman, he was silent. There was nothing for Ransom to say. What he wanted to say was that he wanted the evidence technicians and the crime lab to tear apart Frank Stephens's apartment, and tear apart Frank Stephens's body, and tear apart the very air that Frank Stephens had breathed until they found evidence of murder. But Newman had told him that the case was closed, pure and simple, thereby effectively shutting the door on a stream of emotions and protestations that Ransom could feel welling up inside himself. He hadn't liked the idea of Stephens's guilt with the suspect alive; he liked it even less with him dead.

The inner turmoil Ransom experienced as the door slammed shut on his case brought on something almost entirely new to him: self-doubt. He would have found it difficult to put a name to what he was experiencing. Beyond that were all the unanswered questions that he found spinning through his mind, most of which began with "But what about..." and ended with him shaking his head in disgust. He was painfully aware that he was the only one who entertained any unanswered questions in regard to the whole Stephens affair. Not that Gerald, for example, didn't see any loose ends; it was just that Gerald was more inclined to accept them as a natural by-product of any investigation: just so many questions that didn't bear on the results. For everyone but Ransom, the case was comfortably closed. A great deal too comfortably, to his way of thinking.

Probably the most aggravating part about it was that his case had been solved without him. In the end, he had proven to be extraneous to the outcome. Justice had been done, the murderer discovered, and even the sentence carried out, all without the participation of the man who claimed to be more clever than any murderer.

What was worse was that he had been a fool. He had been chasing phantoms, nameless (or otherwise) suspects created in his own mind, while the real solution worked itself out. He had spent a great deal of time and effort trying to make an unusual case out of what turned out to be mundane. Ransom felt supremely superfluous.

And still there was the fortune-teller. He could still hear Emily's gentle but firm voice asking her pointed question, "Why the fortune-teller?"

"I'VE DECIDED to call her Tam," said Emily, breaking the prolonged silence.

"What?" said Ransom, recalled from an in-depth examination of the fading tiles of Emily's kitchen floor.

"The cat you brought me. I've decided to call her Tam."

"Tam."

"Because of the orange-and-black circle on her head. She looks like she's wearing a hat."

"Yes, she does," he said vacantly.

Emily shifted on the chair and took a sip of tea. The dinner things had been cleared away, and all that remained was her ever-present teapot and two cups. Ransom had managed to arrive for their regular Sunday dinner, albeit late. Emily had kept the glazed ham and steamed potatoes warm for him, but she needn't have bothered. As she had eaten he had merely moved the food around on the plate with his fork with all the enthusiasm of a condemned man who found his last meal to be a TV dinner. Tam was lying in her now usual place in the corner behind the stove. She gave an occasional sniff in the direction of the counter upon which Ransom's untouched meal had been placed.

When Emily felt she'd suffered her companion's silence long enough, she set her cup firmly down on its saucer and folded her hands on the table.

"Are you going to tell me what has happened?" she said firmly.

"Hmmm?"

"Jeremy, even someone who didn't know you well would be able to tell you're distracted. Why don't you tell me what's the matter?"

Ransom glanced up from the floor to his teacup. He took a sip and replaced the cup. His eyes traveled back to the floor.

"It seems," he said slowly, "that I was wrong about this case—the murder of the Stephens woman. I told you about it."

"Yes?" said Emily, her bright eyes intent upon Ransom's face.

"It seems that her husband killed her after all...despite all the loose ends and little irritating aspects of this case that still bother me. I guess I'll just have to learn to live with it, though I'm sure I don't like it at all. But I've been told that the case is closed. So...that's that."

"And the fortune-teller?"

"Killed by Stephens to cover his tracks. Case closed." His tone made it sound as if he were referring to an over-stuffed suitcase that was in danger of springing open at any moment.

"And?"

Ransom looked up at her. "And what?"

"I think there's something more, isn't there?"

He returned to his study of the kitchen floor.

"It seems..." he continued reluctantly, "that I've—somewhere along the way lost my objectivity. Perhaps it was meeting the victim before the murder—God knows that never happened before—but on this case my reasoning seems to have gone haywire.''

Emily waved a gentle, placating hand at him, pursed her lips, and made a "tut-tut" sound.

"I find that very hard to believe, Jeremy."

He paused for a moment, Angela Stephens's face once again returning to his mind. He remembered each delicate feature and each delicate movement. Then the picture dissolved into that of the murdered woman: golden hair fanned out like a halo, marred by a stream of blood.

"She was a very beautiful woman, you know. I...would hate to think that I was blinded by that. If I had been thinking clearly, perhaps I could have accepted the obvious. At least I might have been able to accept that Gerald was right: Just because the woman's story was nonsensical didn't mean it wasn't true. Just because the idea came from a fortune-teller didn't mean it wasn't the real solution. I keep going back to the day that Mrs. Stephens came into my office." He stopped for a moment and then continued ruefully. "I just never would have thought I could lose my objectivity because of a pretty face."

"Even if that were true," said Emily gently, "and I don't believe it for a moment, but even if it were, what of it? None of us are immune to human passions."

Ransom winced slightly as this echo of his own earlier thoughts about the Stephens family returned home to him.

"I'd like to think I am."

Emily set down her cup and laid her soft, wrinkled hand on his and said, "Jeremy, I know I haven't known you all that long, but I do think it's long enough to know that you would not stubbornly fly in the face of the facts, whether or not your 'head was turned' by a pretty face."

Ransom pondered this for a moment, then slapped his hand on the table. "I keep coming back to the fortune-teller. I just can't imagine why Frank Stephens would have hired her."

"Oh, yes," said Emily, warming to the subject, "yes,

well, the fortune-teller must be the key, because she's the one piece that doesn't fit.''

"Stephens said that Angela's belief in that sort of thing was her one flaw."

At this, Emily folded her hands and rested them on the table. Her shoulders raised slightly, then lowered as she exhaled. She seemed to be staring back into the past, searching for something half remembered. After a long silence, she quoted quietly:

"'Carrying the stamp of one defect...their virtues else, be they pure as grace...shall take corruption from the particular fault.'''

"Hmmm?"

"Oh, I'm sorry, my dear, I seem to have *Hamlet* on the brain lately. That's just a little quote about how one fatal flaw can destroy someone, no matter how many other fine qualities they may have."

"Do you really think that's true?"

Emily primly adjusted herself in the chair and looked at Ransom. "I'm sure of it. When I was a young girl, there was a man who lived down the road from us who never brushed his teeth or his hair."

"Well..." said the confused detective, "that's a flaw, but hardly fatal."

"Oh, but *that* wasn't it. His fatal flaw was that he would never look in a mirror."

"I'm sorry, Emily, but...what?"

"You see, he firmly believed that if you looked at yourself in the mirror too long, demons would enter you through your eyes. That one flaw affected his whole life—all of his neighbors thought he was unbalanced, and he became something of a local character and a recluse. Few people could bear to be around him, and eventually all of his teeth fell out."

"Sad, but that still isn't exactly fatal."

"But it was! You see, he developed cancer of the skin, which apparently first appeared on his face. With no friends to point it out to him and never looking in the mirror, it wasn't discovered until it was too late.''

She noticed the detective's incredulous expression and added with a slight shrug of her shoulders, ''It was a simpler time, you understand.''

Ransom declined comment. There were times when he wasn't entirely sure whether Emily was pulling his leg, since almost everything she said was offered with utmost sincerity.

''So what you're saying is that the important thing is how Angela's one flaw really ties into her death.''

''Exactly. That's the key. Of course, we may never know it now.''

''I find it increasingly impossible to deal with an unsatisfying conclusion to a case. I *must* be getting old.''

''Nonsense!'' cried Emily with a smile.

''It's true,'' he said wearily.

''It's nonsense,'' Emily repeated with finality, firmly placing a period at the end of her sentence. ''You are not yet forty years old, are you?''

''Not quite.''

She spread her hands, palms up, before him. ''Then surely you must see what an idiotic thing that is to say to a woman on the nether side of seventy.''

''I suppose so.''

''Really, Jeremy!'' continued Emily, as if speaking to a recalcitrant grandchild, but not without a goodly amount of affection. ''I could half agree with your musings about objectivity and pretty faces and fortune-tellers and all that only if I was forced beyond endurance—but when you sit there and tell me that you're getting older as if your life is over, I cannot sit by in silence. It's just so much poppycock!''

Despite his cloudy humor, Ransom was forced to smile at this.

''And in your brooding, my dear, there is one thing you seem to have overlooked.''

''What's that?''

"The fact that you may be wrong."

Ransom reared himself up with more exasperation than he'd ever before displayed toward Emily.

"But that's exactly what I've been—"

Emily gently put up a hand to stop him. "Oh, I didn't mean wrong in that way. But you now seem to be assuming that because the case is closed and you're forced to move on, that you were wrong. But you should know as well as I do that just because something has been tied up in a nice pretty package doesn't mean that there's something pretty inside."

"Well, I might be being awfully thick, but I—"

"You are, my dear," Emily interrupted genially, "but we can blame that on the weather. I'm reminded of the biblical reference to whitewashed sepulchers: things that may be prettied up on the outside but are quite rotten on the inside." She stopped and took a deep breath, looking as if she were aware that she wasn't making her point clearly enough. "What I'm trying to say is that it's entirely possible that you were correct: that Frank Stephens was innocent and, of course, that someone else was responsible for the murder of Angela Stephens. In that case Mr. Stephens's suicide would be the unfortunate outcome—much as the death of Ophelia in *Hamlet* is, in a way, the unfortunate outcome of the murder of the king. Cause and effect—but the effect can be something totally unexpected. Unfortunately, it seems that this is simply one of those frustrating occasions where you may suspect the truth, or even know the truth, but are unable to prove it, as I'm sure you would realize if you weren't busy feeling old."

This last might have sounded harsh were it not for the twinkle evident in Emily's eyes as she said it.

"Do you really think so?" said Ransom quietly.

Emily nodded, then added gravely, "If that's the case, Jeremy, then that's what you'll have to learn to live with."

IT SEEMED TO Ransom that it had been months since he'd been able to soak in a hot tub with his old worn copy of

A Tale of Two Cities, but it had merely been a day.

He had spared himself his newly acquired ritual of pondering the ravages of time in the bathroom mirror, choosing instead to pour himself a snifter of brandy, quickly undress, and lay contentedly in the steamy water, boiling away his troubles, or at least trying to. Before opening the book, which he noticed with a smile was beginning to yellow with age, he lay quietly, covered up to the neck. Several times he dipped a sponge in the tub and slowly squeezed the water out over his head, letting it trickle over his eyes and ears, running down his face and seeping into his slightly parted lips. He sighed deeply once or twice, letting some of his cares escape with his breath into the moist air of the small bathroom.

But he couldn't stop his mind, much as he tried to achieve a state of mindlessness. Emily was right: An unsatisfactory conclusion was something that he may have to learn to live with. There came to mind unbidden at least a dozen cases of distant memory in which he'd been involved that had similar dangling strings once they were closed (and he admonished himself as old for having forgotten them). It was like putting together an electronic appliance and realizing to your dismay that once you thought you were finished, you had a handful of pieces left over. He reminded himself that one could not hope to go through life with all of one's questions answered, or with a perfect understanding of everything that had happened in other people's lives. Life was, after all, *not* like a Victorian novel, in which all of the heroes were rewarded and all the villains punished in the end. In real life, one had to settle for the best solution possible.

But settling was not something that came naturally to him. In the back of his mind, he was nettled with the questions he had continually asked himself since the case began. At the same time, consciously, he tried to dismiss these very questions, not as irrelevant but with the same argument that Sergeant Newman would use if he could read

Ransom's thoughts: Give it up, there are thousands of other murders to solve.

Ransom filled the sponge again and pressed it to his forehead, the warm water pouring down his face and neck. He smiled. The most annoying thing about Newman's pragmatic argument in this case was that it was true.

He put down the sponge, dried his hands on the tan bath towel that hung by the tub, and picked up his book. He hoped to bury the remainder of his nagging questions in the French Revolution. He took a sip of brandy and settled down to read through Dickens's vivid description of the storming of the Bastille. He managed to get through the marriage of Lucie to Charles Darnay but found his concentration beginning to flag as Darnay set off on his return to France.

Ransom set the book aside, slid further down into the water, and put a hand to his forehead. It had been a long day.

As he toweled himself dry he thought not regretfully that this weariness was not accompanied by a cacophony of conflicting thoughts, as so often happened when he was overtired. It appeared that he'd successfully managed to quiet his mind.

The one thought that did write itself across his consciousness as he settled naked between his clean blue sheets was that he was exhausted enough to sleep the deep, untroubled sleep of the dead, though he wasn't at all convinced that the dead were untroubled.

However, Ransom was wrong once again. As he passed deeper into sleep, he experienced what would be the last nightmare he would have for a long time.

All was complete blackness. He was aware of nothing except movement. The ground, the whole world seemed to be shaking around and beneath him. He realized after a time that he must be in some sort of wagon.

Slowly the sky began to lighten, and he found that he was correct. He was riding in a tumbril, its wooden railings rising only as high as his chest, but still he felt inexplicably trapped. Two huge, black horses, steam shooting at regular intervals from their flared nostrils, pulled the conveyance along the rock-strewn dirt road. In the distance Ransom could see a bright metallic glint in the sky, though where the reflected light originated he didn't know.

Gradually, he became aware of another sound: a dull, troubled rumbling that came to him from across a distance. The noise continued to increase in volume until it overtook the sound of the tumbril's unsteady wheels and the echoing clop of the horses' hooves. Soon the roar was all around him, and the lights came up like the lights on a stage, revealing all around him a teeming mass of peasants, starved and dirty, with hatred in their eyes. And all eyes were trained on Ransom.

"Death!" the enraged faces screamed at him. "Death! Kill all the aristocrats!"

Ransom looked about him, this way and that, in a frantic effort to see if there could be someone else, some other hidden occupant of the tumbril, at whom the wrath of the mob was directed. But there was nobody. He was alone in the huge wooden cage. With that sickening sense of realization so common to our darkest dreams, Ransom became aware with a shock that it was for his blood that the mob thirsted. And there was no escape. Deep inside his dream-self, he was sure of his fate. There was a repeat of the glint that had appeared in the distance; this time it was so close at hand that it appeared as a blinding flash. Ransom looked up, up into the air from which the flash had originated, and realized to his horror that the flash was the glint of the sun off the blade of Madame Guillotine, raised high overhead, honed and polished, waiting to taste his flesh.

He turned back to the mob and yelled, "But I haven't done anything!"

His words fell on deaf ears. Upon each angry face there appeared a demonic grin, as if each of the peasants were possessed of a devil that delighted in the panic of their prisoner. Each of his tormentors looked as hungry for his flesh as the blade. Suddenly, a ripple went through the crowd, and like the Red Sea, they parted. Down the newly formed aisle, lined on either side by solid human walls, there proceeded a hospital bed, propelled forward by an unseen hand. Upon the bed lay Maggie Walker, the dying lover of Lynn Francis, the maid. She looked closer to death than when Ransom had met her. Her eyes had sunken into her head and were surrounded by dark purple circles, giving her the aura of an animated skeleton. Her breathing was labored and loud, a metallic echo making her sound like the machine from which she'd inhaled when they met.

"You have to help me!" cried Ransom desperately.

"I can't even help myself," Maggie rasped weakly.

"But I haven't done anything!"

She tried to manage a smile, but failed. Her once bright eyes seemed dulled with regret.

"Somebody has to be responsible," she said, her faint voice floating like a phantom above the crowd, which hushed at the sound.

She raised two skeletal fists to the sky and sobbed up to the heavens, "Somebody has to be responsible! Somebody has to be responsible for what's happened to me!"

With this the bed and its occupant disappeared into the crowd, and the crowd closed ranks once again. Cries for Ransom's blood rose with renewed vigor. All at once he found himself led from the tumbril by two large men, their faces hidden by black hoods. They led him up the rough wooden stairs to the platform, all of which Ransom somehow knew had been hastily constructed for this very moment. Stretching endlessly into the sky was the scaffolding, the guides to the savagely sharp blade, and at the base an indentation cut to accommodate his neck.

A long rope dangled all the way down the right side of the scaffold. The top end of the rope was tied to the release for the blade. Ransom's eyes followed the rope down, down, down to the platform and rested on the hand that held its end. He realized with a recurrence of that dreamlike dread that the hand belonged to Eva Brinkley.

The look in her eyes seemed to embody all of the malevolence in the world combined. She gripped the rope as if it were a sword with which she would willingly have lopped off his head. Ransom felt himself impelled to look into her eyes, and in those eyes he saw the power over his life and death. Eva's blood red lips spread into a hideous smile that revealed her canine teeth and added a vampirish touch to her contorted countenance.

"A cat may *not* look at a king," she said, twisting the rope in her hands as if she were wringing his neck.

The black-hooded men pushed Ransom forward and forced him down between the scaffolds. The man on his left dropped the top of a wooden stock down over him, trapping his neck in a small hole through which it was impossible to extract his head.

"No matter what you may have heard before," whispered Eva, looming over him, "a cat may *not* look at a king!"

With this an ominous hush fell over the crowd. Ransom could feel the expectation crackle in the air, but could see nothing but the wicker basket that soon would hold his head. He tried to twist his head around to see more of what was happening, but he soon found it would have been better to have remained still. Out of the corner of his eye he saw Eva's hands tighten even more on the rope, until her knuckles looked as if they would explode, and with one sudden, violent motion, she pulled the rope taut.

The scaffold rattled, and there was a loud whoosh, as the blade cut through the air. In the final moment before Ransom and his head parted company, he became aware of a voice, or the approach of a voice. It seemed to emanate from Madame Guillotine herself. It was a female voice, and it spoke only one word, sounding like the whisper of the blade:

"Fool!"

For the first time in his life, Ransom woke with a start, sitting bolt upright in his bed. Though the room was cold from his air conditioner, which had decided, on this occasion, to be hyperactive, Ransom was covered with sweat, and his sheets and pillowcase were soaked. He fought the urge to turn on the lights, admonishing himself for being so disturbed by a dream. He was unsure of what to do next. He glanced at his bedside clock, whose luminous dial showed him that it was three o'clock. He groaned, sure that he'd seen all the sleep he would for the night. After a few more moments of indecision he threw back his top sheet and headed for the kitchen. In lieu of a better idea, he opted for another brandy. But he stopped himself at the last moment, remembering that his last Excedrin had been used to quell an errant hangover engendered by an overindulgence in vodka, the reason for which Ransom couldn't quite remember. He couldn't remember the reason, but he could remember the pounding in his head and the nausea. He told himself wearily that he must remember to pick up more Excedrin the next chance he got.

He returned to his bed and collapsed onto the damp sheets. What little remained of the night he spent staring saucer-eyed at the ceiling, his mind racing.

ELEVEN

The Hanged Man

THE FOLLOWING MORNING was spent in completing the reams of paperwork connected with the Stephens case. Ransom's despondency remained unchecked as he completed his reports, still haunted by the sense of unfinished and unfinishable business. If he had entertained any hopes that he could put to rest his conflicting emotions by the act of completing these reports, thereby formally bringing the case to an end, these hopes were to be frustrated. With little left to do other than dot his i's and cross his t's, the certainty grew that his doubts would always be with him.

It was while he was in the process of performing the aforementioned punctuation that the phone on his desk rang. He answered it with his name and was greeted by an agitated nasal voice with which he was all too familiar. The voice was in midsentence when Ransom put the receiver to his ear.

"Well, you know, when you're in such an all-fired, goddamned hurry for us to rush you goddamned evidence through the goddamn lab, the least you could do is call for the goddamn results!"

Ransom rolled his eyes to the ceiling and sighed wearily.

"Yes, Fergus?" he said, as if the voice had merely said hello.

"I ran all the stuff you sent down—I did it the minute it came, since it was *your* case and since *your* partner told me you were in a goddamn hurry, and it's just been sitting here."

"Sorry," said Ransom wryly, "I've been busy counting bodies."

"I feel like I'm in the goddamn army again!" Fergus droned on into Ransom's ear like the steady whine of a drill. "Hurry up and wait, hurry up and wait!"

"I'm sorry," said Ransom almost sincerely, aware of the hard and heavy workload of the crime lab. But despite himself, he smiled at the visual image that presented itself of the short, overweight, bug-eyed lab technician stuffing his heft into a doughboy uniform. "I really am. To be quite honest, I forgot all about it in the rush. I'm afraid the solution to this case was thrust upon us (like greatness, he thought mockingly to himself), and it won't require going to court."

"Well, ain't that a son of a bitch!" said Fergus. He sounded as if he were disappointed that someone had escaped facing his interpretation of the evidence in court. "What a goddamn waste."

"I assure you," said Ransom placatingly, "that your work won't be wasted. It will, of course, have to be included in the case file."

"Ha!" Fergus barked. He fully believed that a closed case file was second in importance only to an open circular file.

"What did you find?" asked Ransom, more to salve the technician's feelings than anything else.

It was at this point that Gerald White entered Ransom's office, carrying his own reports, which he placed on the desk. He plopped himself down on the couch and watched his partner, trying to gauge whether or not there'd been a change in Ransom's shifting moods. But it was hard to judge. Ransom did little more than stare at the wall blankly and utter an occasional "uh-huh," a sure sign that he was talking to someone he'd rather be rid of. It said nothing of Ransom's mood.

Gerald was totally unprepared, therefore, when Ransom suddenly shot out of his chair and yelled, *"What?!"*

In a split second Ransom's face achieved that burning intensity with which Gerald was so familiar. Ransom listened so intently to the voice on the phone that Gerald was surprised the caller wasn't sucked through the phone line into the office by the sheer force of Ransom's will.

"Say that again!" Ransom put his hand over the mouthpiece and shouted at Gerald, "Get out your notes!"

Gerald pulled the notebook from his pocket, keeping an eye on Ransom all the while.

Ransom's eyes narrowed as he listened, and a smile spread across his face the likes of which Gerald had seen many times before. It was likely to turn a sensible suspect's blood to ice.

"Forget what I said before, Fergus!" said Ransom suddenly. "I think we'll have our day in court, after all!" And with this, he slammed down the receiver.

"My God, what a turn!" said Ransom joyfully.

"Was that Fergus in the crime lab?" asked the bewildered Gerald.

"Yes! That was the fabulous Fergus in our fabulous crime lab!" replied Ransom, looking as if it was all he could do to keep from dancing. "My God, I've been lost and have been found, I've been dead and have come back to life, and this case along with me, to misquote the Bible!"

"The case? What the hell did Fergus have to say?"

"Gerald, my dearest partner," said Ransom, his eyes gleaming, "I was wrong, wrong, wrong when I said that Melina was the fool. I now know why this case has been such a bloody botheration to me! It wasn't Melina who was the fool, it was me!"

"What are you talking about?"

"The crime lab, Gerald! The crime lab! We were so busy plodding through in our flat-footed little way, tripping over dead bodies at every turn, that we forgot about the crime lab!''

"What!'' said Gerald, who would have been exasperated were he not so relieved to see Ransom restored to himself.

"It is at times like this,'' Ransom continued to ruminate happily, "that one is reminded that it is the crime lab that so often is responsible for solving a crime, while we are merely little foot soldiers going about our daily routine.''

"Jer—''

"Who would have thought that a mundane little case like the murder of Angela Stephens would be solved by mundane little evidence!''

"Ransom, will you please stop playing Lord Byron and tell me what you're talking about?''

Ransom fixed his eyes squarely on his partner's, raised his index finger, and wiggled it at him.

"Fingerprints, Gerald!'' he said triumphantly. "Remember? We asked the crime lab to identify the fingerprints from the second floor of the Stephens apartment! Let me see your notebook.''

Gerald handed it to him and said, "And they found something?''

"That, Gerald, is an understatement!'' Ransom leafed page by page back through his partner's cramped but clear notes, muttering, "Saturday…Saturday…Saturday…''

Gerald protested. "But a fingerprint found lying around the apartment doesn't mean anything.''

"This one does.''

"But it could have been left there at any time.''

"Oh, no, Gerald, this print couldn't have been left there at all!''

"Huh?''

"Ah, here we are!'' Ransom read in silence for a moment, and then suddenly snapped the notebook shut, his face fairly glowing.

"What is it?'' said Gerald anxiously.

"What have I always said about presence of mind, Gerald? That a killer always forfeits his presence of mind because once he's killed he has to lie, and eventually he'll get caught in those lies and trip himself up. Well, it's right here!" He waved the small spiral-bound notebook at his partner. "Someone has lied and we have that lie recorded right in your ever-loving, God-blessed notebook!"

"Ransom, whose prints were found in the apartment?" Gerald asked, his exasperation finally beginning to overcome his relief.

Ransom smiled slyly, said the name to his partner, and had the satisfaction of seeing Gerald's eyes widen and his mouth drop open.

"But that doesn't make any sense!" said Gerald when he had recovered himself.

"Oh, doesn't it?" said Ransom disdainfully. "I'm afraid it makes all too much sense. I know now who killed Angela Stephens and Melina!"

"Come on, Ransom, even with the fingerprint, how can you *know?*"

Ransom pursed his lips and looked at his partner through intense, narrowed eyes.

"I saw it in a dream!"

BEFORE BRINGING IN their suspect, Ransom had a hurried conference with Sergeant Newman, who for once found himself in agreement with his superior subordinate. What Ransom had had to tell Newman still amounted to nothing more than theory, but it was an interesting theory, if a little complicated for Newman's taste. Still, Ransom was seldom wrong (and Newman inserted the word "seldom" in his thoughts merely to soothe his own ego), and it might be possible to put this theory to the test. To this end, he dispatched detectives Robinson and Wilke on a little errand that he hoped would bear the fruit that Ransom desired.

"I REGRET HAVING to pull you in like this," said Ransom, oozing the most spurious sincerity Gerald had ever witnessed, "but as I'm sure you've heard, we've been completely baffled by the murder of Angela Stephens, so we find it necessary to go over some of the ground we've already covered."

"It's okay," said Larry Parker, then added with a hint of admonition, "I wish I had more notice. I'm glad I didn't have to work today."

He crossed his slender legs and joined his fingers around his knee. The cuffs of his plum-colored silk shirt were rolled jauntily up to his elbows. He looked pleased, and tanned, and seemed to exude a sexuality that was almost intoxicating. Though he appeared to be relaxed, there was a suppressed energy emanating from within him that threatened to break through his facade at any moment, as if he were a dam trying to hold back a flood.

But to Ransom, Larry Parker looked like a sitting duck: a sitting duck with very wide eyes and very large pupils.

"I'm sorry if you were inconvenienced," said Ransom lightly.

"No problem, no problem," replied Parker. As he continued, words poured out of him quickly and smoothly, like water from a tap that had been accidently left open. "It's just I would have been...I wish I knew ahead of time you were coming, so I could have been...ready...more ready." His smile was broad and careless.

"Well, in a murder investigation, we don't as a rule phone first," said Ransom, returning the smile with one that had no carelessness about it.

Parker laughed. "I guess. It's just, I'm confused. I thought it was all over. I thought Stephens killed his wife and then killed himself."

"You know about that, then?"

Parker rattled on like a drunk in the talkative stage of his intoxication. "Eva told me. I mean, what a useless thing to do, killing yourself. I guess you could feel guilty if you killed somebody by accident, but what's the point when you murder somebody? I mean, he must've known he couldn't get away with it. He must have known everyone would think he did it, or he was a complete asshole. I mean, even *I* thought he was guilty...when Eva told me about it. It was obvious, wasn't it? So, like, I don't understand why you're still...why I'm here.''

"Paperwork!'' said Ransom, thoroughly enjoying himself. "Bureaucracy. Even after a case is dead and gone, we have to fill out endless reports on it and make sure every sentence has a period firmly placed at the end.''

In the spirit of male camaraderie, Parker sympathized with him, then said, "I guess, but I don't see what I can do for you.'' At this point Parker's face took on a sheepishness that was amazing to behold. Ransom was sure that this man could charm his way past anyone. Almost.

"I don't know how I can help. I mean, I'm like what they call an 'innocent bystander,' right?''

Ransom eyed him shrewdly in silence for a moment: just long enough to be disconcerting, then said, "Well, we would just like to go over some of your information once again, and make sure that we've got it all accurately.''

Parker smiled, shrugged, and sat back in his chair as he said, "Anything I can do to help.'' With this he let out a giggle that was neither embarrassed nor nervous. It was simply involuntary.

How much have you had? thought Ransom sharply. *How much of the lovely white powder have you sucked up that fine nose of yours this morning?*

Inwardly, Ransom sighed at the great number of ridiculously attractive people in the world who, one would think, would have all the advantages, who recklessly throw themselves away out of their own arrogant stupidity or boredom. He also wondered how long it would be before Parker's finely chiseled nose would be in need of repair.

But he answered Parker's statement in a tone tinged with wicked glee. "Fine! Could you tell us then, one more time, where you were from Thursday night to Friday morning, the time period during which Angela Stephens was killed?"

"Where *I* was?" answered the startled man with another giggle.

"Forgive me," said Ransom with the casual air of someone apologizing for dropping an hors d'oeuvre on a new carpet, "I meant where the two of you were: you and Eva Brinkley."

Parker rested an arm on the back of his chair and absently twisted his dark ponytail, looking as if he were going over the time period in his head. At last, he said:

"I don't think I can add anything to what I told you before."

"What exactly was it you told us before?"

Gerald coughed into his hand.

Parker's smile spread across his face, his lips parting to show a row of teeth so perfect they might have belonged to a forties-era film star. Ransom chalked up another mark against him.

"I'm glad to help," said Parker again, with a sigh. "I had Friday off. I met Eva Thursday night—"

"What time would that be?" interrupted Ransom.

"Umm...? I worked the day shift...usually I work the night shift, but Danny—one of the other waiters—needed the day off, so I traded with him...." He leaned in to Ransom conspiratorially. "It was a good trade, you know... there's lots and lots of businessmen that like to bring clients and stuff to the restaurant to...impress them, you know what I mean? I mean, they're a joke, but that doesn't make a difference 'cause there's a lot of money in it—they tip big. Lots and lots of money, because the people who come there like to look important, and they think it makes them look important to overtip. You can walk away with a hundred to two hundred bucks in one lunch!"

Parker stopped and sat back in his chair. Ransom eyed him for a moment without speaking, then said, "So you picked Eva up...?"

"Oh," said Parker, recalled to the point without the least embarrassment, "at five-thirty or six. No later than six. No."

"And then?"

Parker shrugged, "Then...we did what anybody'd do, you know. We ate, we went to the movies, we screwed...we did that a lot. I don't suppose you want the details of that, do you?"

"I'll assume you're a gentleman," said Ransom with a sardonic smile.

"That took up Thursday night. Friday we did all sorts of things. I told you all about that." He stopped and then added with a lascivious look that would have been offensive were he not so handsome, "We screwed some more."

"How very energetic of you. And when you had finished exercising, what did you do?"

"We went to sleep," Parked replied with a shrug.

"And the next morning?"

"I went to work."

"So from Thursday night at approximately six o'clock through Saturday morning, you were with Eva Brinkley at all times?"

Parker let out another muffled, involuntary giggle. "With, you know, the usual interruptions for the bathroom and things like that. It's like I told you before, I didn't have my eyes on her every minute—I wasn't keeping her under observation, you know. But she was never out of my sight long enough to run over and kill her sister."

Ransom appeared to consider this seriously, then said, "When exactly did you learn of the murder?"

Parker smiled coyly. "You know that, Mr. Ransom. Saturday morning. Right after the police called Eva, she called me."

"Ah, yes," said Ransom with a wicked glint in his eye, "she called her boyfriend for support and you, of course, refused to rush to her side."

Parker remained unruffled, answering this with the ingratiating forthrightness of a successful salesman. "I explained that to you, man. I'm sorry, I'm really sorry if Eva thinks we're closer than we really are, but it's like that with some women, if you know what I mean. It's an old story."

"The oldest," said Ransom with a look that might have melted steel. "So, Saturday morning was the first you'd heard of Angela Stephens."

"No, of course not," said Parker, shifting slightly in his seat, "Eva told me stuff about her. She told me about when her parents died, and the falling out she had with her sister. That's why this is all so sad for her, you know, because they were just getting to know each other again."

"Yes. I know. Miss Brinkley said something surprisingly like that to us when we interviewed her. You seem to know quite a bit about their old problems."

Parker shrugged, "Hey, you go on dates, you talk."

"You talk," Ransom repeated airily, his gaze traveling to the window. "You talk, you plan..."

Parker drew his perfectly formed eyebrows closer together. "What?"

"I'm sorry," said Ransom with a look that was not designed to give comfort to the unsettled headwaiter. "I meant you make plans. When two people know each other for a while, their talks are bound to get serious—so I'm told. They start to make plans together...for the future."

Parker's smile had vanished somewhere within Ransom's statement. The muscles of his face seemed to tremble beneath the surface, as if his mind could not decide into which expression to mold his fine features. However, Ransom could see one emotion clearly registered around Parker's eyes, or perhaps behind them: fear. Whatever else was going on within Eva's handsome lover, it was clear that he didn't like the direction this conversation was taking.

All at once Parker's face relaxed, his mind having apparently decided that his facial expression should be a combination of amusement and tolerance.

"Like I've tried to tell you before," said Parker suavely, "we didn't have that kind of relationship. I'm sorry if it sounds, you know, shallow, but I really didn't think beyond our next date."

Ransom smiled with the malevolence of a villain from a Disney animated feature.

"It's funny how murder throws people together, isn't it?"

Parker made an unsuccessful attempt to look as if he didn't understand this. He uncrossed then recrossed his legs. "I don't think I'd put it that way, but I think I get what you mean."

"Do you?" said Ransom with one eyebrow raised. "Good!"

Had anyone been watching Gerald, who sat inconspicuously in a corner of the room, they would have seen him pause in his perpetual note taking long enough to look up and smile.

Ransom rose casually from his chair and crossed to the front of the table. He sat on the corner, less than a foot from Larry Parker, which materially increased the headwaiter's discomfiture.

"Now, you've known Miss Brinkley...how long did you say?"

"Around a year."

"And in all that time you didn't meet her sister?"

"No," said Parker with a wary look.

"That's so odd," said Ransom reflectively.

"I've told you over and over, we weren't into a 'bringing-me-home-to-meet-the-family' type thing. I don't think it's so weird that I didn't meet her sister."

"No? Hmmm. Perhaps not. Still, according to Miss Brinkley, she and her sister were making great strides in mending their broken relationship. Miss Brinkley told me, as I'm sure she told you, what a loss it was to have that growing relationship cut short after all that's gone before."

"What does that have to do with me?" said Parker, whose wariness continued to grow.

"Miss Brinkley seemed to want more than anything to prove to her sister that she had changed, and was now the stable young lady that her sister had always wanted."

"So?"

"Well, it's just that I would have thought that Miss Brinkley would have gone out of her way to introduce a fine young man like yourself to her sister as further proof of her stability."

"But she didn't," said Parker, whose brow furrowed in a way that sent unflattering lines across his smooth forehead.

Ransom gazed down at Parker for a moment, then said simply, "Then how did you meet her?"

"Who?" said the confused suspect.

"Angela Stephens."

Parker stared blankly for a moment, then shifted in his chair.

"Jesus Christ, how the hell many times do I have to tell you that I didn't know her!"

"Oh, yes, you did tell us that, didn't you?" said Ransom, his smile growing broader. "Even at our first interview, isn't that right, Gerald?"

Gerald made a pretense of flipping back through his notebook for a moment, then glanced over at his partner.

"Yes, he didn't know her," said Gerald in happy agreement.

"Well, I didn't!" said Parker petulantly.

"You're sure you didn't know her?"

"Of course I'm sure."

"You never met her?"

"Never."

Ransom leaned in toward Parker, towering over the seated suspect, eyes gleaming with delight.

"Then how do you account for your fingerprints being found in her bedroom?"

Whatever reaction Ransom might have been expecting from Parker, it certainly was not the one he received. Though it hardly seemed possible, Parker's pupils widened even further until they were like dark, black moons eclipsing an olive green sun. After a long pause, Parker's full lips spread into a smile that was both coy and ingratiating. One would have thought he'd been caught in a mild schoolboy indiscretion rather than a baldfaced lie in a murder investigation. Perhaps it was the widening of the suspect's pupils that made Ransom feel as if he could see into him clearly at last, but Ransom was sure that in the brief pause that had just elapsed, Parker had determined on a course of action.

"What a pile of shit I got myself into when I met that woman."

"I beg your pardon?" said Ransom with a raised eyebrow.

"I mean Eva."

"Umm-hmmm?"

"Uh, not the way you think. I guess I'm going to have to come clean."

Gerald paused just long enough in his note taking to shoot Ransom a questioning glance. Ransom made a slight gesture at his partner, who then returned to his notes. He turned back to Parker, motioning for him to continue.

"I did meet Angela Stephens, about a year ago—not long after I started going out with Eva."

"Wait a bit," said Ransom, raising a hand, "Perhaps you should start at the beginning by telling us how you came to start 'dating' Eva."

"She came into the restaurant one night, alone. She was nice enough, and kind of wanted to talk, which is a sure sign—usually—of someone who lives alone and doesn't have many friends and usually wants to get laid. So she did what a lot of lonely people do in restaurants—she talked to her waiter, and that was me."

"Isn't La Gioconda a bit pricey for someone like Miss Brinkley?"

Parker smiled at the remembrance. "Yeah, it is. She told me she saved up her money for a while and this was…like a big treat for herself, you know what I mean. It really kind of touched me. She told me later that she chose it because it was the type of place she knew her sister would go to. Anyway, when she finished her dinner, she stayed and stayed and stayed at her table. I figured she didn't have any place to go. And…in the end, I asked her out." He stopped and shifted in his chair again, then ran his hands across his prematurely graying temples, first the right, then the left.

"Very philanthropic of you."

"Not really," said Parker. "I thought it was the only way to free up the table for my next setup. Tips are everything, you know."

Ransom smiled. "Yes, in my business, too."

"Oh, yeah," said Parker, and with this he laughed a little too loudly and a little too long. It was clear that his suppressed anxiety was beginning to chip away at his composure. Now that his tongue had been loosened, the internal pressure combined with whatever chemical recreation he'd been indulging in began to work upon him.

"About your meeting Mrs. Stephens?" said Ransom, attempting to recall Parker to his story.

Parker began to pour out words with the alacrity of a particularly manic improvisational actor.

"Eva and I had gone out a couple of times when one day—out of the blue—she asked me to go with her to a party at her sister's. Well, I wasn't too keen on the idea for a couple of reasons. First, because I didn't know her that well, and second because she had told me a lot...or enough...about their pasts and I wasn't sure how friendly things were between them, you know. But I decided to go with her anyway, because she seemed so...she seemed to want it so badly. It was just like you said. She wanted to have a man with her—I think to let her sister know that she had somebody. And I'm good-looking enough. She wanted someone like me with her, if you know what I mean.''

"Oh, I know," said Ransom with a wicked little smirk that brought Parker up short.

Parker hesitated for the briefest moment, then continued his narrative more insistently:

"She wanted to show me off. She wanted to show her sister she could land a guy like me, like she was proud of getting above herself or something.''

Even Gerald could not suppress a smile at this. Fortunately, neither Ransom nor Parker took any notice of him.

"So you met Angela Stephens..." said Ransom.

Parker's face brightened as the words continued to spurt out of him. "Yeah, and she was something to meet! Now Angela was more my type than Eva. Eva might be all right for a few laughs, but not...she doesn't have...class. She'll never be what her sister was, no matter how much—" He stopped suddenly, with a startled look at Ransom.

"Yes, Mr. Parker? No matter what? No matter how much money she gets?''

Parker looked stricken. It was obvious that Ransom had hit his mark, but Parker was still slick enough to recover quickly.

"No, no, that's not what I was going to say. I was going to say that she'd never be what her sister was, no matter how hard she tries. It doesn't have anything to do with money. Money can't buy class, or taste. You got to be born with it. I don't know..." His voice trailed off. He seemed to be looking for words, feverishly ruminating something, when suddenly his face lit up with a new idea. "Yeah, yeah, I guess I never thought of it like that before. Maybe because Angela had parents around longer than Eva did…maybe that made the difference…I don't know."

Once again, Ransom recalled Parker to the matter at hand. "So you met Mrs. Stephens at the party."

"What? Oh, yeah, yeah, I did. And I spent some time talking to her, the way you do at parties. Nothing too deep or anything like that. Just 'how's the weather type stuff' until…"

"Yes?"

Parker appeared reluctant to answer, almost as if he was loathe to break a trust…or more likely as if he were heading into dangerous waters. He fidgeted in his chair, adjusted the collar of his shirt, and then leaned back in his chair. He stroked his ponytail with his right hand as he continued his story.

"…until later. The party went on and on—the whole damn thing wore on me. It was a pain in the ass hobnobbing with the suits and trying to act interested in whatever the hell they were talking about, and feeling…I don't have anything to be embarrassed about, you know, but feeling embarrassed anyway every time one of those overdressed, overstuffed, upper-middle-class bastards asked me what I did for a living—which was the only thing they talked about all evening. And every time I told them their eyes would just glaze over, and they would see somebody across the room they had to talk to right away. I wasn't in their class, and none of them exactly went out of their way to hide the fact. They were exactly like the type of people I have to wait on at the restaurant. You'd be surprised at how often that type of thing happens at the restaurant. I told you before that lots of people like to show off by taking their clients or friends to a fancy restaurant like ours because it makes them look important. Those same people think it makes them look important to treat the staff like shit. Sometimes...I can't tell you...well, anyway, I think that's why so many of them tip well. It's like throwing a dog a bone after beating him.''

"Angela Stephens?" recalled Ransom again.

"Yeah, right. Well, I got pretty fed up with the party pretty fast, but Eva wanted to stay. At one point—pretty late—I don't know where Eva was, but I went out to the kitchen to get myself a drink and for a break from the 'party,' and who do you think I found there?''

"Angela Stephens," said Ransom monotonously.

"Yeah! It turned out that she'd gone there to get away from them, too. We got to talking—not so surface this time—about life—her life in particular. She was fed up with the party. She was fed up with her whole life. It was dull. Her husband was dull. Everything was dull. I'm just giving you the short version, but you get the idea. And she seemed to hit it off with me and...she was attracted to me. And if you'd ever seen her, you'd know you'd have to be dead not to be attracted to her. So, we sort of went with it.''

Ransom glanced at his watch and then back at Parker. "Right there at the party?"

Parker smiled and assumed his sheepish expression, which was marred by the tiny beads of sweat that had broken out on his brow. Ransom was finding his expression more irritating by the minute.

"No. I went back the next day, and said I left something there by accident. I don't remember what I said I forgot, and it didn't matter anyway, because she knew what I was there for. She offered me tea, and I listened to her...I mean I *listened* to her when she told me about her life. One thing led to another, and the rest, like they say, is history.''

With this, Parker sat back in his chair and laid his hands on his knees. He looked like a student who'd finished his presentation. A nervous student, unsure of the reception he'd receive from the teacher.

After a moment, Ransom slid off the table, walked around behind it, and resumed his seat. He folded his hands and laid them on the table. He looked across at Parker and said with the indelicate precision of a stern father, "I was under the impression that you're still seeing Eva."

Completely insensible to the moral issues involved, Parker babbled proudly, "Oh, it was easy. Since I don't usually work day shifts, and Eva works during the day, it was easy to see Angela during the day and Eva on my evenings off."

Ransom paused, his eyes narrowing.

"Well, this puts everything in an entirely new light, doesn't it?"

The shock of fear that blighted Parker's eyes was unmistakable this time. He was flustered and confused, unsure whether he'd betrayed something great or small. He knew, though, that he'd made an irretrievable mistake.

"What do you mean?" he asked haltingly.

"Just that we've labored under the assumption that Frank Stephens was the only one who had a motive to kill his wife. That was, of course, before we knew for certain that she had a lover."

"Wait a minute, wait a minute!" said Parker quickly, moving as if to rise from his seat: a move that was checked by one look from Ransom. Parker's whole face glistened with a thin layer of perspiration. "I thought you just wanted me here to clear up some things, after the fact, like. Is there any doubt that Stephens killed his wife?"

"I don't know about that," said Ransom vaguely.

"Didn't he kill himself?" cried Parker. "Didn't he commit suicide? Doesn't it tell you anything? It tells me he was guilty about killing his wife." Though Parker said this last with finality, there was a sense of desperation in his tone.

"I've no doubt that Stephens was a desperate man,"

replied Ransom calmly. "He had lost the only woman he loved, he was in danger of losing his career because of it, and he was under suspicion of murder. Far better men have taken their lives for far less reason."

This time Parker jumped to his feet and laid his palms on the table, leaning across at Ransom in an attitude that caused Gerald to check his note taking and be on his guard.

"You can't think I had anything to do with her death! I...I loved her! I did! She was beautiful! And I loved making love to her! I didn't have anything to do with it! I mean, maybe her husband found out about us and that's why he killed her! That sounds...logical to me.... I'll bet that's what happened, her husband found out about us and he killed her! Or maybe he wanted all her money, not just his own, and wanted to be free to spend it! Maybe that's why he killed her!"

"Or maybe," said Ransom as if considering this for the first time, "maybe she realized she was making a fool of herself with you, and decided to throw you over. Maybe you killed her because you saw a potential meal ticket slipping away."

"No!" Parker cried. "She wouldn't throw me over, she relied on me! She was unhappy with her life and her husband, and she turned to me when they were having trouble!"

"Indeed?" said Ransom with interest. "And did she turn to you on Thursday night?"

All movement was frozen in the room like a movie frame that had suddenly jammed. Parker looked much as if he'd been struck on the head with a heavy object, and the shock had yet to register.

"No!" said Parker at last. "No, I was with Eva all Thursday night. I tell you, Angela's husband must have found out about us and killed her!"

"That might be true, but we don't know that her husband knew anything about the two of you, and he did have enough money of his own, and...well, it may seem awfully unprofessional of me,'' said Ransom with feigned chagrin, ''but his remorse over his wife's death seemed quite genuine to me. It's very hard for me to believe that he was the one who killed her.''

''All right...all right,'' said Parker, his mind obviously racing. ''But there's something else...someone else...maybe...maybe Eva found out about me and her sister and killed her! Maybe that's it! I'll bet it is! That's what Eva's like, you know! She talks all that bullshit about loving her sister and how sad it was for her to die now, and that's all it is: bullshit! Because, you see, I know the truth! Eva didn't love Angela, she hated her! She resented her for having everything she couldn't have! Ha! There you are! Don't you see? What if Eva found out that Angela even had *me!* Don't you think that would make her want to kill her?''

''But Eva was with you Thursday night, wasn't she?''

Parker looked stricken, his face wet and pale, his eyes as large as they could get without exploding, and his mouth hanging open. He looked as if his life hung on the answer to Ransom's question, but he wasn't sure which answer would save him. At last he said, quietly and vacantly, ''Yes, she was.''

Ransom allowed Parker's words to hang in the air between them for a moment, then said, ''Compose yourself, Mr. Parker, I haven't accused you of killing Angela Stephens.''

Parker was brought up short by this and looked far less relieved than wary, like a dog that has been tricked by his master once too often and now doesn't know what to expect. He'd given something away somehow, and was tormented by the idea he was continuing to give himself away, but the anxiety and the drugs made it impossible for him to control his tongue.

The exchange was interrupted at this point by a light

knock at the door to the interrogation room. Ransom had a quick, quiet consultation with Detective Robinson in the doorway, while Gerald made a show of rereading his notes. Parker didn't resume his seat, but remained standing with his hands on the table, his head lowered as if it were too heavy for him to support anymore. His silk shirt was so damp now it would obviously never be the same again.

Ransom closed the door and returned to the table, carrying something wrapped in a white cloth.

"Now we're getting somewhere," said Ransom cheerfully.

Parker looked up at him with increased wariness and confusion. Ransom laid the parcel on the table.

"As I said, Mr. Parker, I haven't accused you of killing anyone. We just need your assistance. There is one other little matter I would like to clear up."

Parker's look became less wary and more quizzical. He said with an attempt at his former manner, tainted with his present confusion, "I'll do anything I can to help."

Ransom tapped the parcel with his index finger. "This contains what I think is the key to the whole matter." He paused for a moment for effect, then with a glance at Gerald, he continued. "Any assistance you can be to us in the matter of this little piece of property will be greatly appreciated."

Ransom folded back the corners of the white cloth, revealing a small handgun. Parker looked momentarily startled, then was convulsed in a fit of relieved laughter.

"Oh, God!" he said as he wiped his forehead with a silk sleeve. "Oh, God, oh, God!"

Both of Ransom's brows raised a fraction of an inch. "Do you recognize this, Mr. Parker?"

Parker choked back a laugh and placed a hand over his heart as if to steady himself. He then looked at Ransom with wide, relieved eyes.

"I didn't kill *her!*" he said as if he thought the idea was absurd.

Ransom seized on this triumphantly, like the teeth of a springtrap.

"*Who* didn't you kill, Mr. Parker?"

"The fortune-teller!" he said with a wave of his up-turned palms.

And with these words, Larry Parker's world crumbled around him.

WITHIN AN HOUR after Parker had been "led away in charge" (as the British say), Ransom found himself comfortably ensconced in the creaking chair behind his desk, relating a carefully edited version of the preceding drama to Eva Brinkley. He gave her a shortened version of Parker's ensuing confession, leaving out all mention of the gun, among other things.

"So as it stands," Ransom concluded, "your lover—or I suppose I should say very recent ex-lover—stands charged with murder."

"My God," said Eva with exaggerated incredulity. "You mean that all the time he was carrying on with me he was carrying on with Angela?"

"Umm-mmm," said Ransom with a slight inclination of his head.

"My God," Eva repeated. "I never suspected a thing, the bastard!"

Despite himself, Ransom imagined this line being delivered by Katharine Hepburn. He dismissed this image as uncharitable.

"I suppose," Eva continued with some of the bitterness she'd shown in previous interviews, "I suppose you can believe murder of someone who would be having affairs with two sisters at the same time."

"Hmmm. Perhaps. I do have one stumbling block with

him that I'm sure would be shared by any jury that would hear the case.''

"What's that?'' Eva replied blankly.

"The same thing that bothered me—well, bothered my partner, Gerald, I should say…''

Gerald smiled acknowledgment from his place on the couch.

"The same thing that bothered us about any possible suspect other than Frank Stephens: lack of motive. Nobody else but the husband seemed to have any motive for killing your sister. Of course, at the time we didn't have any idea that Larry Parker was involved in the case in any other way than providing you with an alibi.''

As he spoke these words, Ransom searched Eva's face intently. She paled ever so slightly at the word "alibi,'' and after a moment, she rose from her seat and walked to the window. The air conditioner rattled contentedly in the silence. Ransom was beginning to appreciate the noise as a sign of the machine's steady work on behalf of his comfort. After a moment, Eva spoke with a tone of remorse that might not have sounded practiced to a less trained ear than Ransom's.

"I guess I'm in trouble over that. Well, all I can say in my defense is that you made me think…well, you acted like you actually thought *I* might have had something to do with my sister's death. So I told you that Larry and I were never apart that whole night. I gave him an alibi because I was afraid I needed one. But it wasn't true. We weren't together every minute. Larry got a call somewhere around eleven, maybe a little before, and when he got off the phone he told me he had to go out for a while. He said it was a friend who was in trouble and needed to be bailed out. Of course, I believed it. I thought he meant it literally because…well, I suppose you know by now that Larry's been in jail before, for things like possession of drugs and dealing, but never for very long. And he told me…he promised me that he was off the stuff now and he'd never get hooked again." She gave a bitter laugh at this. "And I believed him. Anyway, he got the call and went out for about an hour, and when he came back he was...he was acting different. He was kind of agitated. I don't know how to describe it. But I only thought that he'd started taking drugs again."

Ransom considered Eva coldly. He felt he'd been present at the first rehearsal of the scene the young woman would play before a jury. Given time she would perfect it, and if she was able to hold her temper, she might even make a favorable impression.

After a long silence, broken only by Ransom's steady tapping of a pencil on the surface of his desk, he returned to his original point.

"So now that you've told the truth we know that he had the opportunity, but..." He allowed his voice to trail off suggestively.

"But what?" said Eva, with barely controlled impatience.

Ransom shrugged and smiled. "That still leaves us with that nagging lack of motive."

"Well..." she said, with an attempt at embarrassment that reminded Ransom of Olivia De Havilland, "I hate to admit it after what you've told me, but we...we talked about getting married. I should say, I talked about it. I...know I look like a complete idiot, but I really am...have been...crazy about him. Maybe he thought if he murdered Angela he could marry me and we'd get her money."

"But that would go to her husband," said Ransom.

"Not if Frank was found guilty of killing Angela," said Eva, as if the idea had just occurred to her.

Oh, how she skirts around the truth, thought Ransom. She's bound to get her hem caught on it.

"Why all the bother?" said Ransom aloud. "Why not just marry Angela and live the way he wanted to?"

"Oh, please!" Eva replied with disdain, "Angela would never have married anybody like Larry! He's nowhere near her class! And she could never leave that idiot she *was* married to!"

Despite himself, Ransom could not help being surprised that even with all things considered, Eva was unable to control her disdain, which was still obviously directed at her sister rather than her lover. After a moment, he said:

"So, you were unaware not only that Larry Parker had become attached to your sister but that he had resumed taking drugs. That he is, indeed, addicted to cocaine?"

She sighed heavily at her own folly. "I guess I was blind. But I was lonely. I needed Larry."

"I have no doubt of that," said Ransom wryly.

"So I guess I closed my eyes to it, if it's true. The drugs and all that. I suppose if you searched his apartment, you'd find the drugs, if he's really addicted."

As she said this, Eva couldn't help but steal a glance at Ransom to see if her suggestion had had any visible effect. She was surprised when Ransom responded to her placidly:

"What else could we find there?"

"What?" she said too quickly to stop herself. "I don't understand."

Ransom reached into the middle drawer of his desk and pulled out the gun with which he'd snared Larry Parker. He laid it on the desk in front of Eva, whose eyes never left it as she came back to her chair opposite Ransom.

"Do you recognize this?"

"It's a gun."

"Come, come, Miss Brinkley. You spent quite a bit of time in Larry Parker's apartment, by both your accounts. I ask you again, do you recognize this?"

Eva curled her lips and eyed Ransom with disdain. "Well, it looks like Larry's gun, if that's what you want me to say!"

"You've seen it before, then?"

"It or one like it. He showed it to me. He keeps it in the drawer in his nightstand."

"Did you ever handle it?"

"No," she said emphatically.

"Make a note of that, will you Gerald?" said Ransom, looking over at his partner, who sat in his place on the couch. The request was superfluous, since Gerald was, as usual, making note of everything. Ransom turned back to Eva.

"You're sure you never touched it?"

"Of course I'm sure!"

Ransom eyed her for a moment. "It *is* Mr. Parker's gun. He identified it."

"Well, what of it!" Eva snapped. "My sister was strangled, not shot!"

Though as a rule he never smoked during an interview, Ransom broke precedent as he broke the seal of a Coronella, lit it, and took a tantalizing drag, releasing the smoke into the air. It was Gerald's turn to elevate his seldom-raised eyebrows.

"That is a good point," Ransom replied at last in a calm and almost purring tone. "Your sister was not shot. And still we have this gun, which leaves us with a dilemma."

"What?"

"The same dilemma we began with," Ransom smiled. "The wild card in this little plot: the fortune-teller."

"What in the hell does a fortune-teller have to do with anything?" exclaimed Eva, her voice managing to sound harsh and hollow at the same time.

"That's what I've been asking myself for days!" said Ransom with a sigh. "And I think I finally know."

These words turned Eva to stone. Her expression didn't change: There was not a move, shadow, or tremor to indicate the transformation, but stone she became, just the same. Her face was frozen in the defiant glare that had become her habitual expression in Ransom's presence. Her midsection retained the power of movement enough to sit.

"Let me tell you a story." said Ransom, with a glance at Emily's picture, "a story with a rather Victorian flavor. I call it, 'A Tale of Two Sisters.'"

"One of the sisters was an aristocrat, who had all the good things in life; the other sister was a peasant who…in a word… didn't. Like most peasants, she hated the aristocracy almost as much as she wanted to be a part of it. And also like most peasants, she was under the mistaken impression that aristocracy and money were one and the same. So she decided the answer to all her problems would be to eliminate her aristocratic sister and claim the family fortune."

"You *know* I didn't kill my sister!" barked Eva, evidently finding her voice again and testing it at top volume.

"Oh, I know, I know," said Ransom, raising a palm to stay the interruption. "Let me continue…. So, the peasant sister enlisted the aid of another peasant: a handsome young peasant, presumably enlisted with promises of future riches that would feed his habits for years to come—whose job it was to insinuate his way into the life of the aristocrat, win her confidence, and when the opportunity presented itself, kill her. By an amazing stroke of luck, the type of luck with which the peasant sister was in no way familiar, the opportunity finally occurred on an evening when the two peasants could provide each other with alibis."

Eva had been regaining something of her old manner, apparently through reminding herself that the story she was listening to was just that: a story. A story that she believed to have not the least possibility of being verified.

"That's very interesting," she said, her lips curling into a sneer, "but it seems too complicated to me."

"Not really so complicated as you might think," Ransom replied evenly. "You see, the aristocratic sister was going through a period of dissatisfaction with her life, as is common to so many people. Many years earlier she had given up a promising career as a businesswoman for a promising career as a wife, which, however much she might have welcomed it, was bound at some time or another to cause her doubts. And she was experiencing the usual, latent doubts that go with choosing one road over the other. Had nobody interfered with her''—Ransom emphasized those words particularly—''she would have gotten through it much the way everyone else does, with time...and either changed her life or reinforced her reasons for having made the choices she did in the first place.

''But she made the mistake—though she was generally wise—of confiding her dissatisfaction to her peasant sister—a sister who had returned to her in the guise of a penitent prodigal after a long estrangement. I'm afraid she welcomes her errant sister back into her life too quickly. We can't judge her too harshly on this score, as she had a tendency to think the best of people, and of course, the reclamation of her sister was something she'd always desired. In a move of sisterly confidence, she told the peasant sister about her dissatisfaction.''

''Still a pretty ridiculous idea,'' said Eva, gaining confidence. ''If this 'peasant' only wanted money, why the hell didn't she just kill her sister and get it over with?''

Ransom leaned in toward Eva, almost in admiration. ''Because she was too clever!''

Despite herself, Eva registered a tinge of pride in the midst of her hostility.

''There were two reasons for this elaborate plan. First, the aristocrat had a husband. In order to ensure her inheritance, the peasant had to eliminate both the woman and her husband in one stroke. What better way than by driving a wedge between them with another man. And it worked, to a point. Being basically honorable, the aristocratic sister couldn't help but register her guilt at her indiscretion, and withdraw from her husband. The husband noticed the change, and even the husband's parents felt that something was wrong. And of course, the peasant sister was more than happy to offer false evidence that the marriage was in trouble. After all, after the murder it would be impossible to verify. This way, when the murder occurred, the husband would be the obvious suspect: So both of the obstacles between the peasant and the fortune would be eliminated at once, at least in the peasant's mind.''

Eva looked momentarily affronted by his choice of words, then, with a desire equal only to the ''imp of the perverse'' to find out how much the detective had surmised, she demanded, ''You said there were two reasons for her plan?''

''Ah, yes!'' said Ransom wistfully. ''And that's where she was stupid. Hopelessly, inexcusably stupid!''

Once again Eva could not stop her face from betraying her thoughts. She turned bright red, and her triumphant smile collapsed into a grimace so full of malice that Ransom was surprised it didn't melt the little varnish that remained on his ancient desk. Really, thought Ransom, if you're going to go around murdering people, you really must learn to control yourself.

''How!'' Eva fairly hissed. ''How was she stupid?''

Ransom replied nonchalantly, ''Like most peasants, she blamed the aristocrats for all her problems. Everything that had ever gone wrong in her life: all the wrongs, the hurts, the disappointments, the frustrated desires—all of these things she laid at the feet of the aristocratic sister.

''It wasn't enough for the peasant to simply gain her sister's money, she wanted to make her sister suffer. She wanted to confuse her and destroy her marriage and terrify her.''

Here Ransom leaned in even closer to Eva, his sharp, concentrated eyes boring into hers.

''That is where you made your mistake, Miss Brinkley. You let your hatred get the better of you.''

"What?" Eva snapped like a frightened dog. "What are you talking about?"

"If you had simply settled for the money, we might never have found you out."

Eva beat her fists against the desk. "You *know* that Larry did it!"

"You knew your sister had one weakness, or flaw, if you want a better word for it. She liked to visit fortune-tellers. So you hired one, a woman named Melina, who was not above selling ready-made fortunes, and directed your sister to her—how? By slipping a leaflet under the door? By telling Angela casually that visiting Melina might be fun. However you did it, you were successful.

"You gave Melina detailed information about your sister's past, and about her present—including the one detail that Angela didn't think *anyone* else knew about, that she was having an affair. Melina used this information to prove her fortune-telling powers to your sister. And when your sister was fully convinced, Melina let fly with your real plan—the prediction that Angela would be murdered, complete with a description that vaguely matched her husband. And all this for the express purpose of punishing and terrifying her." Ransom paused and smiled. "Very, very Victorian of you."

Eva responded only with a stony glare, so Ransom continued:

"The one thing you hadn't foreseen was that Melina played her part too well. Angela believed her so thoroughly that she came to me to report her murder before it happened."

In the silence that followed, Eva seemed to be deciding how to proceed. At last she laughed at him, rose from her chair, and snapped shut her purse, which seemed to have come open merely for the purpose of punctuating her exit.

"I forgot for a minute there, Mr. Ransom—I forgot that you were telling a story. A story with no foundation, that you can't prove. And you seem to forget that you've already arrested Larry. Larry confessed, you told me that yourself! No matter what you might think, you can't prove that I had any connection with my sister's murder...and if Larry tries to implicate me..." She laughed curtly through her nose. "Well, if Larry tries to implicate me, it's just the ravings of a drug addict."

Ransom looked up at her with mock surprise. "Oh, I'm sorry. Did I imply that I thought you murdered your sister? Oh, no no no no no! I know you didn't kill your sister."

"Well, at least—" Eva began, but Ransom cut her off abruptly:

"You killed Melina."

"What?!" Eva shouted, her face breaking into a shocked smile. She choked out between excruciatingly false laughs, "You have to be kidding."

"No," said Ransom calmly, "I'm not. Why did you do it, Miss Brinkley? Did she want more money, or were you just ridding yourself of witnesses?"

Eva narrowed her eyes at him, her anger rising like a forest fire about to burn out of control.

"You're crazy!" she roared. "You can't mean that!"

"Oh, yes, I do. You killed the fortune-teller with this gun," said Ransom, tapping the revolver with his index finger.

"I did not kill her!"

"I'm afraid you did, Miss Brinkley. And I can prove it."

This truly stopped Eva in her tracks. Doubt was written across her brow, along with the feverish speed with which she searched her memory for any possible mistake she might have made. Confused and frightened, she finally said:

"How?"

Ransom shook his head disappointedly and clucked his tongue. "Oh, Miss Brinkley...you left fingerprints."

"I never touched that gun!" said Eva, her volume and pitch rising simultaneously.

"Yes, so you said. You know, that's the amazing thing about this gun, nobody touched it."

"What?"

"It was dusted for prints, and it's clean. Completely clean. There wasn't a single print on it."

"Then what…" Eva started loudly, then stopped herself.

"Not a single print," Ransom continued. "You would think that Mr. Parker's prints would be on it, since it's his gun. He would have no reason to wipe it clean."

"So?"

"It would be my guess…that the murderer was reluctant to wear gloves to commit the murder because gloves would look too… peculiar in the dead of summer. It would be my guess that the killer handled the gun, but was sure to wipe it very, very clean."

"You guess! You guess!" shouted Eva. "This is just bullshit, isn't it? This is all a game! You're just trying to trick something out of me!"

"I assure you, it's not a trick," said Ransom evenly.

Ransom's eyes seemed to become bluer, deepening in intensity until they burned like a blowtorch. His face glowed with triumph as he said:

"Your fingerprints were not on the gun, Miss Brinkley…they were on the bullets."

Eva Brinkley was stunned into immobility. Her expression was a mix of shock, surprise, and dread. After what seemed an eternity, these confused emotions gave way to relief. Eva laughed. She laughed uncontrollably, hysterically, to the extent that Ransom and Gerald exchanged concerned glances. Eva continued to laugh until large, wet tears rolled down her face as she sank back into her chair. She turned her stained, streaked face up to Ransom and said, "Nothing ever goes right for me."

TWELVE

Epilogue with Emily

THE DINNER THINGS were cleared away, and only the tea things and a plate of sugar biscuits remained. Tam rested her chin on her crossed forepaws and purred loudly in her sleep, which she enjoyed beside the stove in the basket that Emily had provided for her, complete with a large, comfortable corduroy pillow.

"You see," Ransom explained, "Larry Parker shouldn't have known about the fortune-teller. If he were, as he called himself, 'an innocent bystander,' he wouldn't have known anything about her. He was so worried and flustered that he was suspected of Angela Stephens's murder that he cracked when I confronted him with his gun. He knew it had been used to kill Melina, so when he saw it he thought we suspected him of her murder as well. So he blurted out, 'I didn't kill *her*'—meaning Melina—but if he wasn't involved in Angela's death, he wouldn't have known about Melina at all. After that the whole scheme came pouring out of him: how Eva had picked him up as a likely candidate for going after Angela; how Eva promised him half the inheritance for his help."

Emily laid her light blue cup on its saucer and turned her bright eyes upon the detective benignantly.

"I'm not sure I quite understand about the money."

Ransom reached for a biscuit and took small bites from it intermittently as he explained.

"I'm not sure I do, either. And I'm not sure that the Brinkley woman did, exactly. From what we could gather from her confession—like so many criminals, she was quite verbose once caught—she fairly reveled in her own ingenuity. Whether or not there was any legal basis for it, I don't know, but she believed that whether or not Angela Stephens left a will, she would inherit as Angela's only surviving relative if only Frank Stephens were put out of the way.

"And he damn near was. It's funny, but for the first time in her life, Eva's luck really seemed to be running in the right direction. First because she and her accomplice were presented with the perfect opportunity for murdering Angela. Angela quarreled with her husband, and he left her on her own. Naturally, she turned to her lover, Larry Parker, for consolation. They were lucky in that this occurred on a night that Larry and Eva were together alone and could provide each other with an alibi. Of course, we thought that Eva was the only one who *needed* an alibi, so we were not quite so circumspect about Parker as we...I might have been, otherwise. And he was all too eager to diminish the nature of his relationship with Eva, to reinforce the idea that he had no strong motive to lie for her. The funny thing is, it didn't really matter when he killed Angela, because there was presumably no known connection between Parker and Angela. But I don't think Eva could resist sending him off to do the deed when such a ripe opportunity presented itself. And she got a great deal of pleasure imagining the look on her sister's face when she was murdered by the solicitous lover to whom she'd turned for solace."

"And no one saw Larry Parker coming and going?"

"Ah, yes," said Ransom slyly, "the necessary security key. Angela gave him one so that, like most clandestine lovers, he could come and go the back way. Unfortunately for him, he couldn't play the part of the lover without leaving a few fingerprints. And with our computerized fingerprint system, if you've been arrested—at least within Chicago—we can identify your prints pretty damn fast."

"So Mr. Parker had been arrested before?"

"Possession."

Emily clucked her tongue.

"Their second stroke of luck was much more unexpected. They had seen to it that Frank Stephens would be suspected of killing his wife: Besides being the obvious suspect to begin with, they had created a situation in which the state of the Stephenses' marriage would be called into question. I'm sure, for example, that Parker purposely called Mrs. Stephens when the maid was there in hopes of the tone of their conversations being noticed, which it was. Even Frank Stephens's parents thought there was a problem in their son's marriage.

"But no matter what they could do, and no matter how damning the situation might appear, the case against Frank Stephens was still entirely circumstantial. They couldn't be guaranteed that Stephens would be found guilty. I'm not too sure he would have lived much longer, if that was the case. It doesn't seem to have been too healthy to have stood between Eva and money. Think of what a plus it was to their little plan when Stephens, distraught over the loss of his wife and perceiving his life to be falling apart, committed suicide. He solved all their problems for them."

"Oh, so he *did* kill himself, then?" said Emily, her eyes expressing compassion for the dead man. "That is very sad."

"Threatening Eva's money was also Melina's downfall. Eva hasn't told us everything yet, but I think she enlisted the fortune-teller's aid by telling her the whole thing was some colossal joke she was playing on her sister, just for fun. When we showed up and told Melina about the death, I think she added two and two and came up with dollar signs—not that she wouldn't have participated if she'd known the plan to begin with—I have no doubt about Melina's lack of scruples. Anyway, Eva *did* admit that the fortune-teller tried to blackmail her. Exit Melina." He paused for a moment, then added, "But I doubt if Melina's try at blackmail sealed her fate. I'm sure her days were numbered the moment she agreed to participate in Eva's scheme. The same fate probably awaited Mr. Parker."

Emily clucked her tongue again, this time with disdain. "It's very fortunate that Brinkley's fingerprints were also on file."

Ransom hesitated. "They weren't."

Emily's eyebrows slid upwards. "Then how did you identify the fingerprints on the bullets so quickly?"

"We didn't. We didn't have time. Oh, there were fingerprints on the bullets all right, but we didn't verify they were Eva's until after she confessed."

"Then how could you be so sure they were hers?"

Ransom smiled coyly, "Intuition?"

Emily studied his face for a moment, her eyes twinkling, then with a satisfied smile she reached over and patted his hand.

Ransom added reflectively. "This actually turned out to be a most unusual case. We don't ordinarily find three murderers involved in the same case. And in another way, it was a very usual case: really solved, as most cases are, by the diligent work of the crime lab—I'm very lucky they were on their toes. Good God, I *must* be getting old to forget the basics."

"Three murderers," Emily ruminated, choosing to ignore his self-deprecation.

"Yes. Parker killed Angela, Eva killed Melina, and Frank Stephens killed himself...if we can stretch the point and consider suicide murder." He paused for a moment and nibbled at a cookie, then added, "Of course, I was lucky, too, that Eva stayed true to her destiny and her luck ran out."

Emily seemed lost in thought as she lifted her delicate cup to her lips with an equally delicate hand and took a sip of tea. When she replaced the cup at length, she said, "It's all so tragic. I can't help feeling sorry for that poor woman and her husband, caught in the machinations of her wicked sister.''

Ransom smiled ruefully at his adopted grandmother.

"And a plot I might have discovered earlier if I'd really listened to you. Although I was right in a way—the motive did boil down to greed—it was you who tried to remind me of that most Victorian of all motives, revenge. God knows there was enough of that in *A Tale of Two Cities*. It was the revenge aspect that muddied the waters.''

"That's the trouble with revenge,'' said Emily. "It obscures everything, including reason. It's a poison that infects everything with which it comes in contact.''

"Without you,'' Ransom continued fondly, "I'm afraid the fortune-teller would have remained a very serious unanswered question, if we had even solved the case at all. And of course, I now have a fuller understanding of 'the fatal flaw' thanks to you.''

"Oh, no. You have the Bard to thank for that.''

"Well, I've been incredibly stupid in this case. I think I owe the solution of this case to you, the crime lab, and to a lovely, very ill young lady who told me about misdirected anger. I didn't see it at first, but I understood it later. I really have to stop back and see her and let her know she helped.''

"You know,'' said Emily with surprising disdain, "the one person I don't feel sorry for in all of this is that dreadful fortune-teller.''

Ransom replied thoughtfully, "Oh, she wasn't a dreadful fortune-teller at all. In fact, she was a very good fortune-teller.''

"Hmmm?'' said Emily, her eyes bright and quizzical.

"The description she gave to Angela Stephens of who the murderer would be fit not only Frank Stephens, it also fit Larry Parker. In a sense, her so-called 'prediction' really was correct, but I sincerely doubt if Larry Parker will enjoy playing the role of Charles Darnay.''

Emily searched the face of her friend, greatly suspecting him of 'having her on,' as the saying goes. Seeing no sign of amusement in his eyes, she decided it was time that they dismissed the topic completely.

''Ah, well,'' she said breezily, ''to paraphrase the Bard, may angels sing them all to their rest.''

Ransom smiled. ''You *will* insist on bringing *Hamlet* into this case.''

Emily returned his smile and said with finality, ''My dear Jeremy, years from now when you really *are* old, you will find that you can successfully bring *Hamlet* into a great many things''

And they finished their tea, talking of other things.

BIRD IN A CAGE
LEE MARTIN
A Deb Ralston Mystery

First Time in Paperback

DEATH FROM ABOVE

Wearing yellow-dyed ostrich feathers, the trapeze artist performed inside a gilded cage high above the dinner theater crowd. Fort Worth detective Deb Ralston and her husband, Harry, enjoy the show—until the cables snap, and acrobat, trapeze and cage plummet forty feet, killing the performer and two patrons.

The victim, Julia Gluck, is a member of a famous European circus family. Beautiful and beloved, there is no apparent motive for her murder. But the severed cables prove someone wanted her dead.

Deb finds the answers buried in a decades-old tragedy, and she searches for a bold and clever killer exacting long-awaited—and deadly—revenge.

"A breathless, high-flying climax caps this lively tale…"
—*Publishers Weekly*

Available in January at your favorite retail stores.

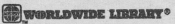 **WORLDWIDE LIBRARY®**

BIRD

A LOVE DIE TO FOR

CHRISTINE T. JORGENSEN
A Stella the Stargazer Mystery

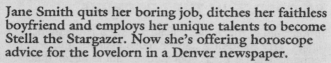

First Time In Paperback

MURDER IN THE STARS

Jane Smith quits her boring job, ditches her faithless boyfriend and employs her unique talents to become Stella the Stargazer. Now she's offering horoscope advice for the lovelorn in a Denver newspaper.

The ink is barely dry on her first column offering advice to a lost soul looking for "a love to die for" when she stumbles upon the body of the owner of her favorite lingerie shop—stabbed to death with a pair of scissors.

Add a police detective she *almost* liked before he accused her of murder, toss in her own uncanny sixth sense and an expressive pet chameleon, and her future is a bit unpredictable...especially with a killer gazing at Stella.

"Stella's quirky humor, human frailties...will endear her to many readers."
                                        —*Publishers Weekly*

Available in March at your favorite retail stores.

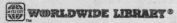 **WORLDWIDE LIBRARY**®   LOVE

A PERMANENT RETIREMENT
JOHN
MILES

First Time in Paperback

A Laura Michaels Mystery

NO CORPSE IN THE BROCHURE

Timberdale is more like a resort than a retirement village. The residents harbor more secrets and scandals than a soap opera does. Life is never dull. But in fact, it is turning deadly.

Cora Chandler, dressed in a pretty blue housedress, her hair in rollers, is the first to die of unnatural causes. But not the last.

Laura Michaels, single mother and sociology student, enjoys her work at Timberdale, despite her wildly eccentric boss or gorgeous, man-eating co-worker. And now Laura's job includes murder. She's accused of the crimes by an Agatha Christie wannabe, bashed over the head...and is unwittingly headed straight for a rendezvous with a killer.

"...an entertaining read with plenty of puzzlement."

—*Booklist*

Available in February at your favorite retail stores.

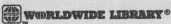 **WORLDWIDE LIBRARY®**

PERM

THE LAST CASTRATO
JOHN SPENCER HILL

A Mystery of Florence

First Time in Paperback

THE UNKINDEST CUT

Cordelia Sinclair has come to Florence to study opera and experience life for the first time on her own terms. But she arrives in a city terrorized by a killer dubbed *Lo Squartore*—the Slasher—as the body of a Roman Catholic cardinal is found with his throat slit. It's the third in a string of prominent citizens murdered with no evidence but the manner of death to connect them.

When a fourth murder occurs, Detective Carlo Arbati begins to make the bizarre connections, recognizing that there is a method to the Slasher's madness.

But neither Cordelia nor Arbati realize the role she will play in drawing out a cleverly concealed killer poised to strike again.

"A frightening climax..."   —*Publishers Weekly*

Available in February at your favorite retail stores.

 **WORLDWIDE LIBRARY** ®

THE CONCRETE PILLOW
RONALD TIERNEY

First Time In Paperback

A Deets Shanahan Mystery

Shanahan wasn't keen on working for an addict.

They couldn't be counted on for either their perceptions or their payment. But something about Luke Lindstrom made the Indiana private investigator take the case.

Perhaps because he remembered when Luke and his brothers were the local high school basketball superstars. Maybe because adulthood had only brought them failure—and untimely death. Mark took a fatal dive off a balcony. Matthew fell off a cliff. That left Luke...and John. Until John takes a deadly tumble.

Now Luke decides to find out who wants him dead—before the killer succeeds. And while Shanahan is all too aware of how tough family relations can be, he's discovering that in Luke's case, it's just plain murder....

"Shanahan is a terrific character, feisty, even noble."
—Publishers Weekly

Available in March at your favorite retail stores.

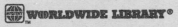 **WORLDWIDE LIBRARY®**

PILL